Angels Strange
and Beautiful

Gina Fiametta

Angels Strange and Beautiful

ISBN-13: 978-1-7357097-1-0 (Paperback)
ISBN: 978-1-7357097-2-7 (Hardback)
ISBN: 978-1-7357097-0-3 (ebook)

Editing thanks to Constance Renfrow

Cover Art by Abbey Konzen

www.ginafiametta.com

For all of the beautiful, ordinary people out there who remind me that it's good to be alive and we have a good God.

The Faith of a Few

Chapter One

There is a song they now sing in Reason, the place where I was born. When I left all those years ago, the story behind its words was only just becoming known. The lullaby made its way to me recently through a friend who'd stayed in Reason. Anyway, it goes like this:

If you must speak, keep your voice to a whisper,
For it grows dark and the leaves are going somewhere,
And the grey-faced man has still not had his answer
Of a pledge in blood; if no one pays it, all will suffer.
Speak not above a whisper.

Keep still, my child, tightly shut your bright eyes,
For it's silent in town and not one child cries.
Tomorrow a madman shall hang for his lies
At last with his payment end the nightly reprise.

Speak not above a whisper.

Be silent and cautious, my darling, and rest,
For the night has just swallowed up one of the best,
Her hair black as shadow, in white was she dressed,
Her quiet grace thwarted, she strayed from the rest
And speaks not above a whisper.

Be quiet, my child, and find peace in your sleep!
For at dawn, all the village will silently creep
Toward the angel that hangs from the gallows, and
weep
Then find in the forest their children asleep.
Speak not above a whisper.

Yes, it is true, most of it. And no one but me knows the whole story. No one but me and a girl named Faith Prescott.

She was beautiful, with inky black hair that, when unpinned, hung past her hips. She had a sweet smile and chocolate-brown eyes that danced like they held a secret. None of the other boys seemed to pay her much attention.

This shy young woman was my first love. We lived a few blocks from each other in a little town called Reason, tucked into the dark hollows of New England. It's about thirty miles north of here. She was a few years older than me and remarkably clever. Everyone knew her name, and with her sunny laugh and shy sort of kindness, they thought they loved her.

Why, then, did she not interest more of the boys?

Was she not sweet and pretty, and delightfully full of secrets? Yes, and that was the catch: a more private young lady you'd never find. She was kind to all, but none were allowed admittance to the walled garden of her mind, and in time she was relegated to the title of "wall flower." Though she was sometimes admired, the others never seemed to see how very special she was.

But I did. And so she was all mine, at least in my own mind.

I'll never forget the first time I noticed her. I was seventeen. Papa had sent me to market with a bale of wool to be sold. Some of the wilder boys were riding through the town on horseback and yelling at the top of their lungs, enjoying their freedom after the melting winter snows.

Suddenly, there she was. Faith had been walking in the road and had to leap out of the way of the riders. She landed a few yards in front of me, resting one arm against the whitewashed storefront.

It was like I was seeing her for the first time. Her peach-hued cheeks had captured the breath of the previous autumn, against which her eyelashes were a shock of black and her slender mouth a stroke of pale red. She pursed her lips and tossed a disdainful glare in the direction of the boys. I decided she was the most beautiful creature I'd ever seen.

She recovered herself in a moment, smiling ruefully and straightening her frame like a little queen. Then she stepped back into the street without so much as a glance in my direction. I concluded then that I was in love.

From that day on, I trod after her like some forlorn pup. She remained apparently oblivious to me, and I kept at a distance for fear she would speak to me. I didn't want to let cruel reality shatter my fragile dream, so I resolved I must never approach. Silly, I was, but devoted.

We were often separated by our respective chores, during which times I suffered great impatience. The instant I was free I was on the hunt for her, hoping to catch just one glimpse of her, or perhaps plod along beside her as she went on some errand, pretending I had some business in the same direction.

She always greeted me with the same solemn politeness she used with most everybody and tolerated my presence, but otherwise forgot about me. I suspect more than one villager had guessed my affliction due to the snickers behind hands, but in my purpose no one molested me. They probably saw it as both pathetic and harmless, and they would've been right.

One busy morning, I overheard Faith's mother instructing her to bring a parcel of freshly-baked bread to the town's dye maker, a man of about thirty who lived a few miles outside of town. Faith's mother made it her business to send the occasional gift to the friendless or the eccentric, so Faith was no stranger to such errands. As for me, I'd never paid them any attention until now. Faith's house was a block or two closer to the town square, which meant I'd previously been relying on chance for us to cross paths. This errand, however, brought her right across my own doorstep, making me the obvious escort. I volunteered at once.

Faith took the parcel dutifully, though none too excited for her journey. As we were leaving town, I received more than one approving nod from the townsmen. I realized to my glee that to escort a young lady on some remote errand was a noble endeavor, and I dared to walk closer to her.

We soon reached the inkmaker's humble dwelling. My little mistress stepped up the neat stone steps and knocked.

"Who knocks?" a man's voice barked from somewhere inside.

"It is Faith Prescott, Mr. Gladstone. My mother sent me to deliver you some bread. Would you like me to bring it inside or leave it out here?"

"Enter!"

I straightened and watched keenly as Faith turned the knob and stepped hesitantly inside. She shifted from foot to foot in the tiny, chaotic entryway. Several wooden and mechanical parts I couldn't identify leaned against the walls, and there were pieces missing from the floor.

"Mr. Gladstone?"

There was a great clattering and muffled stomping before the gentleman himself appeared. His clothing perfectly matched the state of his entryway; he had on a loose white shirt whose tails not only hung out but appeared to have been torn in multiple places, and his bare legs and feet protruded from the bottom of a pair of brown breeches.

Faith recoiled ever so slightly as she handed him the parcel, noticing the brilliantly colored stains on his shirtsleeves. When he saw where she was looking, he caught her eye and quickly smiled, exposing dimples on each cheek and bringing a touch of life to the pale, watery eyes which looked as sad as a basset hound's.

This did little to improve my impression of him. I noted chaotic blond hair and a closely cut beard which defied all sense of symmetry. Faith appeared to share the somewhat alarming impression, though she was polite enough to offer him a sweet smile.

"Your mother is very good to think of me. Give her my thanks."

"Of course." Faith nodded and edged toward the door.

"Well, farewell, Miss Prescott," he added with some disappointment. "And thank you."

She nodded awkwardly again, then made her escape.

This insignificant occurrence was repeated weekly that spring. Mrs. Prescott sent Faith with something different each time: biscuits, muffins, a freshly-baked loaf, or a plate of little cakes.

Each time Faith came to Mr. Gladstone's door, I, her faithful shadow, obtained her permission to accompany her. Her greetings were often initially ignored or unheard, and once he finally did appear, Mr. Gladstone's appearance was continually frightful. It seemed that each week his beard was different, now a full beard, now a half beard, now a goatee, and nearly always uneven. One day, a glimpse of scarring made me realize it was often singed off by chemicals or flames.

As spring progressed into summer, for me the world stood still. Sometimes Faith greeted me after church or acknowledged me when we were at market, but she made no attempt to engage me further. I often traded tasks with others in the village so I could always have an errand to run that brought me in step with Faith. Whenever she seemed to tire of my presence, I bid her goodbye and took a separate route, then circled back to watch her from a distance.

However, one tiny cloud cast its shadow over the summertime. It was a lush summer morning when Faith and I – oh, to hear our names said together! – traipsed through the lush pools of shade peppering the by now familiar path through the forest. She kept a brisk pace, swinging her basket cheerfully in spite of the monotonous task. She'd never taken much interest in these visits, though she dutifully paid them, and always with a smile.

When we got to the cottage, I took my accustomed seat on a nearby stump while she eased open the door and went inside. She had gotten into the habit of placing her mother's gifts on a chair just inside to avoid the necessity of an interaction between herself and the old bachelor. Similarly self-conscious, he had readily agreed to the system. She would merely call out to let him know she'd been there.

Today, however, her customary call was interrupted by an urgent cry for help. With a start, my mistress rushed into the house, hastily tossing her basket onto the chair and leaving the front door swinging. I leapt up in alarm and peered anxiously inside, unsure whether to follow.

The little front room and kitchen were a mess, with pieces of wire and metal stacked in corners and wooden parts leaned up against the walls. Unfortunately, Faith's host was not in either of these rooms and she quickly disappeared from sight.

I darted around to the back of the cottage. To my relief, the back door and windows were wide open, letting in the soft breeze. There she stood in an odd-looking little room lined with bookshelves, apparently no worse for the wear. She held a strange contraption like tree branches which contained several glass vials of fluid in many different colors.

I narrowed my eyes in search of Mr. Gladstone. Suddenly, the disheveled blond head appeared inside. He darted back and forth, hurriedly mopping up some clear liquid which had spilled all over a large wooden desk.

For the next several minutes, Faith worked to help him rescue the other items off his desk and put his chemicals back in order. A strange sight it was, for as clumsy as his appearance had led me to expect he would be, here in his laboratory, his movements were like a dance. He gracefully wove in and out of Faith's path, handing her things and retrieving others, making a wide sweep of the arm to clear a spot here or a sudden grab to move a book there. Faith seemed to notice it, too; whatever she did, he graciously integrated to his purpose. At first she seemed intimidated, but as her clumsy movements were knit into his, she became entranced.

In a matter of minutes, the lab was set to rights. Mr. Gladstone caught up a broom and began sweeping up broken glass. A little dazed, Faith sank onto a high wooden stool to watch him.

"How do you manage all of it?" she finally asked, her eyes wandering over the glass bottles and strange bundles of herbs and little paper parcels, all shelved neatly in hundreds of little wooden compartments.

"As well as I can." He laughed ruefully. "Which, as you can see, doesn't always go as planned!"

She laughed softly. "Well, it's all right." Her eyes had turned bright and thoughtful, and she looked around the room with the discerning intensity I had often noted. "I'd never imagined your work would require so many, um, volatile chemicals."

Gladstone nodded as he set the broom aside and stood back to survey the room. He seemed bigger and taller than he had, standing up straight with his thumbs in his pockets to look about the makeshift laboratory which must have been his pride and joy.

"It can be dangerous work. But it's safe enough if you know what you're about." He flashed his dimpled smile at Faith, and she smiled back. "Though it certainly takes some trial and error."

Faith seemed to remember herself and hurriedly got up off the stool. "Well, I'm glad I happened to be around when that happened. Do- Do try to be more careful!"

His face fell as she edged into the entryway. "Worry not. I am not normally so careless. It was a chance mishap." His eyes followed her reluctantly to the door. "Thank you for your help."

Faith bobbed an awkward curtsy and gestured toward the chair. "Enjoy...my mother's bread."

"Yes, of course. Thank you!" he called out one last time as she made her escape.

I followed her past a clothesline of brilliantly colored fabrics, probably where he tested the dyes he made. As we drew near the town, I chuckled to myself over the mishap. Clearly she was glad to have helped, but probably she'd never want to go there again.

Chapter Two

A week later, however, Faith was on her way back to the woods, and this time she stopped in to chat with the old bachelor. His face lit up with something like relief as soon as he saw her. It was evident from his rapid, fumbling speech and childish delight at someone to talk to that he couldn't often keep a companion.

Faith listened politely, though she occasionally glanced nervously up at a strange-looking bottle or contraption housed on one of his precariously balanced bookshelves. But she reminded me of a gentle mother in the way she followed him graciously through his house, smilingly permitting him to show off and chatter to her about his treasures.

Her delight, however, was unpleasantly obvious to me when he showed her how to work a little trinket from one of his many shelves. It looked like a little acrobat that slowly somersaulted across the table when wound up. Though Gladstone made me uneasy, fascinating her with his strange scientific notions, he was a good host, offering some new item to entertain her while he dug up another project to show.

Half of his explanations, I think, went over her head, for they certainly went over mine and she often looked politely confused, more tolerant than interested. But their interview was a pleasant one, and when she left, the smile did not leave his face until after she'd left the front stoop. Even until we turned the bend, he stood in the doorway, watching us go.

The early summer gradually gave way to the heat of July. Faith still often pretended not to notice how often I was near, while other times she merely smiled. Sometimes she even spoke to me, including me when we were with other young people. Mostly, though, I had to get more and more creative with my reasons for being in the woods near the cabin, where she could increasingly be found. The more frequently she visited, the more awkward it became for me to accompany her. I could easily spot her going past my house, for nothing else was down that path but Mr. Gladstone's cabin, but finding a reason to go with her was harder. I often feigned an errand in that direction or (to my great embarrassment) followed in secret at a distance and either rested in an alcove of trees or visited the nearby creek, then followed her back home once more. Gradually, it became less and less clear whether she knew I was there.

Something had changed between her and Theophilus, however, (for "Theophilus" Mr. Gladstone would have her call him, and indeed, the informal designation seemed to better suit his strangeness), so that even when her mother's gifts began to peter out, Faith began to make her own simple offerings and walk them to the cabin while they were still hot. Within a short period, she and the dye maker took to sharing the treats at his table with a batch of freshly-picked berries and a cup of milk. Then they would take to talking, which often led to introducing or including her in one of his latest projects.

His projects were many and various. I wracked my brains trying to understand them, but even with his explanations, I couldn't keep up. I eventually gave up and either napped or went fishing while they visited, making sure to check in on her every hour. My ear became acutely able to pick up the creak of his front door when Faith was ready to leave.

I should have noticed it then, but several of his projects were less than ordinary. In fact, they may be better labeled as "experiments." He was a scientist, no question, and this should've served us as a warning. His curiosity extended from astronomy to physics to herbology. In fact, his dabbling in plants and their various properties was not limited to professional interest in colors for his inks and dyes.

"What's this for?" I heard Faith ask him one day as she was helping him stock his shelves. I couldn't say why, but the two of them moving in harmless synchrony around the little back room irritated me. She held up a glass bottle of dried leaves.

He took it from her hands and turned over the paper label. "That one has proven effective in the treatment of fevers."

Her eyes widened. "Do you mean to say you've

tested these? All of them?" Her eyes roved the hundreds of wooden cubbies, many of which contained more of the bottles and bundles of herbs.

He blushed slightly, but smiled. "Only on myself and my animals."

So the ever-changing batch of birds and rodents that lived in little pens outside did have a purpose. I'd only ever seen him use the donkey, and that had been to carry his newly-dyed fabrics to town to be sold.

It wasn't until later that Faith and I learned it was also his habit to sell herbs from his garden to the town apothecary. They had a neat little system, an old lady from church chatted to Faith one Sunday; Pearce would ask Theophilus for herbs he needed, and besides selling his plants, Theophilus got a chance to talk herbology and share his speculations. Sometimes, the druggist even seemed interested in his theories or offered him news from other chemists.

Pearce, it seemed, was the only other person in town with whom Theophilus could hold a conversation. The only times I'd seen him in town were on market day, his visits to the apothecary, and at church, where he would slide into a back pew at the last second and slip out the instant the last chord finished reverberating.

I must confess, to my own shame, that for nearly my entire acquaintance with Theophilus, I set the blame for his loneliness entirely on his own shoulders. Having had my own share of shyness and getting picked on to soldier through, it had become my belief that with enough resilience, anyone could survive in this village with tolerable friendliness. In retrospect, I had every reason to know better.

On market days, for instance, it wasn't unusual to spot Theophilus chattering happily about some scientific fact he'd learned or a theory he'd developed, while his listeners gave each other odd looks, bought their fabrics, and hastily made their escape. I had always written it off that they were just as confused or disinterested as I was. But looking back has showed me an undeniable pattern. Though the villagers, especially the womenfolk, held Pearce to an untouchable standard as a trustworthy druggist, they treated most other scientists and their ideas with disdain, fear, or even mockery. Eventually, even Theophilus sensed this derision, though he didn't appear to comprehend the reason, and he retreated into his shell, reappearing only to sell his fabrics.

It must be remembered that this was a small, minimally educated village full of people whose idea of Christianity was whatever their educated leaders told them it should be. The rest of their system of belief was constructed of passed-down wisdom and local hearsay. Anyone who dared present theories contrary to their limited comprehension of Christianity and what their great-granddaddies had taught them was seen as having respect for neither and treated as a threat. It was due to several books that came into my possession later in life that I could even recognize the limited education into which I had been bred.

Theophilus's forced isolation, then, made his gratitude for Faith all the more understandable. In spite of her regular chores in her mother's garden, Faith managed to find time to spend down at the cottage in the woods almost daily. She never mocked or laughed at him, and if she didn't understand something, she would no longer humor him with a fake smile but pepper him with questions until she, too, understood.

By harvest time, I grew impatient with this charitable whim of hers. True, anyone might've pitied his loneliness enough to humor the occasional round of his scientific babble, but since then, he'd become downright friendly with her and, I daresay, took her sweet company for granted.

Indeed, he'd become so comfortable in her presence that he'd ceased to remember to change his shirt before she came so that the brilliant stains from both work and experiments were still plainly visible. Sometimes it was clear he wore the same shirt two days in a row. Both man and cottage were constantly a mess, but he made little attempt to remedy it and allowed Faith to help him reorganize some of his cubbies and piles of rubbish.

For her part, Faith seemed charmed by his untidy habits of leaving his shirttail hanging out or forgetting to put on stockings. The sight of his bare legs and feet grew so familiar to her that she eventually began to remove her own shoes and stockings to wade in the creek with him or work in the garden without getting her things dirty. I blushed at these minor improprieties, but never drew anyone's attention to them. The thought of causing her any trouble never crossed my mind, and besides, she was only humoring a lonely dye maker ten years her senior. I was only a boy, and too blockish to realize she was genuinely interested in their work, or that another sort of interest could be forming between them.

From the villagers' remarks, it was clear that no one else saw him as either a threat or a prospect for a young lady. He was odd and untidy, and not wealthy enough to draw the eyes of well-meaning parents. Furthermore, he had a reputation for taking an undue interest in the natural sciences, one which made him peculiar but not overtly offensive. To cap it all off, his distant look and seemingly all-consuming interest in his experiments and work served as the final factor which blotted him from the list of eligible bachelors. To them, he was an unusual recluse and fellow townsman whom nobody minded.

Faith soon became aware of the town's view of him, as well. Whenever she spoke of him, he was dismissed as quickly as the mention of a particular house or the color of the leaves on a certain tree. He was a fixed object in their minds, whose life never changed and whose feelings didn't matter. Or that's what Faith said, anyway, one Sunday when the ladies in her mother's sewing circle had been making innocently disparaging remarks about him. Faith fled the company on the church lawn, her face turning scarlet.

"She's grown very attached to the man since she began taking bread to him this spring," her mother mentioned, straightening her skirts proudly. "I admit I was a little sorry for him, having no family here, so I thought it might cheer him up to have something nice to eat. The poor soul gets so lonely out there and appreciates anyone who will talk to him. Faith finds great joy in bringing him sweets and visiting for an hour or so. She gets so cross when she can't go!"

"What a little dear!" Mrs. Witherspoon remarked. "The man needs a sensible friend to keep his feet on the ground instead of meddling in all of that scientific hullabaloo."

The ladies cooed their approbation, and it was established: Mr. Theophilus Gladstone was nothing more than a charity case, and Faith Prescott was as his devoted little nun.

Being a thick-skulled young man in the first thralls of love, I didn't know enough to read into Faith's blushing. I couldn't see anything in the man to attract a woman's attention, being lanky and clumsy and full of odd ideas. Besides, he was old, at least to someone our age. However, he had a childlike heart that longed for human friendship, and Faith proved more than ready to provide it. More disturbing yet was that some part of her, long buried, seemed to have come to light when she at last gained a companion who understood.

In fact, I realized a few days later as I made my way to his cottage, the two of them often resembled a pair of enthusiastic children at play. It took me a moment to find them; they were busy laying flat slabs of stone in the clearing to form a walkway leading into their favorite spot among the trees.

I climbed to my "nest," a comfortable spot in a tree near the cabin, and inspected their work. So far this summer, they had cleared out Theophilus's slovenly study so he could use it, reorganized several cubbies, and sent several of the broken wood pieces in the entryway to the woodpile to be used as firewood; I'd heard them chattering happily about having had a bonfire one evening. I hadn't known of this and it gave my insides a twist.

Now I scanned the yard and nearby woods and creek, realizing to my dismay just how many projects they had since instated together. Half the conversations I overheard were the two of them pondering fantastical questions to which nobody ever needed the answers, such as how it felt to be a bug or why flowers turned toward the sun. Some of these questions were just speculation, but then the two of them began trying to find out answers to the ones they could.

For instance, when they'd wanted to know more about a certain type of frog, they'd made an ingenious little live trap down by the stream and had been happily examining a variety of captives ever since. On more whimsical days, the two of them had made a set of windchimes and hung them from his back porch, constructed a kite, designed an unsuccessful puppet theater, and cultivated a miniature village among the protruding roots of a giant tree. Faith's skill at whittling had allowed them to make countless contributions of little houses and furniture. Now they were spreading a sheet over their little alcove with dowels stitched inside. Soon, they could pull a string and the awning would fold or unfurl itself to provide shade.

I found myself less and less assured of the platonic view the church ladies took of the situation. The two did certainly enjoy each other's company; they rattled off their thoughts to each other as though they feared each breath would be their last, and spoke each other's first names comfortably enough to rankle me. What did she want with him, anyway? After all, comforting a lonely man was praiseworthy enough, but this was excessive. If the man needed a mother, then he should have someone in town adopt him, someone without her whole life ahead of her who didn't have a real prospect perched in the tree branches nearby!

However, my young heart buoyed me up with fanciful hopes, and by the end of the day I had decided that I was really in no danger; after all, didn't it naturally follow that a girl like Faith would attract many devoted friends? If she seemed familiar with him, that was because she was so sincerely generous that she enjoyed her times here...within reason.

By the next week, I had convinced myself that she and Theophilus were merely like a sister and brother. To think of him as a fatherly figure was too much to ask, but as siblings the two of them had room for all the affection in the world without ever turning romantic. In fact, I told myself magnanimously, as her devoted lover I was proud to know she had such a good man as Theophilus to look after her until...

Until what? The thought took me by surprise. I had matured in spite of myself and no longer looked on Faith as an ethereal being on some celestial pedestal, but as a woman who could be wooed, perhaps even by me. I was reaching the age at which I could be expected to go courting, and I could think of no one I liked and admired more than Faith. Perhaps it was time to break my old resolution and start talking to her.

However, on the following Sunday I had something like a presentiment that this was not to be. I was out with the sheep when I spotted them. Faith was seated on a grassy hillside overlooking the valley in which our flocks were grazing, with Theophilus stretched out on his back and his head resting on her lap. She held her bible open and read aloud from the Psalms in her clear, low, musical voice. Her tones washed over me, carried on the wind, and I sighed and sat back, trying to forget that another man was laying in the place where I longed to be. *But only a brother,* I reminded myself.

"'He maketh me to rest in green pasture, and leadeth me by the still waters. He restoreth my soul, and leadeth me in the paths of righteousness for his Name's sake.'"

"Faith, do you really suppose that is the kind of faith God wants?" Theophilus queried abruptly. She glanced down at him questioningly. "To be docile lambs, not looking around but following with our eyes down?"

Faith's smile was gentle. "Our Shepherd knows the way. What else would we do?"

He shifted restlessly and angled his eyes up at her. "I mean, do you really think he meant us to close our eyes to all that's around us?" He made a sweeping gesture with his hands. "He says to follow him…"

"Yes?"

His expression grew distant and stern. "But that's not always what our church leaders say."

Faith sounded alarmed. "What do you mean?"

Theophilus returned his gaze to her face. "Our community lives in fear, trying to please God and keep our hands out of what isn't ours to know, yes? We live in such terror of sin that we are sometimes afraid to learn more about the world."

Faith nodded, somewhat reassured but still confused.

He paused for a long time, frowning at a fluffy white cloud that was skittering across the sky. "In the Bible, we are told repeatedly not to be afraid, and yet here we are, covering our heads as though the world God made were something evil meant to tempt us," he mused softly. "Anyone who seeks to understand the world is censured and feared. But what exactly is it that they fear?"

Faith leaned back on her hands and gazed up at the sky, too. "What would you change?"

Theophilus's voice was fiery with passion. "I would stop teaching our children that the study of nature is evil, as though there were something wicked in curiosity. I believe God placed the first humans in the garden so they could enjoy it with him, and that that invitation hasn't been revoked. He gave us the keys to understand our world and to do what we can for each other, and yet it is painted as sin to use those gifts."

He rolled over and sat up. "While it is true that there are ways to pervert these gifts and turn what was innocent into wickedness, to throw it all away in fear is to spurn his blessings. What bothers me the most is that many seem to fear we're going to find something we shouldn't, as if the creation would contradict the Creator."

Faith frowned faintly and nodded. "It seems more to savor of unbelief than it does of faith," she said slowly. Even Theophilus looked surprised as she went on. "As a matter of fact, either God *is* the creator of the world and is bigger than our doubts, or He isn't. I think it comes down to what we truly believe: if we believe in God from the bottom of our hearts, then nothing will ever change that; our understanding of the world will increase and our faith will remain. If we fear that looking too closely could give the lie to our faith, then maybe we never believed at all."

She was looking at the gathering clouds now, but Theophilus was gazing intensely at her, an odd look of wonder on his face. A slow rumble of thunder echoed across the valley, standing out against the buzz of insects. Emotions warred over Theophilus's face, then condensed into an expression of both intensity and tenderness. He reached forward and gently cupped her face in his hands. She didn't flinch.

"You are truly the most extraordinary woman. Surely God has an amazing plan for your life." His voice caught and went deeper. "I hope I am permitted to…watch it unfold."

I rose abruptly and hiked deeper into the valley. After a minute or so, Faith's voice read on.

"'Yea, though I should walk through the valley of the shadow of death, I will fear no evil; for thou art with me: thy rod and thy staff, they comfort me…'"

I knew not what to think; I was afraid to think. Theophilus had played his hand; now it was her turn.

Chapter Three

That evening, when the sheep were safely penned, my feet took me against my will to the path in the woods that led past the Gladstone house. I wasn't sure if she'd be there; it had been a long day and the sun was setting. But as soon as I reached the cabin, I knew she was. Something about her presence made the lights appear brighter, and Theophilus's laugh was heard through the open windows. Declining to go to my nest, I instead paced outside, taking out my frustration on some nearby trees with a fat stick.

Eventually, the front door opened, sending me leaping into the underbrush, ashamed of my spying. The two of them stepped outside, reluctantly bidding one another goodbye. But when Faith looked out into the growing twilight, her face lit with a smile even I couldn't help but mirror.

"Oh, how beautiful!" she breathed.

Both of us looked about, following her gaze. Faith pointed, happy to make him see what she did.

"Look there, Theophilus! The fading light makes

everything seem to glow! Oh, and the spots of light look like pearls suspended in the air!" She clasped her hands and sighed contentedly. "Oh, it makes me so happy I could just dance if only to be part of it."

Theophilus leapt to the bottom of the steps and grandly offered his hand. Faith laughed and began to protest that she didn't know how to dance and wasn't sure it would be proper, but she slowly descended the stairs regardless. He drew her to him and began the first steps. Her complaints died away.

"Here we are, celebrating the beauty of creation, and do you think the Creator looks down without a smile?" he asked, his blue eyes dancing.

Faith's only answer was to laugh with delight and let Theophilus lead her in a wide arc around the little clearing, trampling the trodden-down grass.

A strange combination of joy and heartache assailed me as I watched her laughingly turn in Theophilus's arms, her cornflower skirt twirling outward and ink-black hair catching those very pearls of light she had mentioned. How happy she looked!

The first raindrop splashed on my nose, awakening me to reality. The two of them remained oblivious, spinning all the more energetically until at last, the rain fell steadily enough for them to notice. They pulled to a brief stop, looking up at the woolen grey sky.

"Oh, no!" Faith sounded so terribly disappointed that I almost wished their dance had not been disturbed.

Almost.

But Theophilus didn't give up so easily. "Shh, Faith!

Look," he said. "Come! It's still beautiful. Just take off your shawl and whatever you don't want to get wet."

Faith hesitated, but even I could see the ready shine in her eyes. It was as if she were asking for just a little more encouragement. The eagerness in them made me rip out handfuls of the grass beside me.

"Go on!" he said again.

She complied, giggling as she dashed to the house. She shed her outermost layers and stowed them under the protection of the overhang. She glanced up at the sky and hugged herself as the rain poured down harder, but still Theophilus stood there, holding out his hand and grinning an invitation.

Faith ran to him. As he took her hands once more, the heavy rain became a deluge, soaking us instantly. The two of them laughed up at the sky, happier than ordinary people would have been in full sun. Her drenched skirts clung to her legs, allowing a distressingly clear view of her alluring shape.

As they splashed through the standing water littering the lawn, my heart sank. More than rain wet my face. I didn't yet know real heartbreak, but I was stung as though someone had thrown scalding water on me. It was all too clear that Faith knew what man she wanted; his untidy presence had imprinted itself upon her heart.

All at once, Faith twirled into him. Their arms got so tangled they were forced to stop for a moment. They were still laughing softly when Faith lifted her face to look up into his.

It happened as naturally as breathing. They leaned in and pressed a kiss on each other's lips.

A huge clap of thunder made me jump. As they pulled slowly back, Faith's face was a gorgeous canvas of pink and white, deeply tranquil and glistening with rain. Theophilus's visage clouded with a dozen different passions, filled with a longing so intense that it nearly burned me to see.

Theophilus appeared so solemn that he looked almost angry or sad, but then Faith's lips began to spread into a smile. His eyes brightened and his countenance lifted with happy surprise, and soon his arms were slipping around her waist, drawing her in closer. Her color deepened and she slid her hands up to gently cup the base of his neck.

I took a moment to absorb the situation. Faith was in love with Theophilus. Theophilus was in love with Faith. Her family had no idea. The townspeople hadn't thought it a possibility. I sat back against a tree trunk, my head reeling.

All at once, the storm was right above us. Lightning and thunder came within the same breath, and the wind whipped Faith's hair against Theophilus's cheek like a slap. They jerked apart and stood still, taking in the severity of the situation.

Suddenly, Theophilus took her hands again and they spun, looking like a majestic pair of dancers from the Old World. Faith's laugh rang out across the clearing. Theophilus suddenly looked powerful, standing tall with his arms spread wide, guiding Faith to turn again and again, his lively steps directing her own. The dance from that first day she'd run inside his house had recommenced with all its vitality. Suddenly, the vivid stains on his cuffs, the wild tangle of hair, and his towering height all mingled together and almost blinded me, both beautiful and terrifying.

I turned to Faith to strike a contrast, for solace from his wildness, but she looked completely different from the girl I'd known. Her hair had broken loose from its pins with the heft of water and the wind so the long black tresses hung down and swung enchantingly against her back. Her flashing eyes, black lashes, pale peach skin, and red, laughing mouth clashed as violently as the aspects of Theophilus had, and suddenly I was running.

The lightning flashed all about me and I almost didn't know where I was. I couldn't see through the pouring rain and the flurry of leaves and pine needles. The wind howled as though it shared in my despair.

After several frantic minutes, I found the creek bed and followed it, slipping in the mud and landing on my rear. At last, I reached home and dashed up the stairs, not wanting to think about what I had witnessed. I flung myself on my bed and didn't move all night.

The next morning dawned clear and red. When a lurid shaft of light pierced my lids, I realized I was abed an hour later than I should be, which was sure to earn me a whipping. As I rushed downstairs in the same bedraggled clothes I had worn the day before, I heard several hushed and urgent voices below.

I hit the bottom of the stairs and glanced around, frowning. My father was inside, which was unusual at this hour, and what was more, two men from the village stood in our doorway. Papa's arms were tightly wrapped around Mother, holding her as if afraid she'd slip away.

Then the group of them started out the door of one accord. I pounded after them.

It was the first time I'd seen anyone dead. The victim was Mr. Barham, the local barber. What was left of him has been left lying by the roadside just a few yards past the bend in the road, shielded from view of the town by pines. He'd been a mere fifty yards from the nearest house when he breathed his last.

By evening, he'd been hastily laid to rest in the churchyard after a quiet funeral, and his family gathered in the parson's home for comfort and a hot meal. The rest of us milled about outside, shell-shocked. Several men stood in a cluster at some distance, sternly discussing the horrific occurrence.

"He was torn apart," the doctor said at last. His voice was empty, stunned.

Released from the silence, one woman began to weep. Several friends drew together, and many children were sharply sent home. They swiftly obeyed, detecting the note of fear in their parents' voices.

"Did you hear what they're saying?" another woman whispered loudly to her friends. I edged cautiously away from my parents to hear more. "Some of the men are saying there was a man here last night, someone not from town. Several people saw him on the edge of the forest, walking about in the rain."

A few women recoiled or turned to each other worriedly, but many weathered mums of the village only nodded solemnly.

"Aye," one woman said. "Zadok was bringing in the livestock when he and the boys spotted him. They said he was tall and dressed in black."

"It was nobody *we* knew," our next-door neighbor put in timidly, cuddling her infant daughter closer.

The postmaster, who was standing near me, frowned. "Ladies, ladies! All this talk about a mysterious stranger and we already know who was walking through town last night."

Everyone stared at him, uncomprehending.

"Mr. Barham!" he exclaimed, motioning uncomfortably toward the fresh grave we had just left. "Maybe the only person anyone saw was him, and shortly afterward an animal killed him."

"But they said the tall stranger was wearing black," said a girl close to my age. "Mr. Barham was well-known and wearing white when they found him."

"How could you tell?" I murmured, remembering the mess of gore I had seen. I still can't forget it.

"Ugh!" Amity, one of the popular girls in town, shuddered and pressed herself back against her beau's chest, taking advantage of the atmosphere for a little canoodling. His arms tightened around her slim waist. "I want to move! When can we leave town?"

Another girl snorted. "And where would you go?"

"What if the man in black follows you?" added one of her lesser comrades.

"*Or* what if he's not real?" susurrated another snide voice.

Everyone straightened. Primrose Everly, the queen bee of the town, tossed her chestnut curls, which she'd "not had time" to put up in her hurry to see what was wrong. All of the boys struggled to keep their eyes off her and a few snickered to each other.

"*I* don't intend to throw away my life here just because someone says they saw a ghoul in the forest," she purred contemptuously.

"Maybe it's not safe to- "Amity began, but she was sharply hushed by the others.

Bored of this crowd's speculation, I scanned the crowd for Faith. I spotted her parents at the fringes of the men's circle, as reticent as she was. Then I saw her swath of black hair speeding through the crowd.

"Oh, thank goodness!" She raced to greet Theophilus, who had just arrived with the rest of the stragglers. In her relief, she threw her arms around his neck and kissed his cheek. This invited a few startled looks, but everyone quickly dismissed it, perhaps attributing it to overzealous neighborly concern. I rolled my eyes.

Theophilus blushed faintly and released her, trying to look into her face. "Are you all right?"

"Yes." She pursed her lips bravely, no doubt banishing the same gristly images which stained my own memory.

"Oh, Faith!" He pulled her close again, gripping the back of her head with one massive, spider-like hand. He allowed himself to rest his chin on her head and close his eyes briefly.

"Mr. Gladstone!" Mrs. Prescott called.

Faith's parents rushed over. They, too, appeared relieved to see him, and several other neighbors drew near. Faith wisely extracted herself and allowed the others to take over the discussion. Theophilus listened with interest to several different accounts of what had happened as everyone made their way toward town hall. The villagers seemed to relish the relief of unburdening themselves to someone to whom it was all still fresh.

He nodded a few times, looking thoughtful. "Have they already buried the body, then?" he asked with a tinge of what sounded like regret.

The question took everyone aback. A few people stared at him in surprise and dismay. It was Mr. Mueller, the town magistrate, who spoke up.

"Of course they did. It wasn't right to leave it out for everyone to stare at," Mr. Mueller replied, looking down his nose at him.

"Did you get a good look at it?" Theophilus was persistent.

"Yes! No. It is terribly inappropriate to be asking such questions, Mr. Gladstone, especially so soon after the burial!"

Theophilus frowned and stopped in his tracks. His voice was oddly soft and penetrating. "A man was killed outside your very door and you don't care to know how it happened?"

Mr. Mueller froze and turned to face him. His gaze was ice. "He was eviscerated, Mr. Gladstone. Tore the flesh from his limbs. There was barely enough of him left to give a clue who he was."

Theophilus's face went ashen. "Dear God," he murmured.

A few of the matrons clucked over him sympathetically, while others exchanged triumphant looks at someone having momentarily curbed his unhealthy curiosity. Mr. Mueller snorted, straightening his suit jacket, and went to join the other men.

The rest of the day was spent in subdued quiet. My chores flew by, the terrors of the morning making me long for the sweet absorption of normalcy. Many of the other youths met or whispered to each other, but Faith remained out of sight, whether at home or with Theophilus I didn't know.

Throughout the afternoon, three shifts of men patrolled the woods with muskets, looking for signs of an animal that could have thus destroyed a man, but with each shift's return, we received another sober shake of the head and downcast eyes.

Before evening, messengers were sent to the neighboring villages to see if they had any news of either beast or murderer. Per the second suggestion, all young people were corralled indoors promptly at sunset and not permitted to even walk to the neighbors' alone. It was a silent night, but nobody slept a wink.

At dawn, everyone gathered in the commons within half an hour, and all anxiously watched Mayor Hart speaking agitatedly with the small group of messengers. No one had been sent out alone, so there were six of them in all, exhausted from the journey and blanched white.

At last, Mayor Hart held up his hands for quiet. His face was florid and damp with sweat in spite of the morning chill, and he fidgeted with his collar.

"Yes, well. Our messengers have all done their duty, and we thank God for their safe return." He sounded choked, as if he had only wanted something to say to give him courage.

He cleared his throat and took a step forward. Everybody unconsciously leaned in.

"Well," he began again, "In Three Oaks, they have not heard of anything like what we've seen this week in Reason. But," he licked his lips and stared out over our heads, "it would appear that our friends in Templeton and Clayton have both had similar incidents. One person, a woman of about thirty, was killed just outside of Clayton a month ago, and before that there were four suspicious deaths of the same nature in Templeton. No one witnessed any of the crimes but," again he cleared his throat, "but rumors consistently point to a tall man in dark clothing seen prowling the edge of town around dusk."

There were several gasps and cries of fear. The mayor struggled to speak above the uproar.

"Though many have given a description of this man, no one knows who he is or has ever seen him except at a distance. Estimates of his age have widely varied, but the color of his skin has been consistently described as, well…grey."

With that, the mayor nodded nervously and allowed chaos to ensue. He had nothing further to add at the moment, and one of the messengers was gesturing furiously to him.

While the crowd squabbled over what this information could mean, I watched Mayor Hart curiously. He hurriedly joined the group of messengers, who appeared to be hotly disputing something. The messenger who had summoned the mayor put an arm around him and drew him in, whispering urgently in his ear. The mayor was shaking his head.

"Horatio!"

I jumped. I hadn't heard my father approach.

He laid a hand on my shoulder and murmured in my ear, "Be a good lad and take your mother home. She's badly frightened, but I need to stay here and keep an ear out for news. Go on, son."

He gave me a push, but I turned back to throw my arms around him for an instant. His gentle tone told me more than his words did; he was badly shaken. He embraced me tightly before letting go and turning quickly away to join the other men. I took a deep breath and held out my arm.

"Come on, Mum. Let's go home."

As I threw one last glance into the crowd of our frightened friends and neighbors, I caught sight of Faith standing on the other side of the commons. Her own face was tense with fear, but she had her arms wrapped around her mother and was rocking her reassuringly. Her father was talking with the group of men. For a moment, Faith's and my eyes met. We were both afraid, but we had families to be strong for. Without a word, I turned down our street and hurried my mother home.

Chapter Four

The following week was dreadful. A more commonplace tragedy might have proved an interesting topic of conversation, but this incident was far too gruesome and unearthly to be enjoyed. Every interaction was carried out in a tense hush that made one want to scream. The adults became agitated and overprotective to the point of driving us mad. The youths both chafed against the increased restraint of their movements and yet remained terrified as children.

Still, there were no more attacks, and the week passed in relative safety.

During the first few days after the attack, Faith's visits to Theophilus had to be more and more discreet. I benefited because her parents would never allow her to travel into the forest alone and my services as her escort were often appreciated. I did not always venture to go visiting *with* her, per se, as she clearly wanted to be alone with Theophilus, so I often told her I would be in the area and come back when she was ready to go home.

Though determined to see her friend, Faith was no fool and always made it back to town before sunset. My own mother, too, occasionally started a row at our house, but I managed to tame her fears by always making it back before dark. I wasn't yet ready to discuss my tenderer feelings with my own family and didn't mention Faith, though by now I'm sure they knew. But whenever we spoke of my evening journeys, it was referred to as my evening stroll. *An evening stroll with Faith.* What a lovely thought!

One night, however, the threat of the intruder became chillingly real to us.

After a veritable feast of produce from Theophilus's garden, the two had gotten carried away with talking, and I was too abashed to try and hurry them. Still, the sunlight glimmered orange over the horizon as Faith and I set out at a trot for home.

One minute we were hastening through the forest with only shadows among the trees, and the next an outline was startlingly visible: a man in black stood not thirty yards away, separated from us by underbrush and a tangle of trees.

Faith stopped, and the figure slowed as well, mirroring her. She paused for a long moment, and it turned toward us, though we could not see a face. Suddenly, she broke into a run, I upon her very heels. The figure set off, as well, but like no living being I'd ever seen. While we leapt over roots and dashed through small depressions in the dirt, he seemed to glide, and sped up until he had shot past us and out of sight. Neither of us turned our heads once until we had left the forest behind us at a sprint.

When we'd reached the main stretch of houses, both of us bent over, gasping.

"Did you see it?" Faith exclaimed. "Did you see it?"

I glanced over my shoulder and shuddered. For once, I didn't want to prolong the conversation with her. "We need to get home. Now."

As I walked Faith to her door, I hardly heard a word she said. Word spread throughout the village with such urgency that the news reached home before I did. I was forbidden to take any more walks just before dark.

Soon, reports of similar incidents began to multiply. Following this, Faith only managed to get away to visit Theophilus three or four days a week at most. She was twice as reluctant to leave his side for fear that his living so far outside the town would place him in harm's way and she fussed over him until he was quite exasperated.

Since their display in the commons after the first attack, both were more reserved in their affection, but the warmth between them was painfully evident as they clasped each other's hands across the kitchen table. Theophilus was most afraid for her safety, and I came to see that his irritation when she worried over him was because it pained him so to see her distressed. Many a cup of milk and eventually, as the days grew colder, many a mug of hot chocolate was shared amid somber discussion of what could drive a human being to such savagery. Many of their theories were uncommonly disturbing and I won't repeat them, for they still make my hair stand on end.

The attacks marked where Theophilus's path began to diverge from that of the rest of the town. While everyone gibbered over wild animals and murderers and fear for their children, he pursued his own ends, writing to colleagues in the other towns and receiving replies startling in both quantity and rapidity. He was unwilling to speculate with the rest of the town and soon drew some petty resentment. I heard many spurious conjectures about his lack of fear, but for once I took no satisfaction in their disapproval of Faith's lover, for I knew the truth. His actions were governed by one great fear that was dear to us both.

Eventually, however, even he and Faith began to argue. Theophilus's contacts appeared to know more about the attacks than anyone else in town, but this did little to allay his or Faith's fears. His explanations were partial and mysterious and only begged darker questions than before. He tried to impart what he knew without frightening her further, but the more he said, the more alarmed she became.

At last, Theophilus gave up explaining himself altogether, though he did not cease his inquiries, and he took to soothing his frightened love instead. My temporary peace with him was sharply tested when his long, tanned fingers stroked the backs of her graceful hands, he quieted her tears with ample kisses, or even had the audacity to pluck her off her chair and set her on his knee. Faith responded tenderly to these unseemly advances, and I occasionally considered abandoning my post altogether. She was with another man; why should I care what became of her now? But my young heart wouldn't be so easily turned aside, and I maintained my watch over her.

Only three weeks passed between the first attack and its sequel. The second victim was a young man from the opposite end of town whom I didn't know very well. He was delirious for three days before succumbing to his wounds. The marks were the same, deep gouges made as if by claws all over his body, concentrated around his neck and shoulders. He would tell us nothing of the attacks but repeated over and over that his attacker had hissed like an animal.

This obviously increased the level of terror in the village, and I heard Faith had had a dreadful fight with her parents in order to maintain her visits to the cabin. Even then, she only managed to go once a week.

Faith began to scare me, seeming weepy and distracted when she had always been sensible and focused before. The direness of the situation made me dare to converse with her when I could, probing for some indication of her state of mind, but she shut me out with everyone else, dodging underlying questions with her usual skill. It made me wonder how Theophilus had managed to coax out the intensely inquisitive, almost exotic side of her nature in the first place. How had he known it would be there? Somewhere in my heart after all was said and done, I understood: he had offered her a glimpse into his world, and the similarity in their spirits had drawn them together. As for the way he smiled even when she exasperated him and she looked past his flaws, love had done the rest.

Late one evening, Faith had managed to wrestle herself away from home about an hour before sunset.

Theophilus beckoned her to sit with him in his back room. The back door was open, letting the crisp autumn air in without leaving them bereft of the kitchen stove's warmth. Though I had told Faith I was going fishing, I planted myself a mere ten yards from his door, hidden by underbrush. She sat across from him on a low wicker basket, wrapping her cloak more closely around her. He was ensconced in a dark wooden chair with high arms and a deep green cushion, one gangly leg crossed over the other and a piece of paper in his hand. It was clear he had something important to say.

He gazed down his nose at her from where he rested his head against the corner of the two walls, then seemed to think better of it. He rested his forearms on his legs, purposely setting the paper aside, and held out his hands. She took them and forced a wary smile.

"Faith, some disturbing news has reached me that will quickly reach the town. I wanted to tell you before anyone else so you would not be shocked and could offer support for the others. This letter I have here is from an attorney in Marbury, far north of here."

Faith nodded; we knew the place. Theophilus took a deep breath as though assessing her, then wrapped both his hands around one of hers, stroking it deliberately as though willing her to understand.

"Faith, it's not a happy story, nor one which is easy to believe."

Her eyes widened and she sat stock-still, her face white. His fingers stopped their stroking and tightened around her hand until her fingers turned pale.

"Upwards of twenty people have been attacked the

same way in the past year. Some are saying the culprit is a creature."

Faith frowned. "I thought you said it didn't match any animal you'd ever studied."

Theophilus nodded gravely. "No animal did this. I speak of a monster."

Faith slowly shook her head. "A monster? You mean...a person who is out of his senses?"

"No," he said sharply. "I mean a creature of evil, perhaps something spoken of in myth and legend."

Faith looked mystified and not sure whether to believe him or laugh.

"I wouldn't have believed it without this." He handed her the letter. "The signed testimony of ten sane, reasoning people, some of whom I know, corroborating the same facts. Where this tale began, it's consistent, and that is not a common feature among tall tales."

Faith's lips parted and her head nodded slightly as she read. Incredulity replaced confusion as she looked back up at Theophilus. "Do you actually mean to say you believe this? That something from the spirit world is stalking our village?"

He raised his palms, fixing her with his stare. "What explanation is left?"

She forced a laugh and gestured vaguely. "An animal, or a deranged man!"

Once again, Theophilus shook his head. His seriousness made his words the more horrifying. "Every report of its behavior sets it at once somewhere between man and beast and somewhere beyond both. Think, Faith. If it were an animal, it would either be defending its territory or hunting for food. Based on where the attacks have taken place and what remained of the bodies, clearly neither is the case."

Faith's voice quavered. "Then a man," she said softly, but with less conviction.

He raised one pale eyebrow incredulously. "A deranged man might use a number of methods of attack, but slashing with claws is a new one on me. He kills people left and right, spanning many miles, without making any attempt to hide what he's done. He takes nothing from them and leaves nothing behind. How could such a person pass through several villages, murdering townsfolk, and never leave any trace of himself?"

"The people saw someone-"

"Yes, and so did you." Faith froze, and Theophilus added gently, "Did that thing that chased you and that boy seem at all human to you?"

She trembled but made no answer. Instead she asked, "What do *you* think it is?"

Theophilus sighed and rubbed the back of his neck. "Once a few more of my colleagues' contacts reply to my letters, I shall know more."

"But *you*- You really believe that some monstrosity out of a myth is coming to get us?" she murmured.

Theophilus's jaw tightened. "Myths are the stories people tell to explain what they don't understand. There is too much evidence for this to be a hoax. Something is out there killing innocent people, and I want to do something about it!"

Her eyes narrowed in horror. "Like *what*?"

"Search for facts!" He paced, gesturing sharply with

his hands. "Talk to people who know more about the attacks. Learn who the victims generally are. Scrutinize the marks the monster leaves behind. Track where it hunts. Sooner or later, some pattern or clue is bound to arise."

"But *why*?" She sounded frantic. "What good will it do you?"

He put his hands on her shoulders. "A known evil is easier to face, Faith. There are plenty of stories about how to banish or even kill evil beings. Plenty of them are probably superstition, but there may be something we can use. We will study the poison to produce the antidote. The tools may be within our reach!"

"And then what?" she challenged. "Are you going to hunt this monster?"

"Maybe!" he shot back. "I'm certainly not going to cower behind a band of villagers with pitchforks and wait for the situation to resolve itself!"

Faith shook her head, trying to calm both him and herself. "Theo, you don't have to do this. Once the rest of the town learns about the other attacks, the mayor or- or Reverend Thornton will mobilize everyone. I'm sure they'll figure out what to do. We'll all face this together."

Theophilus pursed his lips but said nothing. He stood stiffly and prowled into the kitchen.

Faith watched him uneasily. "What?"

He turned toward her. "Faith, you know where we live. This is Reason. Where people are taught the necessities of life and a few scraps of Scripture. How can such knowledge stand up against the unknown, even the occult?"

"Theophilus," she began, trying to calm herself, "what do you think this is? Truly."

He sighed in exasperation but lowered his voice. "Every culture has its name for the things that go bump in the night. The Bible tells us of demons and other spiritual powers. All we know is that there is evil in this world. And sometimes it takes a form that is neither animal nor human." He leaned forward and took her hands. "But when one of the Enemy's fiends takes a step into the light, be it man or monster, I choose not to shrink back, but to learn about the enemy before engaging it."

She shook her head. "I don't like this. This is the work of ministers and hunters, not of people like us."

"The leaders of the village, ministers included, will have enough to do to keep the people from panicking. Some would be too afraid to even find the answers if they knew where to look. It has to be me, if only because I am willing to face the facts."

Her voice had gone shrill. "And maybe they're right to fear! Leave this madness before something worse happens."

"Something has to be done!"

"Leave this!"

"No." It was like a thunderclap.

Never had he so flatly contradicted her. Her face blanched with anger, but in spite of herself, her flashing eyes welled with tears. "Theophilus, this is more than science. This is the supernatural. If it's as you say-"

He took her arms and bent toward her earnestly. "Then we're going to need every defense we can manage!"

Her lower lip trembled even while it was pursed with rage. "-this is something much more powerful and dangerous than the stars in the sky or the animals in the creek! This is blood and spirits and if you get caught up in it, you'll be poking about in practices our Creator forbids with good reason. If you cross a line, it could all turn out worse than just a monster. I don't want to lose you!"

He tried to talk over her, but she persisted, drawing herself up so that they were almost nose-to-nose. "You're playing with fire, Theophilus! You're going to put us in danger of-"

"We're already in danger!" he shouted, pulling away from her. "And that's not going to change until we do something about it, something other than leaving the future in the hands of a group of frightened parents who think if they study the earth that they reject heaven!" He rested his fists on the tabletop and struggled to control his ragged breathing.

Faith's eyes were wide and the tears had started to leak down her cheeks, but her gaze burned, burned until I thought it would light the collar of his shirt on fire. "You're going...to get...yourself...killed."

She stalked out of the room, her heels rapping deliberately on the floorboards. Theophilus's head shot up as she yanked open the front door.

She turned back to look at him, her eyes still smoldering. "And then where will *I* be?"

With that, she stepped off the porch and marched for the edge of the clearing. I trailed after her just outside the clearing, uncertain whether to make myself known. Only once she had gone a few yards did she allow herself to burst into sobs. Still she held her head high and let the tears stream down, unapologetic.

All the anger had drained from Theophilus's face, leaving only ashen fear in its place. His big hands started to tremble. In a split second, he had cleared the doorframe and was striding across the lawn faster and more smoothly than anyone I'd ever seen. He easily outpaced her.

Faith did not turn or slow down. She was quite near me when Theophilus tried to step in front of her, but she easily slipped around him. In that second, I saw that the blue fire was gone from his eyes, leaving behind only sadness and undisguised longing.

He started after her again, this time grabbing hold of her hand and spinning her around to face him. She met his eye fiercely, but he gripped her arms and pressed her to his chest. He wrapped his arms around her tightly and rested his cheek on her forehead, like a child holding onto its last and dearest comforting plaything.

"Faith..." His voice trembled like that of someone half his age. "I'm trying to do what I think is right. It's dangerous, but everything is. Doing the right thing is dangerous. Living's dangerous."

He paused, still not letting her go. He even rocked a little from side to side. Still silently weeping, she was softening.

"I try to keep my relationship with God strong, but the way these people live seems contradictory to the loving Maker I know. Sometimes," he lifted his head and looked down into her face, "sometimes he works a miracle through the prayers of holy men and women, but sometimes he puts the tools within our reach long before we know we need them. If there is anything I can do, I need to know I tried to find it. Even if it's risky."

His eyes sought the horizon. "I've read about creatures like this. In Europe, usually, but there are myths, legends. Information we can use. The reverend will quickly be on the right track, but I don't want to wait for the common folk to panic and start burning villages. They will. They always do." He looked down at her again. A tear dripped from his eye onto the bridge of her nose. "We're in danger *now*. I can't let it hurt you, because then it would be my fault. I would know that I could have tried something to keep you safe and I didn't, and life would be insupportable. I've crossed the threshold, Faith. There's no going back."

Faith's eyes were pierced with sorrow, and she gazed lovingly at her man. Theophilus dropped his face to the top of her head, burying it in her hair. "But I can't do this without knowing that wherever you are, you're behind me. Without your support, I won't be at my optimum, and I'm going to need everything I've got. Faith, do I have your support in whatever I have to do?"

When he lifted his face again, brushing at the tendrils of hair he had loosened with his nuzzling, she was nodding.

"I will be with you," she promised softly. "You will never be abandoned by me."

The scientist heaved a great sigh and drew her closer, engulfing her.

A small smile touched her lips. "And I will help you with whatever-"

"No," he murmured tenderly, kissing the bridge of her nose.

Faith frowned in alarm and pulled away so she could meet his eye. "Theophilus, I will not let you do this alone!"

"I said I needed your support, and now I have it." He met her gaze and kissed her furrowed brow. "But I'll not have my angel going where even fools know to fear to tread."

With that, he tucked her against his side and slowly walked back to the cabin, all the way sneaking kisses on the side of her head. Faith raised one eyebrow and said nothing, but the instant they were inside she was armed with new arguments.

In the end, it was Theophilus who prevailed. He made her swear to keep a list of foreboding rules, all meant to keep her out of harm's way. Faith, however, inevitably managed to locate its loopholes.

Together, their studies took on a nature that, if known, could ruin the reputations of them both.

Chapter Five

The following week was a trying one, for as soon as Theophilus was packed the following morning, he set off, keeping his destination quiet and his absence almost secret. Faith was in charge of continuing certain parts of their projects while he was out. For my part, I couldn't even guess what she was up to, and she said nothing to anyone about it. Several parcels were sent to the house under Theophilus's name, and she secreted them carefully in the cubbies.

In these times, I paid less attention to what Faith was doing in my concern for the woman herself. She looked gaunt at times though her flesh remained healthy, for it was her spirit which suffered in her lover's long absences. In the space of a month, he had gone away three separate times for a week or more each. Upon his return, he was always careful not to say a word about it until he and Faith were carefully shut up inside the cabin. This meant that for the first time, I was ignorant of their plans. The cold also kept me from staying long, so I often settled for just walking

Faith to and from Theophilus's cottage.

To make matters worse, the rumor of a sort of vampire or some other supernatural being reached the village. That wasn't the extent of the stories from the north, however. The messengers had at last managed to distill a singular message, corroborated by several people.

They all said that the killings had begun in Marbury following the death of one Archibald Carter. Carter had been an old innkeeper and unremarkable enough. Some ten years ago he'd found himself in dire straits, losing money faster than a man with a hole in his pocket. One night, he had gone out for a walk alone, oddly shaken when he left. His wife spent the night waiting in terror, cursing herself for not insisting she go with him.

When he came back in the morning, however, he was a different man. He grew strong and cheerful, all signs of the hard years gone from his visage. No more did he worry or obsessively count money, but slept like a baby and dressed like he was going somewhere important. It was as if he had the energy of a younger man.

No one could figure out where the money was coming from, though many tried. Mr. Carter seemed utterly confident in his good fortune. He repaid his debts and became fabulously generous with his friends and neighbors. Within another week, he was speculating in real estate.

The only other odd thing was that he'd begun to always wear a bandage on one wrist. Discreetly covered by his sleeve, it wasn't noticed until one day a friend of his spotted blood leaking through. When he'd mentioned it, Carter had gone ghastly white and become uncharacteristically hostile, practically threatening him if he said anything about it while simultaneously swearing it was nothing.

Some time later, his wife noticed another distressing pattern. Before every turn of good luck, Carter not only seemed to know it was coming, but had a ritual: the very night before, he waited until he thought his wife was asleep, then slipped out of the house and came back a few hours later looking grey and worn. He rewrapped his arm, then went to bed, and in the morning, they always awoke to good news about one of his investments. Once, she decided to follow him, but whatever she saw, she never spoke of it, only becoming quiet and grave and asking even fewer questions about her husband's money.

But then, several months ago, Carter was visiting the owner of a coal mine and was killed in an explosion. Carter was given a rapid funeral and his money fell to his widow and portions were sent off to their grown children.

It was around then that the tall, darkly clad figure first came calling. It was seen pacing agitatedly beside the wreck of the mine and Carter's fresh grave. Some said the being sniffed like a dog as though it were searching for something. If anyone tried to address the being, it fled into the woods without turning back. After about a fortnight, it was no longer seen beside the house or the graves.

Then the killings began. Within a month, four people had been murdered, torn apart like old Mr.

Barham and the others would later be. Some said Archibald Carter had sold his soul to the devil in exchange for his fortune, but as more and more people began to turn up dead, that theory was upstaged by the theory of the vampire. None of the victims' blood had been drained, but several people had seen the monster crouching beside his victims, frantically sniffing at them before giving up and disappearing with a snarl.

It was a puzzling narrative, and a macabre one, and met with a volatile mixture of skepticism, uncertainty, and outright terror. You can imagine the frenzied prayers, rites, and superstitions in which many townspeople engaged. Doors and windows were tightly fastened from dusk to daylight, social calls were curbed, and all visitors to the town were regarded with scathing distrust. Even so, by the beginning of October, two more victims had been buried.

Nevertheless, Faith valiantly planted daffodils in the garden of briars. She began to gradually introduce Theophilus to her family after church on Sundays. Soon, he was invited to share meals with them. I knew she was grooming them to accept him as her suitor, perhaps one day her betrothed. They seemed to like him well enough and showed a polite interest in his work, but I suspect his more radical ideas were mostly kept between him and Faith.

All seemed to be progressing nicely (for her, not me) until her happy little vision was shattered by the obliviousness to Theophilus in which her family was rooted. One afternoon she ran into Theophilus's arms at the cottage, unable to speak for several minutes through her sobs. When at last he managed to get the truth out of her, he, too, was stung: her family had introduced to her a young man they pronounced her first suitor. I, too, felt this blow, for my own sake. It meant that both our interests in Faith had gone unrecognized. In my case, it was understandable given my attempts at secrecy, but Faith had done everything in her power to introduce Theophilus as a possibility. If her father wouldn't acknowledge Theophilus's suit, it was as good as outright rejection in the public eye. Though the girls of Reason were known to choose their own beaus, when it came to marriage the town was remarkably serious, and Faith dearly wanted her parents to love her husband, too. And so, Faith and Theophilus's romance was forced to weather its first bitter frost of rejection.

The town, meanwhile, had grown first paranoid, then vigilant, later restless, and finally bored. Weeks passed with no sign of danger, and life more or less resumed its accustomed pace. But the fear never left a single threshold; desperate for any change in circumstance, people were all too willing to find someone to blame. Suspicion engulfed the village like a silent inferno, burning trust and companionship like chaff and kindling every petty dislike or vague impression into something near hatred. It was always there, ready to lunge at the first sight of a stranger. Every eye pierced like a hawk's, tearing aside normalcy and trust until I felt gloomy and hunted merely from having breathed the pungent vapors of universal suspicion.

Somehow, Faith still managed to help Theophilus

with his research. The two had become increasingly secretive, but even the little I had seen would be enough to cause public outcry. Once, I heard them fighting about certain books which had arrived.

"You may not have been before, but *now* you're dabbling and I want you to stop!" Faith said shrilly.

Theophilus's voice was calmer and harder to hear, but I did catch this much: "Studying and participating are two very different things, my dear. Don't worry about me."

"But if your intent is to track down some kind of manifestation of evil and- and confront it or something, isn't that participation?"

Again, Theophilus remained oddly cool. "Summoning or communing with evil is witchcraft. Sending it back where it came from is biblical, and that's all I intend to do."

Faith's voice had turned pleading. "But isn't that something for a minister to do? What if you can't face it yourself?"

Though I couldn't see him, I could imagine him counting his reasons on his fingers. "First, I intend to go in prepared. Second, some things must be done by whoever is willing. Third, if I can't, I trust you to call in the cavalry."

We both knew on the latter point that he was being facetious, but it quieted Faith for the moment. She helped him unpack a strange-looking suitcase inside. I had kept my distance, drawing in the dirt with a stick, but as Faith's exclamations grew louder, I stood up, intending to investigate.

That was the one time they acknowledged having

spotted me and invited me in to share hot cider. The suitcase had been whisked away by the time I entered, and I tried not to betray my familiarity with the place as I moved about.

It was an awkward meeting, one in which they chatted merrily and I tried to figure out whether they knew how often I spied on them. They said nothing of their dark studies, but as I was leaving I saw that several of the letters on an end table were from Marbury. That must have been where he'd been going. How like the scientist to go straight to the source.

One night, however, I was at last able to hear their theories. Faith was daring enough to slip out after sunset, for she had been tied up with chores all day. I would have missed the opportunity had I not heard her promise him (for they had crossed paths in the market that day) that she would come that night, come hell or high water. Hoping she wouldn't but knowing she would, I waited by my window with my jacket in my lap and took off as soon as I saw her slip by in the growing gloom.

Upon her arrival, the two of them gathered a couple of old blankets from inside the house and disappeared into the back. For a moment I dared question Faith's integrity. Moments later, however, I saw them scampering up onto the roof from the back of the house. They must have climbed up the woodpile. Grinning like a pair of truant schoolchildren, they spread out a blanket and reclined side by side, leaning back on their elbows to look up at the stars.

For some time, I can imagine what they were saying. Their faces were soft with happy smiles, and each often found an excuse to brush aside a wisp of the other's hair or straighten their companion's collar. When their expressions turned serious, however, I crept near enough to hear.

"What I've come to believe," Theophilus said slowly, absentmindedly piling the bits of grass which clung to the blanket, "is that while our creature *is* a vampire of sorts, it is not limited to any one place during the day, and since it chased you at sunset, it must not be harmed by the light."

Faith bit her lip. "But the creature deviates from the mythical vampire in other ways." She cracked a smile. "But I suppose you've thought of that."

Theophilus nodded, a faint smile of approval on his face. "I've got a theory."

He flipped over onto his stomach so he could gesture with both hands. Faith copied him and scooted closer. To my annoyance, the familiar stab of jealousy returned to torment me.

"According to my friends in Marbury," Theophilus continued, "the place Carter went was known by locals as a haunted place, a deep, dark stretch of woods full of the supernatural and all manner of evils. No one in their right mind would go there after dark, except those who were later tried as witches. Carter was raised on those stories and he went there knowingly. When he left home that night, he was up to his eyes in debt, but upon his return, all was suddenly and without explanation restored." Theophilus raised one eyebrow grimly. "Immediately following his death, this vampire begins haunting the village. What does that sound like to you?"

Faith frowned, her eyes glowing keenly. "Strange that it would only appear *after* he'd died," she said. "But it sounds like his wife saw him leave for a visit to the woods every time he wanted something. And the blood on his wrist...Is that why you think it's a vampire?"

Theophilus shook his head. "Not a vampire exactly, but something like it. Vampires aren't the only mythical creatures that drink blood. Some ancient rulers even drank their enemies' blood in order to gain their abilities. Some especially dark spells," he said carefully, watching her, "also involve blood. It's closely tied, both physically and metaphorically, to life."

She pursed her lips. "Do you think they had some kind of bargain, Carter and this being?"

"That's exactly what I think."

"So Carter was selling his lifeblood for monetary gain." She tilted her head from side to side as though debating how it sounded. "It's plausible. But what about the other victims?"

Theophilus pursed his lips. "It's difficult to say. It's possible it *did* drink their blood. Since Carter was, we have to assume, only bleeding at the wrist for that purpose, it must not need too much."

Faith sighed in exasperation. "What I don't understand is why the creature only started appearing outside of the forest after Carter was gone. Do you think the being *was* Carter?"

Theophilus shook his head decidedly. "No. If it had been anyone they knew, the townsfolk would have latched onto that. It was a stranger."

She nodded. "Why didn't it begin hunting as soon as Carter summoned it or set it loose or whatever he did?"

Theophilus shrugged. "It probably knew Carter would keep coming back. But once he was dead, it set out to find him." He suddenly sat up straighter. "Wait. Do you remember what the stories said about the beast kneeling beside its victims? No one ever saw it drink their blood, but several sources saw it sniffing around their neck and then leaving, seemingly frustrated."

Faith's frown deepened. "So...what are you saying?"

"I'm not sure yet. It's just the beginning of an idea. But the creature is seemingly content to stay in the forest and have Carter bring it his blood, yes? And once Carter stops coming, the beast emerges to search, stopping at the place where Carter died. Add to that the seeming desire but inability to drink its other victims' blood, and it seems like..." He threw up his hands at the incomplete thought. "Somehow it has to be Carter. For some reason it needs *his* blood in particular."

Faith sighed impatiently. "But Mr. Carter is *dead*! There is no more blood! Why does it keep hunting for him?"

Their conversation trailed off. For several minutes, the only sounds were the chirps and rustles of the woods around us, too much like the place Theophilus had described for my liking.

Suddenly, Faith whirled to face Theophilus. "Didn't you say Mr. Carter had three grown children? They have his blood! Do you think that counts? What if the creature finds them?"

The two huddled closer and silently held each other for a moment while the terrible thought sank in.

Theophilus shook his head, reassuring himself as well as her. "They- they live far away. It won't be able to find them. As long as they stay there, they'll be safe."

Faith gazed at him soberly. "And what about the rest of us? It may not be able to sustain itself from our blood but it's been willing to kill even so, maybe just for spite!"

Theophilus was silent for a moment. He tucked Faith's head under his chin and absently rubbed her back. "We'll think of something," was all he said.

A horrible scream rent the night. Both of them sat bolt upright and Theophilus grabbed for his knife. For my part, I didn't stay to witness the rest. My instincts got a hold of me and I ran for home with all the strength I possessed, and I didn't stop until I was hidden under my covers.

In the morning, however, I heard what had happened. Another victim had been claimed, and practically on Theophilus's doorstep. At the sound of the scream, Theophilus had stowed Faith inside before sprinting out after the monster like a plain fool while the villagers tended to the victim. He came back the next morning worn out and dew-soaked, but none the wiser.

The victim was Hester Williams, and miraculously she had survived. She was carried back to town, murmuring deliriously about how a creature had tried to bite her neck. The wounds on her arms and body were bandaged, and by morning she didn't remember a thing. But Theophilus had his theories. I know; I made sure to tail Faith back to the cottage the instant she went, because they were the only ones who didn't stink of garlic during this madness and I wanted to know what they thought.

Theophilus was fidgeting about the garden, impatiently awaiting her return. "I've got a theory!" he said the instant she drew near. "The wounds from the more recent victims were notably shallower than the previous ones, yes? And this time Hester's wounds weren't even enough to kill her! As it travels south, its attacks have grown less frequent, though more desperate. The longer it goes without nourishment from Carter, I propose that it grows weaker. It's weakening, Faith!" He stood beaming at her triumphantly.

Could it be? The weight on my heart to which I'd grown accustomed suddenly shifted. What if it really was this strange man whose theories would save us all?

With that, they went inside and I heard no more.

Chapter Six

For a week, our little town's somber condition remained stable. No new bloodied corpses were found, no dark strangers were seen prowling the village at night, and every tenuous suspicion was left to root and fester.

Near the middle of October, that mock-stability was shattered, and to this day the town of Reason has never quite righted itself. Everyone went to bed one night in a typical state of health. When the town awoke, however, eight young ladies about Faith's age lay bedridden with a mysterious sickness.

Theophilus's predictions of panic did not go unanswered. At noon, a crowd of women had gathered just outside the church, begging for God to save their children and to rid the village of this menace. Under ordinary circumstances it would be supposed that some sort of plague was sweeping the village, but the illness's concentration in young virgin women fit too well with the vampire folklore in constant circulation. By evening, the reverend had been called to more than one young lady's bedside for fear she would pass in the night.

Tense days followed. God must have heard the mothers' prayers, however, for at last morning dawned upon a village mostly relieved of the pestilence. The young women rallied, though some but slowly. It was later discovered that some young men had also fallen ill, but had been treated as another case entirely, in favor of theories that a vampire had overtaken the young ladies' will.

Pearce, the town apothecary, had been at his wits' end, dashing from house to house in those first days. When at last the crisis had died down, however, and he'd had time to collect himself and review his notes, he pronounced a dreadful conclusion: the victims had been suffering under the effects of ricin poisoning.

Made from the same plant as castor oil, he said it was powerful enough that consuming even one whole castor bean should've killed the strongest. As sick as it made them, the youths must have consumed a truly minuscule amount to have recovered.

Many thought it must have been an accident. Young people were careless; maybe they had eaten something that looked like a berry out in the woods. But Pearce averred that it was impossible. If anyone had eaten a whole bean, which they would have done if it had been an accident, they would've certainly died. The low concentration in so many of them meant it must have been in something they had all partaken of. Besides, the plant was extremely rare this far north. It would be too much for the poisoning to have been anything but deliberate.

The druggist carefully examined each of the patients to look for a common source from which they had eaten or drank. Failing this, he tested several communal food sources and the water from every well, but to no avail. The source of the poison was nowhere to be found. The plant, however, would be easy enough to spot. It was rare and distinctive-looking, and given its African origins, one would have to go to some pains to acquire it.

Only Theophilus Gladstone was known to possess one. In the face of ireful questioning, he replied that he kept it for making castor oil and because the spiky red plant fascinated him on its own merit. This single piece of evidence was enough to unleash the entire flood of fear and anxiety of the town upon his blond head.

When the findings were announced in the square, a gasp arose. Faith clung to Theophilus's hand, but soon a flock of angry parents of victims was bearing down on them. I shall never forget the cry Faith emitted when he was torn from her, and the childlike sorrow and utter loneliness in his eyes when they were separated.

With some difficulty, he was wrested away from the angry villagers and carted off to the jail, perhaps more for his own safety than theirs.

Twelve grueling hours of questioning ensued while the whole town held its breath. Evidence was scant, and a hopeful Pearce affirmed that with the right knowledge, anyone could have made the poison. Theophilus's plant grew in a special box on a windowsill where it could absorb sunlight without being chilled to death, so it was just possible that someone had taken a bit without his knowing. Theophilus's unique scientific background, however, worked against him, and the entire town had been ravenous for a culprit for too long.

Finally, Pearce demanded that Mr. Gladstone's house be searched for further signs of his having prepared the poison. While Theophilus was not popular, he was not utterly disliked. More than one family smiled at each other in relief when the search was proposed. Soon the truth would be uncovered and his innocence revealed, and quite a store of motherly clucking was likely in his future.

When the investigators returned, however, their faces ranged from scarlet to ashen. They were escorted into the town hall to present their findings, but it was quickly known that now they must consider a different and far more dire charge: Theophilus was accused of witchcraft.

At this, Faith lost her senses. She paled until I thought she would faint, then frantically shouted to everyone in the vicinity that his studies would only look suspicious if one didn't understand them. She cried out that Theophilus was not dangerous. He was her friend, a Christian, and would never engage in witchcraft.

The bailiff exited the town hall and wordlessly wrapped his arms around his wife. She murmured a question and he shuddered. Even Faith's voice died away amid the murmurs. Soon her family had whisked her silently away.

Through the neighbors, I learned that in their terror that she would be tarred with the same brush, her family overwhelmed her with prayers and pious tasks, insisting on making her innocence as visible as possible. She wore pastel colors and took communion every day. Her downcast eyes, however, contained a misery from which no one could free her.

I must admit, my own nerve almost broke during the ensuing days. It was all too much for a daydreaming boy of seventeen, and the involvement of my sweetheart made it worse. Everything I knew was shifting under me and nothing felt certain anymore. How I longed to return to the languishing summer days in which I had merely followed Faith around, pretending she was mine and unaware of anything more than Theophilus's name.

I was pasturing the flock when Theophilus was brought before Mr. Mueller, the respected old town magistrate. Only adult men were allowed to attend and virtually every townsman was present. I did not want to view the proceedings; I'd had more than enough of fear and accusations for my taste, and I couldn't look again on that bowed head and hopeless gaze. Knowing as much as I did but almost certain I couldn't prove anything filled me first with guilt, then despair. I planned to ply my father for details when he returned home.

On my way to drink from the creek, however, I found Faith sprawled upon a small rise. It was the place where I'd once found her reading to Theophilus. Arms, hair, skirts were splayed in a gesture of defeat. It looked like she had fallen and simply neglected to rise.

At the sound of my footsteps, she hastily sat up.

Seeing it was me, however, she remained where she was, wrapping her arms around her knees and wiping at the helpless downpour of tears with the back of her hand. My breath at last returned to me in a shuddering sigh.

"Oh, Horatio," she quavered as fresh tears fell. "They've sentenced Theophilus to death."

I dropped my waterskin and dashed to her side, falling upon my knees. My arms reached out of their own accord. With a rasping sob, she collapsed into me. I held her, and yet I felt no magic, heard no heavenly song, only the splintering of a human heart.

All at once, the spell which had been cast upon me sometime in the spring was broken. I clasped her tighter, amazed as a few silent tears spilled down my own face at the unfairness of it all: of unrequited love and of love that was returned and yet still doomed, of daydreaming summers followed by ghastly autumns. For several minutes, I held Faith Prescott not as a lover, but as a friend.

That night I went to bed utterly spent, and in the morning I rose from restless oblivion to another day of dread. I had not asked Faith any questions; she had not been up to it. Now I resolved to find my answers. I dressed in my warmest cloak and went into town.

The commons were a battlefield of sordid details, of which I gathered as many as I could though I took no pleasure in it. When they had come to search Theophilus's house, the investigators had found no evidence of his having concocted the poison. Instead, they had found a map of the creature's attacks with dates and descriptions, several bundles of herbs and unrecognizable concoctions, an enormous quantity of salt, and a huge stack of books and letters on the subject of vampires and the occult.

The damning detail, however, consisted of a sketchbook filled with anatomical drawings of the most recent victims, along with the carcass of an animal apparently killed in the same way. To make matters worse, they had discovered a patch of freshly-turned earth in which was buried another animal victim.

Theories varied wildly as to what he'd been doing, but the evidence was enough to condemn him. He was to be hanged in two days' time; no one wanted a dabbler in the occult to remain long in their presence. A few reasoned that he'd been summoning or even controlling the monster and that once he was gone, the creature would leave us alone. The majority, however, remained convinced that he *was* the monster. Garlic was gathered from wherever it could be found, and many walked with silver crucifixes around their necks.

Eventually, I tired of their speculation and left. I had to see Faith. I found her in her parents' barn, stowed away at last from their attempts to evince her innocence. She was seated on an overturned pail and looked even worse than the night before. Her bent form was the picture of despair.

"Faith," I started softly.

She rounded on me, her wild eyes starting out of their swollen red sockets. "Don't you dare tell me what you think of him!"

"Faith, no." I came nearer to her, even though I saw her eyeing her father's riding crop and knew she was too frenzied to shrink from using it. I took a seat beside her.

Gradually the tension eased in her rigid frame. She was not calm, only distracted and absorbed by her cares enough to forget me.

"He seemed like a good man," I offered half-sincerely.

"Oh, he is!" she burst out, but the tormented darting of her eyes never ceased.

I licked my lips. Someone had to talk this through with her, someone who knew the truth. "But the evidence..."

She barked a tortured laugh. "Oh, it wasn't the *evidence*, Horatio!" she spat bitterly. "Anyone can acquire a book that will frighten a priest. No, it's because he confessed!" With that, she dropped her face in her hands and wept heartily, at last having released the pent-up source of her grief and desperation.

I stared at her dumbly for a moment. *"What?"*

Defeated, she slumped sideways against me. *"He did it to save me!* He was afraid they'd start suspecting me because I've spent so much time with him. Horatio, I helped him with-"

"Hush!" I snapped harshly. "Don't say anything about that! Not to me, not to anyone."

A strangled sob rattled her entire frame. "They questioned him for *hours,* Horatio. And nothing he said made any difference. They would've found him guilty no matter what he said because they were so desperate for an answer." She was so quiet for several moments that I was afraid she'd stopped breathing. "And then when they started asking about me..."

For a moment she was overtaken by ragged, gasping sobs. At last, she shook herself and grated out, "Up until then he fought to defend himself. He stayed strong even though they were accusing him of unspeakable things but when they came after me-" she hiccupped, "he knew that they would never stop- and he- he-" She put her hand over her mouth. "He thought they would decide I was a witch and he did it to stop them. They interrogated him about me and he confessed. He confessed to it all."

A few peaceful minutes passed. She sagged, utterly spent. I kept my hand on her back to steady her but waited, watching the dust dance in the shafts of dull sunlight filtering down under the eaves. Shudders occasionally passed through her little body, but eventually she was calm, having told the worst of the news.

At last, she sat up again and dried her eyes. "My cousins were at the meeting when Theophilus testified. They said he'd been patient all day, even tried to reason with them and explain what he'd been doing, but then- as soon as they began to ask him about his relationship to me, he started wildly fabricating. He made up this whole story about how he had met with the devil and been given this power and he- and he said he'd cast a spell over me. He said I didn't know what I was doing, that I was *bewitched*."

I had thought the story was over, but she turned slowly to face me. She wrung her hands but forced her glistening eyes to meet mine. "And then they called me in to testify."

"Oh, Faith, don't-"

"No," she sighed. "I have to confess this to someone or it shall torment me forever. If he dies, it will anyway." Her face crumpled again as bitter tears washed away the brine of desperation and replaced it with tormented grief. "As soon as I went inside, I could feel his eyes on me. He was so forceful – his gaze scorched me and I was afraid. They started asking me questions and I knew what he wanted me to do. But I *couldn't*. I couldn't tell everyone I know that he'd put a spell on me to make me do things I didn't want to do!"

She shook her head miserably. "I said that I'd been visiting his cottage every day for over four months now. They asked about the spell, asked me if I'd been meaning to do the things I'd been doing. I said yes, because I couldn't *bear* to bear witness against him, even if he would've been convicted anyway." She sniffled. "I'd tried to avoid his eyes because he was scaring me, but then I couldn't help it- I looked up and- He looked so frantic and demented that I started crying."

Faith dragged her sleeve across her eyes. "But Theophilus got his way in the end," she said thickly. "When I looked at him and couldn't speak, they took that as confirmation of what he said he'd done, that I was under his control. And then he started shouting nonsense and gesturing wildly at me until they took me away because they thought he'd kill me. Now he's condemned to die. He's dying for me."

"Shh! Faith, stop." I pulled her into my arms. "No. He's dying for- for-" I floundered, then finished softly, "He's dying for what they said he did."

"But he didn't! He's innocent..."

"I know." It was the first time I'd admitted it to myself, but I really believed it.

"I wish they would hang me, too!"

I pressed her face into the front of my coat, hoping to shush her because I didn't know the answers. I held her for what felt like hours, rocking her occasionally. She'd made her confession. That was enough.

I didn't register the crunch of footsteps outside until the door swung open. Her parents stood there looking at us for a second, surprised to see me.

"Hello, Horatio," Mr. Prescott said.

"H'lo, sir."

Faith sat up and swiftly wiped her eyes. I offered her my handkerchief, which she refused. Her parents stepped inside and shut the door. In spite of my fears that they might even suspect her of involvement in Theophilus's alleged crimes, they turned compassionate eyes toward their daughter.

Faith's mother knelt in front of her. "Faith, darling." She took her hands and pressed them between hers, smiling sadly. "None of this is your fault. You visited a lonely man. It was my fault you ever went there in the first place! None of it is because of you."

Faith fell gratefully into her mother's arms and accepted the comfort only a mother can give. Mrs. Prescott patted her back and rocked her. Mr. Prescott, too, looked down on her dark head with pity.

"Mama…" Faith sat back and raised her head.

I flinched. I knew what she was going to do. I slipped my arm behind her back and gently pinched her arm. She didn't know what she was about, or what it would unleash.

"Theophilus is my-" She winced at the pain in her arm. "I-"

I pinched her viciously, and at last she turned her mournful eyes to look at me. She silently pleaded, but I shook my head ever so slightly. I would silence her by any means necessary. She would not follow Theophilus Gladstone to the gallows, no matter how much she loved him.

She lowered her head in defeat. "I- I care about him," she said finally.

Her mother touched her hand and her father smiled gently.

"You have such a good heart, my dear. You couldn't have known he would turn out this way, and the reverend even said he doesn't blame you. You did what good you could, Faith, and for that we're proud of you. You can't save a man, though, and all this was his choice, not yours."

She slowly raised her head, unspeakable relief in her eyes. It must have been terrifying to never truly know whether her family blamed or even suspected her of involvement. But when her father held out his arms, she did not move.

"Soon enough that monster will have gone where his kind deserve."

"How can you say that?" Faith's tortured eyes pleaded with her father. "Theophilus is innocent. I of all people know that for certain. I want to go to him."

"Think of what he could have done, Faith. I'll not have you near that man."

Faith's color rose. "Any person can come to Christ at their darkest hour. Who's to say his time of salvation won't come before they put him to death?"

"The minister will see to that." Her father's face was hard but not unkind. "But you will not go back into danger."

"And what good will that do?" she snapped angrily. "What is a visit from one more person who believes you to be a servant of evil? What he needs now is a friend, and I believe I may be his only one!"

"Faith, enough!" Her father shook his head, his own dark eyes flashing in turn. "Reconcile yourself that you will not see him again. All will be well."

Faith fell to her knees in tears of impotent rage. She drowned out her father's voice for several minutes and was unable to reply to anyone. In vain Mrs. Prescott wrapped her arms around her daughter, and at last she turned pleading eyes upon her husband. I stood frozen, flushing both in embarrassment and irritation that no one could help Faith.

"Faith." Her father's voice was anxious and gentle. He hesitantly knelt in front of her and touched her shoulder. "Faith, heaven only knows what you've been through at the hands of this man. Why is it so important to you to save him?"

Faith's fists clenched. "BECAUSE HE WAS MY FRIEND!" she thundered. "Deny it all you like, that's what you don't understand! I *cared* for him-"

"Oh, sweetheart!" Mrs. Prescott folded Faith against her and patted her back. "He did seem like such a sweet man, so cheerful and almost childlike. He looked like he needed a friend."

Mr. Prescott nodded. "I know," he said softly. "We all liked him. But behind that mask was a terrible, godless man who tried to use you." He was cut off by a wail. He knew not how deeply he cut. "You are a sensible woman. For him to have fooled you, he must have been crafty. Under any other circumstances I would trust you implicitly, but with him you are not in your own power."

"I will go to him," Faith said in a strange voice. "And that is a promise."

I stared at her face, feeling not for the first time that I didn't even know her, that I'd never known her at all. In spite of her father's shouting and her mother's pleading, I knew. Even if they locked her in her room, she would find a way out, and she would go to the jail. It wouldn't surprise me if she did something desperate.

At last, I stepped forward, in a frenzy to calm her. "I will go with her."

Mr. Prescott's gaze cut straight through me. I knew it was an unwelcome suggestion and that I would be perceived as a threat. But somehow, knowing I had already lost my chance to be Faith's beau through other means, I no longer cared what her parents thought of me. I just needed her wretched crying to stop.

The Prescotts looked at each other fearfully. Mr. Prescott rallied once more. His voice was heavy and stern. "I will not allow it."

Faith raised her face slightly and spat out, "You can forbid me all you want, Papa, but that man is condemned unfairly and I will not have him see through his last days in despair!"

"You would disobey your mother and father to visit

a condemned sorcerer?"

Faith sat up, her tears ceasing suddenly. "Condemned does not mean guilty." She rose regally and brushed at her dusty skirts, then met her father's eye. "Theophilus was and remains my friend. He is innocent of what they say about him. He only confessed to keep them from turning on me as well."

Mrs. Prescott blanched and clung to her husband's arm, and he unconsciously drew her closer. Tears shone in his eyes. Faith nodded.

"Then it is even more important that you don't go to him!" Mrs. Prescott said shrilly. "The villagers are still afraid and they may-"

Faith's face darkened. "I will not let my best friend die not only innocent but alone."

"But sorcery..." her mother persisted. "You didn't know you were under a spell."

Mr. Prescott's eyes were full of sorrow. "Faith. Please."

"No, I *will* go, and you will not stop me." There was no threat in her voice, only resolve.

In the silence, Mr. Prescott's breathing was audible.

"All right, Faith," he said quietly. "All right. We'll go tonight, you and I. After supper. Your mother will stay here while Horatio and I," he glanced at me, "will escort you there and let you pray for your old friend for an hour at the most. But if he says anything to you, we will leave at once. Understand? But first," Mr. Prescott rested an enormous hand on his daughter's shoulder and met her eye gravely, "I require your promise that if I go with you to visit this man, you will not speak a word to him of your friendship, nor assert his innocence in anyone else's hearing. Do I have your word?"

Her lip curled bitterly. "Yes, Papa."

Chapter Seven

The night was a blanket of darkness through which the chill seeped. I had the sense as we made our way through the town that evil was so near that it mattered not whether it was out in the night or contained in the jail, for either way we approached.

A handful of militiamen were gathered outside the jail with muskets. I didn't know whether they were there to keep Theophilus contained or to make sure the villagers didn't finish the job before dawn. Two stood guard while the rest prepared their evening meal, and all gave us suspicious looks as we passed. Mr. Prescott bore it admirably, nodding to the men as he passed. When they saw who it was, many offered signs of respect or pity, but a few sneered.

For a moment, Faith seemed to lose her nerve. She trembled before the den which held her beloved. She backed away from the militiamen until she bumped into the cauldron of stew the group was making for supper. She yelped at the faint splash. Her father held out his hand, and she took it, her other hand hidden where she clutched the prayer book. A tiny spatter of stew clung to her sleeve.

We stepped through the heavy door into the compact brick building. The jail itself was a tiny, dimly-lit room with a desk in the middle and one cell on each of the three sides. All were empty except for one. Faith clung to her father's arm as the turnkey led us to the back of the dismal place.

Theophilus's frame was a mere silhouette in the darkness of his cell, but when he saw Faith, he gladly hurried toward us.

"One word to the lady, and it's as good as your life," the turnkey warned.

Theophilus's face fell, but still he pressed against the bars. His eyes played tenderly over her black hair, somber clothes, and the little prayer book she held in her slender hands. Just the sight of him made me want to spit; I knew not whether his strange studies were really sorcery, but under the circumstances his devouring gaze roused my anger. How dare he have brought her into this? Why couldn't he just live out his lonely days in the woods without causing her trouble?

"Go on, girl," Mr. Prescott whispered. "Do what you came here to do, and be quick about it."

She cast one resentful look over her shoulder but nodded and went upon her knees. Her hands shook so hard that the pages of her prayer book rustled. Theophilus eyed her as closely as a panther, and I saw Mr. Prescott stiffen as though fighting the urge to sweep up his daughter and not look back. Still, she held herself bravely upright and lifted her chin though she kept her eyes upon the prayer book. There was something unreadable in her gaze.

"Theophilus Gladstone, they say you are a sorcerer, and without a doubt you are a sinner like any other man."

Her tone was even, but here her eyes dared flick toward his face for an instant. Some tiny movement signaled a change in his own expression. Pursing her lips, she turned a page.

"But I also know you to be a scientist and a scholar of Latin." She licked her lips nervously. "So though we often recite this prayer without knowing its meaning, I want you to meditate upon my every word."

Realizing she meant to pray, we all removed our hats and awkwardly bowed our heads. All of us, however, kept our eyes on Theophilus.

The prayer she said was vaguely familiar to me. She read it in a firm, deliberate tone, emphasizing every word. Whether it was from the situation, the evil which stalked our poor town, or merely the way Faith's voice resonated in that desolate and half-empty room, chills danced up and down my spine and made me shiver. Mr. Prescott glanced at me as if he understood. He pursed his lips as though willing her to finish quickly. Gradually, however, he closed his eyes in respect, seeming to will the condemned man's salvation almost as much as his daughter did.

After a while I stopped hearing the words and let my eyes wander. Theophilus's face was softly radiant, and of a sudden his expression was filled with undisguised love and admiration as his piercing eyes rested caressingly upon my little love.

Then she said a phrase that sounded distinctly rocky compared to the others. I was sure it was not part of the prayer, at least not the one that I knew.

"*Amen.*"

When his eyes opened, Mr. Prescott startled visibly. His eyes, too, were fixed upon Theophilus's face. Mr. Prescott reached toward his daughter, then restrained himself so as not to startle her.

"It's time to go," he said softly.

For a long moment, she didn't move. Still staring at her book, she enunciated, "Seek God's mercy, Theophilus, and you *shall* be with us in the end."

For a long instant, their eyes met and both released a pent-up sigh. With that, Faith slapped the book shut and almost lost her balance. The turnkey glanced at Mr. Prescott, but the latter raised a hand to steady him.

Mr. Prescott took Faith's hand and helped raise her to her feet. All the bravery in her face was gone, and she trembled violently all over. For a moment, her father wordlessly hugged her.

"So that's it, then?"

Everyone started when the prisoner spoke. He stared at Faith, his expression completely altered from tenderness to furious disbelief. His fists clenched and unclenched on the bars, turning his knuckles white, then red, then white again.

The condemned man's eyes cut into Faith, hard as steel and sharp as daggers, and she stood transfixed, as though she were seeing a ghost or fiend. Her lips trembled and her bright eyes shone with something like horror.

"Let's go now," Mr. Prescott commanded.

Mechanically, Faith's feet started toward the door. Suddenly, Theophilus slammed one hand against the bars so hard that Faith jumped and screamed. The turnkey reached for the dagger at his waist and turned to face the prisoner.

"Did you hear me, princess?" Theophilus's voice sounded tortured and belligerent, desperate. "Is this the end for me? Is this it?"

Faith's father gave her arm another pull, but she was rooted where she stood. All the color had drained from her face. I reached out to touch her, then stopped. I glanced back at the cell. Theophilus had the true look of a madman now; he jerked the bars of his cage as though trying to rattle them. His odd face had never looked wilder.

"Tell me, Faith! Do you know what happens when a hanging takes place?" he shouted. "Did you know that the neck doesn't usually snap? That's what's supposed to happen." He emitted a hysterical chuckle. "That's what's supposed to happen! But it doesn't usually go that way. Usually the victim will die of strangulation-"

"Shut him up!" Mr. Prescott shouted at the jailor. He stepped toward his daughter, shielding her from the terrible sight. "Faith, it's all right. He can't hurt you." He took her face in his hands and gently rubbed it as though to get the blood flowing back into her hollow cheeks.

The jailor let out a yell. We whirled around to look. Theophilus had one arm around the other man's neck and was crushing him against the bars. He looked to me as no earthly being ever had, lost inside his own head and past desperation. Faith screamed.

Mr. Prescott sprang toward the cell and seized one of Theophilus's hands. Theophilus was surprisingly strong, but he was no match for Mr. Prescott, who twisted it backward until at last the prisoner cried out and submitted.

The jailor pulled away from the cell and took several ragged breaths. He opened his mouth to thank Mr. Prescott, but then fixed on something behind me and nodded. "Look to the girl."

Mr. Prescott hurried to Faith's side. She was sprawled on her back, stunned.

"Sorcery!" murmured the jailor.

Mr. Prescott shook his head. "She's in a dead faint. Bring me some brandy, quick!"

Hurriedly, the turnkey took his own flask from his belt, and Faith's father angled her upward so she could drink. With a few drops between her lips, she began to stir. Her terrified brown eyes were as soft as a fawn's.

"It's all right, Faith. He won't try it again." Mr. Prescott had the look of a bull about to charge. I didn't doubt Theophilus would stay quiet now.

In fact, he seemed anxious and subdued. He continued to twist his hands around the bars of his cell, shifting from foot to foot so he could get a look at the fallen woman.

I glanced back at Faith just in time to see her hand back the flask. Her other hand was curled into her sleeve.

"Come." Her father's voice brooked no argument. He barely let the turnkey take his flask before he'd bundled his daughter into his arms and out the door.

Theophilus strained longingly to catch her eye one last time, but she never turned. I hid my face from him as I left, feeling as if those terrible blue eyes would rake away the flesh and pierce into my very soul. I never wanted to see a prison again.

Within a few minutes, the chill had done its work and Faith was able to walk on her own. Mr. Prescott insisted on seeing me home. All things considered, I was still young and he wanted me safe.

When we rounded the bend, Faith gradually fell behind her father and into step with me. She looped her arm through mine.

"Thank you," she whispered. "I don't think he would've let me go if you hadn't volunteered."

I blushed. "It was nothing." Then I studied her moonlit profile, all blacks and whites in the darkness. "Are you-"

"I'm fine," she said sharply.

She was silent for the rest of the walk. At one point, something crunched under her bootheel. It hadn't sounded like a twig, almost more like glass. I turned to ask her if she'd dropped anything, but she stared straight ahead as we passed. I chose to say nothing.

As we parted ways at my door, she pressed my hand and gave me one of her sweet smiles. "Thank you, Horatio. You've been a good friend. Be well."

Before I could reply, she was gone with a swish of skirts and a flash of inky black hair. I watched until she and her father were out of sight.

I slept in surprising peace. Perhaps it was because the general feeling of ill-will had passed, leaving both a common enemy and a sense of relief. I could not but grieve for Faith, and I sent up a prayer for Theophilus. He and Faith had succeeded in thwarting my understanding of each. I would leave them both to God now.

I stirred sleepily a few hours later. I had no desire to return to sleep or to wake fully, for I was enjoying that rare feeling of complete restfulness. I gazed contentedly around my room. It was filled with a silver glow. Remembering it was a full moon tonight, I lifted the drapes. The moon was the most beautiful I've ever seen, a spotted silver plate unobstructed by clouds.

This must be why Faith and Theophilus like watching the night sky, I thought sleepily. Then I felt a slight pang. He would hang in mere hours.

I started to pray for him, but then my eye was caught by movement.

A chill ran down my spine. I blinked my eyes, praying I was dreaming or imagining, but to no avail. A black silhouette like that of a human was creeping into town.

I threw off my covers and pulled on my shoes and trousers. Then on impulse, I peered out the window for a closer look. As the figure drew even with a whitewashed storefront, I relaxed. I would know that gait anywhere.

Faith.

A strange sensation like a cloak covering my whole body and being drawn shut over my face cast its spell upon me, and I crept downstairs without waking my family. I took a lantern but didn't light it. I felt no need to bring a weapon, but slipped my knife through my belt just in case.

The night was as peaceful as broad day, and more so because I was the only one on the road. The only one except Faith. Somehow, I didn't even wonder what she was doing. I just followed with a strange, detached peace in my heart. It was as if I was meant to witness whatever was about to happen.

As we entered the town, however, the hairs of the back of my neck began to prickle, and I cast about for a threat. In a moment, I saw what was amiss and jolted to a stop. The militiamen. The entire group lay motionless in the grass.

Not just a few resting while the others stood guard. All of them.

Another icy finger of fear grazed down my spine as Faith calmly picked up her skirts and stepped over them to the door of the jail. I followed, my heart pattering in my throat as I slipped into the shadows of the prison yard. She gripped the enormous door handle, then paused and lifted her ear to the door and rapped lightly. She tilted her head this way and that, listening. Then her shoulders sagged in relief and she yanked the door open.

I crept closer, slipped the toe of my boot inside to keep the door cracked, and peered inside. The jailor lay with his face upon his desk, flask still gripped in one hand. Faith paused beside the desk and picked up the flask, shaking it to see how much remained.

"Faith," a man's voice called softly.

The tenderest of smiles blossomed from Faith's eyes to her mouth. She almost rushed to his cell right then, but she caught herself. She knelt down and undid the jailor's belt. When she again approached the cell, she was carrying the ring of keys. Oh, Faith!

Theophilus watched her with a disbelieving grin. "Am I to assume you drugged his flask?"

Faith jerked an enormous skeleton key around inside the lock and grimaced. "Not nearly enough, I'm afraid. My hand shook so much that I wasted most of it on the militiamen's supper. I thought for sure I'd failed."

Theophilus shook his head with a smile. "Nay, sweet liberator, when mixed with alcohol, even a mouthful will do. It compounds the effect. He may sleep the longest of them." He laughed a little giddily, shifting eagerly from foot to foot as she gave up on one key and tried the next. "Never, never have I been so glad to have taught you a bit of Latin! And to think you spoke our plans aloud while the jailor himself looked on."

At this, she allowed herself a wry smile. "Not really. I just told you to trust me and asked you to make a scene. Suggestive, but only to a minister...or a scientist." She winked at him, though the keys still rattled in her shaking hands.

I stared at this little raven-haired minx, dumbstruck. The prayer, the argument, the faint...she had been a clever little actress, and all to get ahold of the jailor's flask and slip the drug inside. I recalled the object she'd smashed once we were outside. I was a little alarmed. Who was this girl beside whom I'd grown up? Clearly I didn't know her at all. None of us did.

Another wrong key. Faith wrenched it out and fiddled for the next.

Theophilus' grinning white teeth gleamed in the dying firelight. "What cunning! What courage! And who would've thought: little Faith, the darling of Reason, become a lawbreaker for the sake of her sorcerer lover!"

When she brought it to the lock, her hands shook so hard that the other keys jingled and she nearly lost her grip. Theophilus's big hands wrapped around both of hers.

"Oh, Faith," he murmured tenderly. "Oh, Faith. What a risk you've taken on, and for me!"

"Faith is trying to concentrate," she grunted. She muttered a few impolite words and shoved the key home. It turned with a loud screech and the rusted door popped open.

Theophilus sprang from his prison, wordlessly scooping her up and twirling her around the room. His face was buried against her neck.

Then he set her down and took her face in his hands. "You've done it, Faith! You've saved me. I- I owe you my life!"

She smiled primly. "I intend to collect in full! Now come, we've got a long way to go before daylight."

He pressed a fervent kiss on her lips. "Then I'd best be off. Get on home before they notice you've gone."

Faith froze, thunderstruck. "What?"

Theophilus tried to pry the keys from her hands, refusing to look at her. His eyes briefly caught the moonlight coming through the window, glistening.

"Faith, you have people here who will love and care for you. I'm a wanted fugitive who only escaped the gallows through the love of a girl I had no business falling for. If you get out of here now, you can start again without leaving home. I'm the only one in town besides Pearce who could've drugged the girls, and Pearce has a wife and children and a brother who can vouch for him. They'll easily conclude I acted alone. Now go."

Faith caught him by the arms and frowned up at him like he'd lost his senses. "Theophilus, there's no way you could've gotten out on your own."

"I'm a sorcerer, remember? I'll have thought of something cunning."

She almost laughed, but her eyes pleaded with him. "Dearest, the militiamen, the jailor's keys – there's no way they will believe you didn't have an accomplice. Don't talk nonsense! Let's just go. Together."

He tried to pry her fingers from his sleeves, but a stray tear managed to wet his cheek. His smile was reassuring even as he refused to meet her eye. "Faith, you've been the truest love a man could ask for, but it's time for us to part. I will slip out in the night, and you'll be found in your bed, innocent as-"

She renewed her grip and violently shook him. "Theophilus, everyone knows I came here and spoke to you! Let me come with you or I swear they will know-"

Theophilus grabbed her hands so suddenly that she jumped. He met her eye fiercely. "Tell them I made you do it; I renewed my spell when you were here earlier. Now go."

She shook her head. "That *won't work*! They're ravenous for witches-"

With sudden strength, he caught her by the back of

her head and pressed her face against his coat, muffling her squawks. With the other arm, he scooped her up like a doll and carried her outside. I ducked around the corner of the building and knelt, peering at them through a thorny bush.

He set her on her feet hard, then gripped her shoulders and looked into her face. "Faith, I will not have you take blame or lose your life – your life here – for this! Now here's what we'll do: you'll sleep in the front of the jail. No idiot would ever stay behind if they'd freed a man of their own accord. You'll say you don't remember anything and pretend you'd been under my control. Faith, will you do this for me?"

She was still shaking her head and talking over him. Tears ran down her face. "Theophilus, please don't leave me! *Please!* I love you…"

"Faith, I need you to listen!" His face softened in tenderness as he wiped her tears with his thumbs. "I love you, too, my darling, and I will never love anyone again so long as I live! But you have to do this for me now. What could I offer you, forever on the run? What if they found us one day?"

Faith was sobbing violently. She stamped her foot and dared to raise her voice. "*No!* I will not let you do this!"

He gripped her close to him and hissed a mere inch from her face, "Shut up now! If they find you here, they will hang us both. Tonight!"

Faith's voice began to waver dangerously. "You will come with me now. You will bring me along and we shall escape together or I shall scream at the top of my lungs and they will surely find us both. They will kill me, do you hear? Either we both leave, or we both die. It's your decision."

Theophilus's face went taut with fury, but Faith left us in no doubt that she would carry through her threat.

He tried one last time, forcing cruelty into his words. "I could gag you…"

She shook her head triumphantly. "They would find me and they'd never believe me. I wouldn't act a part. I'll confess, like you did! I'll hang by myself while you run free." Her eyes blazed at him as she gripped his collar as tightly as he'd gripped hers. "Now take me with you and never speak of this madness again!"

He hesitated a moment, then took her hand. A prison yard seemed an odd place for the wild joy on both of their faces as they ran.

Chapter Eight

I hid in the bushes to let them pass. I couldn't go after them without knowing for certain whether what she'd said was true. As soon as their footsteps faded, I crept swiftly into the yard of the jail and knelt beside one of the militiamen. He was alive. In fact, I discovered, every last one of them was breathing. I released my own pent-up breath; I couldn't have stayed quiet if Faith Prescott had really killed someone.

I hurried back out into the moonlight. I'd seen which way they went, an old road leading away from town. As I neared the edge of the village, I tried to think what would be this direction. Nothing but a handful of cottages, and Theophilus's wasn't among them.

In spite of Theophilus's long strides, I was able to catch up. Faith seemed oddly encumbered and slowed them down. After the third stop, Theophilus took two packs out from under her cloak and insisted on carrying both.

In about half an hour, we came upon a log cabin in

the forest with neatly trimmed hedges and a light glowing in one window. I couldn't think who would be up at this hour, but I did know who lived here: Reverend Alston, an old curate who used to teach us Sunday school. He'd retired some years ago and had been abroad in recent months. I hadn't realized he'd returned.

Sure enough, however, the door opened and the portly, snowy-haired man stepped out to greet them. He expressed hushed surprise at seeing Faith, but he'd clearly been expecting someone. I crept a little closer, then dared go no farther when Theophilus glanced behind him.

Faith was clinging to his hand. "*I* sent you that letter, Reverend. I need your help."

"Well, child, you could have used your own name-"

"No, I couldn't."

In a minute she had given him a brief explanation of the town's belief in Theophilus's guilt. She sidestepped actually admitting to having sprung him from prison, but she emphasized that they were on the run and had to move quickly.

"So you see, in trusting me, you will have saved an innocent man's life."

"And if I'm wrong to do so?" The red-cheeked old fellow cocked his head, gazing at her curiously but not unkindly.

Theophilus's eyes flashed. "Are you threatening to turn us in?"

Faith went upon her knees, pleading with him. "Please, if you do not help us now, then no one ever can. We can go on without it, but you see, this may very well be our last chance. Once our names get out..." She shook her head. "It will be much easier for us to travel if we are married. Please. If I was ever good to you, if ever you had reason to think I had a good character-"

"Now, now, there's no need for all that fuss." He patted her hand consolingly and helped her rise.

The lovers glanced at each other.

He went on. "You were a good child, Faith, and I see the signs about you of a wise woman. This is a strange case indeed, but I have no reservations about performing the marriage, as long as you can each answer a few simple questions for me first. I would much prefer to spend more time making sure you're ready to undertake these vows, but given our short time," here he glanced up at the moon, "I shall try to make it fast. Theophilus."

For several minutes, Reverend Alston plied them soberly about their faith, their love, their plans to support one another, and how they hoped to raise their children. He probed gently into the accusations against Theophilus, but aside from gently chiding him for his dangerous curiosity, seemed to hold no wariness against the scientist. The couple answered his questions breathlessly, taking each other's hands unconsciously for strength.

At last, Reverend Alston nodded his satisfaction. "A strange case," he repeated, "but not perhaps the strangest I've ever beheld. Now, where shall we-?"

He and Theophilus glanced around, but Faith smiled hesitantly. "I'd hoped we could do it, you know, at the church where my grandmother-"

Reverend Alston's face crinkled with a smile as he finished for her. "In the old churchyard! How lovely!"

Faith beamed.

"Now, just let me get my book and vestments…"

As the old man frowned and lumbered into the cottage in search of the needed items, Theophilus and Faith grinned at each other.

"I'll go scout a place for us." She planted a quick kiss on Theophilus's lips. He bent toward her to prolong it, inebriated. She smiled and gently pulled away. "You help the reverend find his vestments. We need to be quick." She glanced meaningfully at the old man and Theophilus smiled and nodded. He stole another hearty kiss before they parted ways.

All was ready in short order. Faith led them to the place she'd chosen. The tumbledown church near the reverend's cabin had burned before Faith's mother was born, but she was fascinated by the old place, and in the sparkling moonlight, tonight it looked its very best. For a moment as the three picked their way through the old wrought-iron fence and through the crumbling headstones, it occurred to me how very strange it was for me to be witness to this.

As they hiked deeper into the old churchyard, I realized they would soon slip out of sight. At first I was intimidated to be crawling around a graveyard in the middle of the night, but with the clean, pure moonlight and the joyful hush ahead of me, I felt my fears melt away. I followed them through knee-high grass until we came to a great stone arch. I shivered and hunkered down in the grass where I could see. I'd never been this far into the old graves.

"See? Isn't it lovely?" Faith smiled hopefully. But Theophilus had eyes only for her.

As Theophilus softly kissed her, the reverend looked around and nodded with satisfaction. Behind the arch lay the oldest section of graves. Despite the mottled silver-green of the rest of the yard, the three stood in the midst of a sea of blood-red leaves. For a moment, I thought it looked like rose petals.

"A good choice, my lady. Well done. Now, let's get down to business."

He grunted inarticulately and fluttered his hand at Theophilus. The lovers smiled and parted. The reverend took his place between them, then settled his book on top of a headstone. For some reason, this struck them both funny. They were probably somewhat hysterical from their narrow escape, which was not yet completed.

At last, it was time. Theophilus held out his hands, but Faith took a step back from him and with a sly smile on her face, removed her voluminous cape.

Theophilus was dazzled. "Oh," was all he said.

Indeed, Faith was a vision. She twirled a little, and the white folds of the wedding gown swished about her feet. She smiled shyly up at him, and I saw that under the hood of her cape, her hair had been braided into a crown on top of her head with a few ringlets to frame her face.

With his eyes glittering, Theophilus stepped forward and took her hands. The reverend raised his hands and began.

The whole world seemed to hush. It was over in a few minutes, but as they signed the marriage certificate, it was clear that neither saw anything but each other. Their soft eyes were constantly seeking each other, and as Faith signed, Theophilus stood behind her, restlessly pressing kisses into her hair.

At last, it was done. The reverend embraced and kissed them both, then followed them out of the churchyard.

"Where will you go now?" he asked.

Faith smiled and shook her head, then wrapped her arms around his neck. "Best if we don't tell," she whispered, her voice raspy. "Thank you. We shall never forget you or what you've done for us."

The reverend wordlessly returned her embrace, then shook Theophilus's hand. "Be safe, my children. Rest assured that truth will always triumph. And Godspeed!"

The two took a circuitous route back to town. It seemed an odd move, but they probably planned to leave town from a different direction.

They stopped suddenly, and I drew near.

"What shall I do with this? It was my mother's. I could never take it from her, though I could hardly-" Faith was fighting tears. "-could hardly bear to be wed in anything else. It was selfish of me to take it."

"No." Theophilus wrapped her in his arms. "She would've wanted you to wear it. She'll feel better knowing you never forgot her or your family. She knows you love her."

Faith buried her face against his chest and wept. Theophilus held her tight as he surveyed the town. When she raised her face, his eyes were heavy with sorrow.

"I'm sorry." He stroked her cheek with his thumb. "I'm so, so sorry. Here you are, with this beautiful life-" She shook her head, but he continued to stroke her face. "I'm taking it all away from you, taking you away from it. I'm a thief!" He laughed bitterly.

Faith watched him intently until his hands stopped moving. She took a step closer until his feet were hidden under her skirt and slipped her arms round his neck, forcing him to look down at her.

She pursed her lips coyly. "Does it count as stealing when the gold jumps into your pocket of its own accord?"

Theophilus took her face in his hands and nuzzled kisses all over her hair.

I decided it was time to let them alone.

I headed home, back through the slumbering streets of Reason, letting the tears stream unchecked down my face. My little romance was officially buried, having met its end in the old graveyard. It weighed so heavily upon me that the walk home seemed interminable.

Somewhere in my heart, however, kindled a thrill of joy. I knew they loved each other, and Faith would not begin her life having already lost the man she loved.

I took a few moments by the gate to compose myself. Even as I made my way up the creaky old wooden stairs to my room, nobody stirred. The rest of the night passed in peace.

I awoke to a clamor of noise outside. I didn't immediately move. I kept the covers over my head for a minute, silently preparing myself to face the people of Reason. For a moment, I was wracked with dread that the newlywed fugitives hadn't made it. I pictured them dragging Faith back, kicking and screaming, calling her a witch and preparing a spot beside her husband on the gallows-

I kicked off the covers. It was time to find out the truth instead of torturing myself with speculation. I discovered I still had my trousers on from my midnight escapade and put on the boots I had kicked off beside the bed.

When I got downstairs, Papa was gone, but Mother was in my brothers' room trying to calm them. I peered through the shutters to see several townsmen running for the commons. Shrugging on my jacket, I rushed out after them.

At least a hundred people were gathered in front of the jail in the predawn chill, most of them pressing closer to see while the rest stood in little pockets and chattered wildly to each other.

I dodged through the outer layers of the crowd, searching for anyone I knew well enough to question.

"-was always an odd fellow, but never thought he'd go an' do something like that!"

"...said there was animal blood..."

"How long had she been going to see him?"

In spite of myself, my heart started to pound when I heard them talking about Faith. I looked around wildly, then gave way to impatience and began shoving my way through the masses closest to the jail, and to the gallows.

The militiamen were still sprawled on the ground, but now Pearce and many of their wives were crowded around them, covering them with blankets.

Pearce looked frazzled and a tad desperate as he calmed one after another of the frantic women whose husbands slept on.

"It's as I said, Mrs. Maddock, they've been drugged. If it were the type to kill them, it would've done so a long time ago. He will recover, have no fear."

Restlessly, I pushed my way through to where the main commotion was focused. I heard the mayor's perplexed voice calling over the rest. He stood beside the platform while several others worked to find him answers.

When I saw, I fell to my knees.

Chapter Nine

My hand went to my heart as though to staunch a physical wound. I felt so dizzy that I leaned forward and braced myself, afraid I would faint.

Her white skirts flapped lifelessly in the breeze, swaying gently back and forth in the shadow of the scaffold. Everyone was gathered around, staring and gabbing excitedly as if they had come here just to be entertained. I could no longer distinguish individual voices; I heard only the inarticulate cawing of vultures.

My ragged breath warned me that unconsciousness was near when the crowd shifted. A large farmer moved just a step to the side, but it was enough. My line of vision was left clear all the way to the gallows.

It was the wedding dress. She'd hung it from the gallows prepared for her husband.

A strange fit of both terror and relief overcame me, and I burst into tears. The crowd around me was so preoccupied with the mysteries before them that few even noticed my crouching form, and I was the better for it. For a few seconds, I buried my face in my hands and abandoned myself to the shuddering sobs. They had made it. They'd made it!

In a moment, my vision began to clear, and as I wiped away my tears, my attention fixed upon a tall, grim-faced man standing closest to the gallows. He was reaching up toward the delicate white gown. He ignored the scolding of those nearest him and plucked something from the high lace collar. Instantly, he strode toward the mayor and held out the little folded card, murmuring and gesturing toward the dress that hung from the gallows.

The mayor snatched it up eagerly and read it. He frowned in bewilderment and handed it to the man next to him, asking something I couldn't hear. The other man pursed his lips and shook his head, then called out and motioned for someone. Whispers snaked through the crowd that he was looking for Reverend Thornton.

He quickly arrived and was handed the piece of paper. By this point, the crowds were pressing in on them and demanding to know what the paper said. The mayor shook his head uncertainly. His aide, however, guided both the mayor and the reverend up onto the platform to give them some room. He motioned for everyone to quiet down.

Reverend Thornton cleared his throat and solemnly read the letter, his pulpit voice carrying across the commons and resonating off the houses on the other side. "Dated yesterday evening, it reads, 'To the People of Reason. God bless you all, though you have done us both a great and irreversible wrong.'"

There were murmurs of dismay.

"'We applaud the energy with which you have endeavored to protect our village, but you've accused and ruined the life of an innocent man.'" Reverend Thornton swallowed some strong emotion. "'You will not find us. We shall build a new life somewhere far from here. As for you, you are free to do with the beast what you like. Theophilus has done all he can by tracking the beast and learning its properties. Unfortunately, he was unable to finish his work due to your interference.'"

Many people hissed or booed, but others snapped at them to be quiet. The whole assembly pressed forward until the edge of the platform dug painfully into my legs with the weight of them behind me.

The reverend was frowning as though he were seeing through the paper to wherever the young couple had gone. "'As to the poisonings, I (Faith) have a theory. It was introduced to my mind by the memory of a curious incident in town when I was frantically studying ricin poisoning after Theophilus' arrest.

"'As a couple of you may recall, Mr. Wilson's dog died suddenly after becoming violently sick just after the first poisoning victims became sick. I had seen him only that day when I passed the pool behind the church where we do baptisms and saw him lapping out of it. No one thought much of a dog falling sick, and most food and water sources had been sampled to no avail. But the baptismal water was never tested because no one would think to drink from it.

"'I went to the pool to have a look around. Sure enough, there were fresh shoe prints leading to and from the pool. But we hadn't had a baptism in months, and the trails did not lead to the church. One led into the woods, while the other trailed off where it met a back road.

"'This led to more questions. First, why would anyone drink from this pool instead of the wells? The only reason I could think of was that they didn't want the noise the wells' pulleys would make. This pool is fresh, hidden from view, and may be accessed easily without using a pulley. The second question is who. I had no way and no time to search for clues, so in my hurry, I did something somewhat extreme.

"'I took what remained of the drug I had set aside for the jailer and the militiamen and emptied it into the baptismal pool. Whoever has been using this water and for whatever means, you will find them sleeping, hopefully caught in whatever guilty act led them to this secrecy in the first place.

"'Now all that remains is to give our love to the Prescotts, and to bid farewell to a town which has cast us out as witches. May we never again tread its soil.'"

"What traitor has done this?" shouted one of the men. Several answering shouts peppered the crowd.

"Didn't you hear?" old Mrs. Nelson crowed. "It was that Prescott girl!"

"That would be it," one man snorted malevolently. "She was in deep with the old devil. Probably helped him make his spells."

"No! Faith would never!" someone cried.

"But she certainly spent enough time with him to-"

One impatient voice called out above the rest. "Reverend, was it Faith Prescott?"

The reverend cracked a quizzical smile. "Yes, and

107

yet no. This note is signed by a Faith Gladstone."

The entire gathering was stunned. A tiny smile began working its way onto my face.

Then the whole assembly became an uproar. Everyone knew Faith often visited Theophilus. Many knew she'd become fond of him. A handful were willing to believe she'd gone to bed with him. But nobody could fathom that she'd run off and married him.

"But-" One young woman shook her head. "But why? He wasn't handsome!"

Another lady laughed and shrugged. "Maybe not, but she was always an odd one. Maybe she imagined she saw in him what nobody else would! She was a lonely girl, that was plain enough."

A stifled sob drew my attention across the commons. I recoiled when I spotted Mrs. Prescott, but not soon enough to deflect the image of perfect wretchedness. Mr. Prescott held her as though they would both collapse, grief and shock written in their faces.

"So then it's official." Mayor Hart nodded, surprisingly calm. "She has run off with the town sorcerer."

"Where's Amity?" a voice said behind me.

I turned nonchalantly to see Mrs. Braxton, Amity's mother, anxiously scanning the crowd. Her face was ashen. "I can't find her anywhere!"

"Can't find her?" Another mother turned in surprise.

Mrs. Braxton wrung her hands and shook her head. "No! She said good night to me last night and then went to bed. That's the last time I saw her."

"Primrose, too!" another voice added.

Other voices shrilled similar pronouncements. It was soon established that all of the missing were near my age, and none had been seen since the previous night.

A chill crept through the assembly. Missing children were the last news we needed.

"How many youngsters are we missing?" Mayor Hart demanded of the group.

Questions flew through the crowd like sparks in the straw. Neighbors knocked next door to inquire after other villagers' youths. Within a quarter of an hour, it had been ascertained that upwards of fifteen young men and women were missing.

"Wherever they are, they may be together." Mayor Hart regained control. "Split up and search! Look anywhere you think they might be. Men, bring your guns. They may have gone outside the village, and nothing good has come from those woods in recent times. Hurry! I know not what sinister game is afoot."

The assembly rapidly splintered off, women to search homes and other property, men to go out into the fields and forest. Being old enough to hold a musket, I was among those sent into the forest, and not without some trepidation. With Theophilus gone, most of the townsfolk now imagined we were safe, but more than a few of us felt we had cast out our best defense. If the latter, now might be the time we paid for our sins.

Even in the late morning light the forest was swimming with shadows. Every hum of wind, every rustle of leaves or crack of a branch kept us on edge.

Every familiar place we passed brought a lump to my throat. The woods were filled with memories of toddling after Faith, and I would see her no more.

We meandered through the underbrush, calling out names, but to no avail. I began to feel dizzy from fatigue, and at last the men called for a halt. We reposed for ten minutes, during which several fathers quarreled and struggled to cast blame.

Then we heard the horn blast. Everyone sat up. It was the signal; one of the missing had been found.

We barreled back through the forest, making enough noise to drown out any monster's approach. I tripped once, and the man behind me nearly stepped on the backs of my legs as I struggled to rise. Nobody knew what we would see, but we shared a universal sense that some horror was about to be unmasked.

We were one of the last groups to reach town. When we arrived, we had only to follow the caravan of others walking into a different part of the woods. With so many of us, one could almost miss the traces of an ancient hunting trail beneath our feet, nearly lost among the frostbitten grass. Several men had brought scythes to help widen the narrow track, but still we filtered in like water through the tiniest crack in a pail.

Soon, I became aware of a powerful smell. Those around me began to pull up their collars over their noses. My heartbeat quickened until it hurt. Someone had been this way and we were about to find what had become of them.

We reached a clearing. Though the old hunting trail had been lost some distance back, the clearing's grass had been flattened by hundreds of footprints. We stood around the fringes in complete silence.

I had been preparing to hear the agonized screams of mothers, the shouts of fathers, and the horrified whispers of others, but I wasn't prepared for the nothing, nothing except the laughing breeze flying through the treetops above us and ruffling loose clothing.

The ground before us was littered with fallen youths. Some lay reclined against a friend or a pile of cloaks, while others looked like they'd fallen in the midst of a dance or conversation. Many of them lay in pairs, clasping hands to dance, leaning against one another in comfort, or entwined in an embrace. Several had mugs still clutched in their hands, and more mugs littered the ground.

Mr. Clarence, an elderly gent from the village, laughed softly beside me. "Looks like we know what they wanted the water for!"

He pointed. I cocked my head at the big metal contraption, uncomprehending, but the others murmured disapprovingly. I glanced up at Mr. Clarence. He eyed me without turning his head in my direction.

"Moonshine, boy. From the looks of it, I'm a little amazed they didn't pass out like this until their water was drugged!" He chuckled again in genuine amusement.

Other parents were taking it less well. Several wandered into the clearing, staring uncomprehending at the young people laying on the ground.

"But- But Michael wouldn't do this!" one mother asserted shrilly.

Mr. Clarence grunted. "And so it begins." He draped an arm around my shoulders and turned me away from the clearing. "Be glad you're not mixed up in that crowd, Horatio, because they're all in for a good whipping." He chuckled again. "Strikes me ironic that this is the thing Faith Prescott *didn't* get mixed up in! Guess sorcery was more to her liking. Eh! Take your pick, eh? Can't win 'em all as a parent!"

I glanced quickly up at him but decided to let it pass. We had only gone a few steps when he jerked me to a stop and flung his handkerchief at me. "Cover your eyes!"

I did as he said. I heard him dash away from me, then whistle to a few of the other men. Moments later he returned, grunting at me that it was safe now. He steered me away from the direction he'd gone, but not before I caught a glimpse of Mr. Everly covering something with his cloak. His face was scarlet. As we rounded the bend and I got a better look, I almost let out a hoot of laughter. Some of the bare limbs sticking out from under the cloak belonged to Primrose. The others belonged to a young man.

We were halfway to town when Mr. Clarence ran smack into Mrs. Paxton.

"Mrs. Paxton! Terrible sor- What's the matter?"

The poor lady could only shake her head, her eyes hollow with horror. She trembled so hard that the ribbons on her cap jiggled. "Please help," she whispered. "Oh, it's so awful!"

Mr. Clarence glanced back toward the clearing, then shook his head. "Leave them to look after the kids. They've got enough to do. Horatio and I will help you.

Come on!"

We followed Mrs. Paxton back into the village. Heart hammering away, I prepared myself for the third shock of that wild morning. Mrs. Paxton led us to Mr. Mueller's house. The door of the magistrate's fine house stood open. Our steps echoed deliberately as we slowed on the porch and she turned around to face us.

"I keep house for Mr. Mueller since his wife passed away, but this morning I came in a- a- and...I found them like this!"

This time, there was no shielding me from what we saw. I followed Mr. Clarence slowly into the madness.

The kitchen was a wreck; there was shattered glass everywhere and the whole place stank of the alcohol that stained the carpets, living room furniture, and even the walls. Somewhere, a pillow had exploded, and now the feathers that weren't floating on the slightest breath of air were sticking nastily to the spilled wine.

"Someone's had a nasty fight," Mr. Clarence remarked.

Mrs. Paxton let out something between a giggle and a gasp, then turned and fled. I heard her outside retching violently as we went into the bedroom. The door caught on a rumpled rug and we had to force it the rest of the way open.

"Oh," was all Mr. Clarence said.

If the kitchen had been a mess, the bedroom was worse. Here we found the remains of the broken pillow, alongside the remains of a broken love story. A woman's unclothed body was sprawled across Mr.

Mueller's bed, tangled in sheets spattered with wine.

I was numb. Distantly, I noticed her skin was an odd purplish grey and she lay utterly still. A pillow covered her face, and judging by two stretched and rumpled spots on either end of the pillowcase, it must've been held down. Her arms lay outstretched in front of her, and there was blood under her nails.

For a moment, I thought I was going to retch, too. A welcome cold breeze hit my face as Mr. Clarence opened a window.

"Dreadful smell," he muttered, keeping his sleeve over his face as he approached the woman. With a coolness I'm sure he didn't feel, he yanked the other pillow off her face.

"Mrs. Denton," he said miserably. "How in the world did a sweet schoolteacher like you get mixed up like this with an old magistrate? And what about your poor husband? Such a shame."

Without thinking, I turned and looked over the rest of the room. "Where's Mr. Mueller?" I asked woodenly.

Mr. Clarence looked at me, then both of our eyes locked on the outer door at the same time.

"Didn't think this used to be the bedroom," Mr. Clarence said, nodding. "Looks like he put a bed in what was the back sitting room. I suppose the door was for…"

I glanced down, noting the lurid red drops at my feet. My gaze followed them to the back door, which was drifting back and forth in the breeze.

"Don't go out there," Mr. Clarence said roughly. "With a past as proud as Mr. Mueller's…After this, I don't like to think what-"

My feet shuffled through the door. Outside was a pleasant little arbor enclosed by trees. They made an excellent screen, so that any neighbors would have to walk within sight before they could observe its occupants.

Not twenty yards away lay Mr. Mueller, face down and shirtless. As I got closer, it looked as though he had been in a kneeling position and fallen forward, never again to rise. One arm was tucked under him while the other had flopped limply alongside his prone form. There was little doubt that he had smothered Mrs. Denton with the pillow after their fight, but who had killed him?

His one exposed arm was covered in human nail marks, but it didn't explain the blood pooling beneath him. I hesitated for a moment, then took a deep breath and held it while I turned him over. It was the dreadful stiffness that did it; I went several steps away from him and vomited.

Chapter Ten

When I once again had the strength to return to the corpse, Mr. Pearce, the apothecary, was there.

"If I didn't know any better," he mused, "I'd say this looks like a sloppy version of the beast's work." He was pointing to a vicious set of teeth marks on his throat. It looked like the creature had made one last desperate attempt at claiming its victim and had torn the flesh in its fury.

I nodded. "I once heard it theorized that it was weakening as it went farther south."

Pearce laughed. "I wonder where you heard something like that!"

When I looked up, his whimsical green eyes were boring into me though he genuinely smiled. I hesitantly smiled back. My secret was safe with him; he and Theophilus had been friends.

Then Pearce became serious again. He squatted down next to the body.

"The one thing I don't understand," he said, "is that he didn't fight back. Look." He showed me the marks on Mr. Mueller's arms. "These are nail marks. They're probably from Mrs. Denton when he was trying to smother her, but there are none of the defensive wounds we saw on the creature's other victims." He shifted his feet over a bit, then pointed to the neck. "But *that* I know to be the beast, *and* it's what killed him." He was silent for a moment. "He was already lying here facedown when the beast came, and he didn't even move."

"Are you sure he wasn't already dead?"

He pursed his lips. "As I say, that neck wound is the only one that would've killed him. There's no other sign of harm."

I heard footsteps behind me. We turned to see Mr. Clarence holding a teapot. "I don't suppose that sleeping drug Miss Prescott put in the baptism water would boil out?"

Pearce paused, then cracked a smile. "And I suppose a married woman and a wealthy widower who were having an affair would number among those who wouldn't want to draw attention."

Mr. Clarence handed him the teapot. "Would you be able to tell if it had been drugged?"

Pearce stood and dusted off his trousers. "I don't suppose it much matters at this point, but I *would* like to know if one of these two was the poisoner."

He strode into the house.

Mr. Clarence glanced down once again and shook his head gravely. "As I expected," he said, kicking something out from under Mr. Mueller's body where he'd been holding it in his right hand. It was a pistol. "Mueller may have been willing to dally with a married woman, but he wouldn't have been up to hiding a body. Looks like he meant to kill himself and the creature beat him to it. That, and the drugs took him down before he could pull the trigger. Better for the poor bastard that he went in his sleep."

We walked quietly inside. Already, several other members of the village had gathered and were examining the remains of Mrs. Denton. One of them looked at me and started to say something, but Mr. Clarence jerked a thumb over his shoulder.

"Magistrate's dead. He's out back."

That was enough to send them running.

Mr. Clarence draped an arm around my shoulders. "Catch your breath, now," he murmured without turning his head. "Plenty of time."

Suddenly tired, I shifted to lean my weight against him like a child with its father. Where *were* my parents?

Everyone went silent as Mr. Pearce reappeared. He held something behind his back as he made his way with slow deliberation over to the desk. He set the teapot down hard.

"Drugged, as expected," he said curtly, nodding to Mr. Clarence. "Mr. Mueller and Mrs. Denton were the other party using water from the baptismal font. Clearly they'd been having a lovers' quarrel; the kids must've been caught in the crossfire. Explains why all the kids got a week off of school when only a few of them were sick; Mrs. Denton must've gotten sick from the poison, too."

Then he placed a coffee tin beside it. Without saying a word, he popped the lid off and stood back, nodding at each of the men to come take a peep inside. Several of them blanched, while more than a few frowned and whispered in confusion to one another.

"Castor beans," he said gruffly, then gestured vaguely in the direction of the two corpses. "There's where you'll find your poisoner." Then he turned and strode quickly from the room, but not before a few tears slid down his face.

There was a pause as everything sank in.

"Oh, Lordy." Mr. Clarence patted me on the shoulder. "He must've been truly desperate if he had to throw it straight into the baptismal pool. Maybe he couldn't sneak it straight into her drink, either because she was watching or because he couldn't look her in the eye while he did it." He shook his head in disgust. "Thirty kids nearly died for his carelessness. He couldn't have known someone else would be drinking water from that pool, but still, it was terribly reckless to poison it. Imagine if someone had been baptized while it was poisoned and managed to take a swallow. They'd be dead and not know what hit them."

My stomach clenched. Without another word, I turned and walked out of Mr. Mueller's house. I had seen enough.

I meandered the streets for hours without knowing where I was. I'd never seen a person dead before this dreadful autumn, and I'd just seen two. Worse yet, nearly three dozen people's reputations had been ruined, not even counting the man we'd nearly hanged and the girl we'd driven out of her hometown.

My throat clenched up, and I forced myself not to think about her. Faith had been a good person. No doubt she would make him a good wife. *But will they get far enough before someone recognizes them?*

My nose twitched. There was a strange burning smell, not like woodsmoke. Almost as if-

I turned. The towering cloud of smoke told me I was right, and I took to my heels.

I'd never run this path so quickly. I'd never planned to tread it again, at least not until I was grown and had a wife of my own; then maybe I'd be brave enough to face where I'd been when my heart had been pierced by jealousy for the first time.

When I reached the clearing, I pulled to a stop.

The cabin smoldered angrily. All around it, men and women from the village were tossing torches into the inferno. Windows shattered. People shouted. The smoke cleared for a second and I recognized my father among them. The tendons in his neck stood taut as he yelled for more torches. Women cackled and young men whooped as they threw rocks to break whatever was inside.

In that moment, as I watched smoke pouring out of the windows, as they smashed stepping stones and wrecked fairy cottages, as I watched Theophilus's cottage burn, something strange came over me. It was not a feeling, rather an absence of feeling. In that instant, the village of Reason was for me as dead as Mrs. Denton and Mr. Mueller and all of the beast's other victims. Numbly, I turned on my heel and walked back to town.

My mother was in the kitchen with my two youngest brothers, so she barely noticed me when I passed. I went into my room and stood at the window, staring down at the village where I'd always lived, the people I'd always known. Then I quietly filled a knapsack and went downstairs.

To say briefly, that day I kissed my mother and brothers goodbye and didn't turn back until I had left Reason well behind me. The only place I knew was south and west, so my final exit brought me past the burning cottage again. I tried to give it wide berth, but the stink of burning chemicals poisoned the air for miles and I couldn't help but turn back to look at the forlorn black cloud forever painted above the roof of the once happy home.

Epilogue

So there you have it: the love story of Faith and Theophilus, or rather, the story of Faith, Theophilus, and poor Horatio.

There is no need to tell you how I've passed my life from that point to this; Faith and her strange love affair were by far the most exciting feature. However, I may perhaps tell you what became of the beast.

A group of young people in Marbury were walking late one evening when all of them swear they saw a ragged black cloak billowing in the breeze, almost see-through. Full of the news of the creature, they charged after it, hoping to catch a glimpse. They described the same unearthly speed Faith and I had seen when it chased us from the forest. The thing led them straight for the old woods where the entire frightful story was said to have begun.

But before they could reach the trees, the creature suddenly sank to the ground with an otherworldly screech and seemed to fold into itself. As the group came within a few yards of it, it shriveled and shrank until it disappeared, floating away into nothing like ashes on the breeze.

The young people would not have been believed, I presume, had not the people of Marbury found a set of footprints leading toward the woods, separate from those of the young people, stopping right at the claw marks gouging the earth right at the spot they'd watched it disappear. Oh, plenty of people like to blame the old beast for any accident or dead livestock, but the true story of the creature has since slipped into legend.

As for Faith and Theophilus, though I think of them often, I never saw them again. But I've never been able to shake the sense that in some small way, they've never forgotten me.

On the day I left Reason, I didn't cease walking until well after dark. You would think that after the terror in our village I'd have had more reverence for creatures of the night, but by this point I was so tired and empty that to be assailed by a beast might've given some relief, if only it would make me forget or else separate me from those thoughts forever. But no such attack came, and I nearly collapsed in the doorway to an inn. I paid for one night with what little money I had and took supper, then went straight to bed.

The room was stuffy, so I opened a window before retiring. I knew not whether I was awake or asleep for what seemed like hours.

Sometime after midnight I awoke and found myself staring at the ceiling. The breeze had ceased, and I considered shutting the window.

Suddenly the window was pressed against the faded wallpaper by a powerful gale. I sat up in surprise and turned toward the window.

Something was coming in!

As tired as I was, I yelled in fright and leapt from the bed in an instant. I made an unsuccessful grab for my trousers and settled for scrambling for a light.

Then, as suddenly as it began, all was quiet again. My hands shook as I lit the candle. I dashed to the window and slammed it shut, then whirled around to face whatever had entered.

The floor was littered with dead leaves. As I drew near with the light, I saw that they were brilliant red, bright as blood and yet beautiful. I frowned slightly. There were no such trees in the area; I knew this hamlet and had seen it as I'd come in.

Picking up one of the leaves by the stem, I reopened the window and leaned out. The night was cold and peaceful, a dead October dusted with moonlight. The breeze came again, gently this time, and in spite of myself I smiled, breathing in the sharp smell of autumn air and dead leaves. Still, I saw no red trees.

I climbed back into bed, wearily dousing the candle. I placed the leaf on the nightstand and lay down, gazing at it until my lids grew heavy. What was it about this leaf that struck me so? I had seen plenty of pretty leaves before.

I was almost asleep when another breeze as soft as the brush of a hand wafted in and caught the leaf from my nightstand and brought it to rest upon my pillow.

Somehow, the appearance of the white fabric contrasting with the blood red brought me bolt upright. I feared I was about to sink into memories of the ghastly scenes that morning as I had many times that day, but no. Instead, a feeling of peace came over me, as if someone had wrapped a fresh, clean sheet around my shoulders.

I picked up the leaf. I remembered now. There had been thousands of leaves like this in the churchyard where Faith had been married. It occurred to me then that I had held the key to their fate last night when I had stood witness to their escape and wedding. Never once had I thought of betraying them.

Another last breath of air sent the leaves on the floor twirling toward me, and I found myself smiling. *Thank you*, it was as if she was saying. *Thank you.*

Hope in a Rain of Ashes

Chapter One

The trouble in Riversedge began with the fire at the cathedral.

No one knew how it started, but the church was badly damaged, the rectory was reduced to cinders, and the beloved old priest who had led the parish for decades was left bedridden from burns and smoke.

But life must go on. There was nothing to do but rebuild. After some discussion, it was agreed that as long as construction was needed, other additions should be made to prepare for further growth of the parish, from functional rooms to a pretty little chapel with plenty of stained glass. From the ashes, they would build for the future.

"Hence, we shall begin with blocks of stone," read a snippet from the associate pastor's letter to the parish. "Just as one dissenting flame can grow until the bastions of a beloved rectory burn and collapse, so may a united community of faith rebuild on a firmer foundation and become strong enough to face whatever the future might bring."

At the time, I knew nothing of the matter. I was an orphan child of London who'd never considered what joys and sorrows might occur in a New England city. But around the same time as the fire, my last tie to London—indeed, my only tie in the world—abruptly snapped. That is, the grandfather who had been paying for my keep at this dismal London school, little more than a nursery for children my age, passed away. Thus, I was sent to live with a pair of cousins in the New World, who would receive the remainder of my grandfather's money for my keep.

I don't have many memories from my life in London, since all I knew there was overcrowded rooms, overworked nurses, and squalling babies. Perhaps that was why I didn't speak, Papa has since mused to me; there was enough noise in that place to put one off of speech for years.

But I remember all that happened in Riversedge when I was but a lost little child. All this time spent inside my own mind allowed me ample chances to see and listen during an age when children were to be seen and not heard. This allowed me to absorb much more than the adults around me ever realized. My moments of muteness also helped them to forget my presence and to say perhaps more than they intended.

The intense happenings around this time also aided my memory. Other events were recounted to me until I formed memories as strong as my own, of scenes which I never could've witnessed. Unfortunately, my silent mind also absorbed and imprisoned within itself several monsters too disturbing for me to fight alone or comprehend, leaving me with fits of nightmares, sometimes calling forth screams of terror from my wordless mouth.

So what touch of fate connected my world with that of a burned cathedral? The fact that my cousins had sent for me to meet them in Riversedge would have meant nothing, had the cathedral's parish not decided to hire the stained glass maker from the valley.

His work was said to be beyond compare, practically sublime. Visitors remarked when the church was finished that it was because of the strange titles he gave to his creations. Others thought it was the evocative nature of the scenes he depicted, and truth be told, that was a large portion of it. But everyone knew that the first aspect to arrest the hearts and imaginations of his viewers was the colors.

When first they saw his blood-reds, daybreak lavenders, flaming yellows, and blazing whites, the delegation from the parish had had to stop and catch their breath. Had he instilled the reds and violets with some of his own lifeblood? And where did he find the means to dye the waters in his pictures as deep and blue as the ocean? Indeed, it seemed the very honeyed warmth of a sunset had been bidden to coalesce to form the materials for one of the panes he was making.

A brief discussion among themselves, and they decided he would do. They sent for the associate pastor's approval to bring him before the poor bedridden priest. This was soon accomplished, and the deal was struck. He would do the work and stay the first winter among the droves of stoneworkers gathered from all over the territory for the reconstruction. This brought the glassmaker and his family to Riversedge seven weeks before my own arrival.

It took me and the two stiff nurses who accompanied me six weeks on a cargo vessel to cross the ocean, and I'm told I cried the whole way. I only remember it was cold and windy and rainy and I was sick just about every day. The first mate would pick me up and walk up and down the deck, patting the back of my little head with tobacco-stained fingers. He would often whistle or talk to me and shield me from my caretakers when they drew near. I'll never forget the tune of one sea chanty he hummed over and over to me when I wouldn't sleep one night, though I can't recall a single word. How I wish I could remember his name! When they took me away from him to disembark, I heard the captain say kindly that the first mate had been missing his own children and that he had found solace in comforting me.

We then took a stagecoach to the city, several landlocked days of misery. Though bereft of my defender, I was somehow sated and felt I could endure the trip more peacefully, having once experienced so much love. My two big-boned nurses either clucked away to each other or sat bolt upright in an attempt to keep their faded dresses neat.

I remember very distinctly that as one of the bonneted women lifted me down from the stagecoach, as soon as my feet were on the ground I felt that I was in a new phase of my life, as well as a new world. The air was cleaner here than in London, and the sky here was so big! I stood gaping up at the vast expanse of pale blue when one of the nurses he yanked me by the wrist to walk beside her. Then we sat down on a bench to wait.

And for the next several hours, we never moved. That is, *I* never did. The nurses took turns to go look for someone or bring us a bite to eat. Still I was quiet, which probably saved me from many more painful experiences; perhaps from the stress of our travels, the nurses had an unfortunate habit of taking my every movement as misbehavior.

When sunset came, however, and I was beginning to shiver with cold, the older nurse frowned and shook her head.

"This is ridiculous. The Brandons *ought* to be here by now!"

She stood up and went to the office window, but returned looking no more enlightened.

"It's no use. They will get here when they get here. Let's go at least up to the cathedral. It's not far from here or the docks and we'll at least be warm!"

The younger of the two helped me to unbend my stiff legs and both chafed my hands uncomfortably, and then we were off. They both walked so briskly that my little feet, still weary and unsteady from the carriage ride, tripped over and over across the pavement. Still, I was able to look up and about me, taking in this strange new cross between the city and what I had seen of the countryside. It was not nearly big enough, nor dirty enough, to be anything like London, but on either side of cobblestone streets the buildings were closely packed together, row upon row of thatched roofs and dark wood, like identical somber faces pressed against the street.

Yet still, all above was sky. It was as if I had entered a miniature city where someone had taken the top off so that some great being could peer attentively down from the sky, and he would sometimes pull away from it so that the fresh, pine-scented breeze could sweep through its streets. As I walked, frog-marched as I was, my brow started to lift and my steps started to lighten. This was lovely, or at least it was interesting. I decided I liked it much better than either London or the sea.

As they hauled me deeper and deeper into the town, the sharp voices of my nurses betrayed what I was too young to recognize as wariness with a touch of fear. Near the heart of town, they steered me toward a crowd of people. All were somber and well-dressed, men and women wearing beautiful colors and murmuring to one another. Already wary of crowds, my heart began to hammer and my lower lip took to quivering.

All were flocked around a tall, soot-colored building with grimy sheets flapping from some of its upper windows. It was so tall by comparison to its surroundings that it reminded me of a big ship, its high, peaking roof reminiscent of a sail.

But the closer we got, the more my distress grew, for an entire side of the building and what was left standing of the ruins beside it were marred by clawmarks left by fire. The pile of rubble beside it was, I was later told, the rectory, or the priest's home.

Docile up until this moment, I stopped in my tracks,

frowning in disapproval at this massive and imposing edifice. The nurses were yanked to a stop, and they looked down in surprise. Then one of them knelt down near to me. Her breath was still short from our rapid trek from the outside boundaries of the city, and she pressed one hand against her side.

"It's all right," she told me, more cautious to avoid a fit than eager to comfort me. "That big building is a church. It was burned by a fire a few weeks ago, but they're going to build it up again, and it's going to be a cathedral. Now come on; I've left word so your cousins will know to look for us here. I do wish they'd had the courtesy to be on time!"

With that, she raised herself up, and we pressed on. But as the crowds grew thick about us, my heart began to hammer once again. I'd never liked crowds, since they savored of noise and loneliness, but ones made up of adults were infinitely worse. Everyone was so big and I was afraid I'd be stepped on! Besides, these people were not like the other people I'd seen; I was entering a world I'd only seen from a distance.

And the church! Oh! The closer I got, the more I could smell the rotting cinders; it stank of sorrow and smoldering rage. The black hulk of its flank rose up before me, for due to the construction at this point we could enter only at the side door, and my panic became too great. Just before the steps, I planted my feet, lifted my angry pink face, and let out a scream that echoed off every building in the vicinity.

Mortified, one of my nurses snatched me up and charged into the building. I've since been told that anyone with a child knew it to be a screech of impotent rage, such as only a very frustrated child can emit. Numerous looks of astonishment and disapprobation followed us. Stately women covered their mouths with handkerchiefs; men held up a glass as if to examine the frightful tot. Some parents even cuffed their children preemptively as if to discourage such a display.

Two people, however, a couple with a child, tried to stifle their laughter, but they were swept from my view in a trice.

I screamed the entire way up the steps, through the entrance, and across the large, echoing hall until we came to an alcove where we were hidden from view. Here, my nurse gave me a hiding which turned my screams into sobs but did not accomplish submission. I stood thrashing aimlessly while she held me by one arm, speaking harsh words I no longer heard. I hated it; I hated everything! This big black church was abhorrent to me. I feared crowds and I missed Annie.

(Though I cried for her incessantly, to this day we have not discovered the identity of "Annie." We suspect she must've been a favorite playmate back at the orphanage.)

Presently, the little alcove was flooded with more parishioners leaving the sanctuary. This did not deter my nurse from administering a few more admonishing whacks, but she gradually subsided, nodding reverently to those who passed, a little embarrassed.

"What could all these people be doing at church at this hour?" she hissed as if to herself. "It's almost night!"

It was at this distressing moment that the nurse was approached by her comrade and, to our surprise, the couple who had laughed.

The man was taller by far than most people around him, and his apparent unconsciousness of the fact made him appear even more awkward. Men and women alike gazed at him as they passed, taking in plain but attractive clothing, though marred by several brightly-colored stains on his otherwise white shirtsleeves. He was apparently known to them, however, for instead of hiding whispers behind fans, his neighbors exchanged with him a hesitant nod of recognition or a tip of the hat.

The man himself seemed pleasantly relaxed, however, and this, too, made him stand out. An easy closed-mouth smile seemed to melt through the cold, sharp air and shine down upon me like sunlight. Indeed, his hair caught the slightest bit of light and gleamed like gold atop his high, faraway head, and still he smiled! Oh, he had lovely eyes, so very blue, and he cocked his head as though listening. Listening, and not making noise. I stared back up at him, my mouth frozen in a little round "o."

But between my nurse's painful grip on my arm and all the troubles which were facing me, I soon became overwhelmed. I tried to scamper behind her, shielded from that peculiar blue gaze. She rewarded me with a sharp twist of the elbow that made me whimper.

"Good evening to you, madam," the man was saying.

I liked his voice; it was deep and gravelly, standing out in sharp contrast to what I had known in both pitch and tone. But the way he spoke his words was strange to me, for I had never been outside of England before.

"It sounds as if someone has not been having a very good day." His smile was sympathetic, not accusing or derisive.

The nurses hurriedly dropped a curtsy and uttered some slanderous remarks against me. But I was caught up in gazing at the lady who stood beside the remarkable gentleman. She was beautiful, but not in a way I had ever seen before. The lovelies of London who appeared in pamphlets and picture books were always blond, curly-haired, and blue-eyed, but the petite woman before me was crowned with a sleek mane as black as shoe polish.

She gazed kindly at me, but I hid beside my nurse, shielding myself as well as I could with her hand. The black-haired woman laughed softly. Still curious, I pinned my eyes to the hem of her cornflower skirt, wondering who or what she was.

"Our daughter gets the same way when she's restless," the woman said to the nurses. She, too, pronounced her words strangely. "I've not met many children who handle long periods of sitting in silence very well. Which is in fact why she is out playing with the other children in the courtyard!"

"This one's been a holy terror ever since we left London," the other nurse grumped.

It was at this point that the angel-man got down on his knees and tried to talk to me. I, of course, made no answer, but he says I stared at him with sad eyes that would bring the coldest heart to weep. My nurses briskly announced my stubbornness or stupidity to everyone within earshot, as they did whenever I embarrassed them by staring dumbly when questions were put to me.

But this man and the black-haired lady were unfazed. They seemed to know that I was not refusing to speak out of stubbornness or because I was stupid. Even when I couldn't coax a single sound out of my throat, both continued to speak to me. Their gentle voices were to me like the cooing of doves.

Overwhelmed by the attention, I felt my face blush and chose that moment to break free of my bondage. I dashed up some stairs and disappeared from their view, but remained watching from behind a banister.

"Drat that child!" my older nurse exclaimed.

"She's unbearable," spat the other.

Tears sprang to my eyes. But when the nurses gripped their aprons in preparation of hot pursuit, the man and woman stepped forward with smiles and shaking heads.

"Leave her be," he said, to my surprise. "Perhaps she will come down when given some minutes alone to compose herself."

"I'll alert the doorkeepers not to let her outside." The lady nodded around her at the gaping hall. "This may all be very overwhelming to a little child, especially one who is tired from traveling. Come, you can meet the associate pastor of this parish. We've just been to a meeting about the reconstruction and everyone is making their way outside."

She glanced meaningfully up at the stairs, and I could've sworn she winked at me. Terrified at having been spotted, I sprinted away, delving even deeper into the maze of upper stories.

I had not gone far when I encountered my first pane of stained glass. I say that even though I had glimpsed cathedrals out the windows of carriages, because I'm a firm believer that until one has seen the work of the mysterious glassmaker of the valley, one has not lived. I drew silently near, gazing up in subdued awe.

"She's an orphan girl from the middle of London," I heard the younger nurse's voice carrying up the steps and into the gallery where I was exploring. "We've brought her to deliver her to some cousins of hers, the last who would take her."

"Oh, how dreadful!" the lady's wonderful voice murmured sadly.

"You misunderstand, ma'am," the older nurse said. "She's been an orphan since she was about a year old. She doesn't remember anyone."

"It was her grandfather who was paying for her to live somewhere decent, but the poor man has died," the younger one added.

The pane was not fixed in place yet, and stood on the floor supported by a wooden frame. It began at the bottom as a rectangle, but at the top it curved into peak that towered high above my head. The open window was partially covered by another piece of dirty muslin which flapped in the wind. A heavy piece of fabric which was probably supposed to cover the glass lay on the ground in a heap. As I stepped closer, a beam of pale sunlight escaped the surrounding grey, woolen clouds to pierce the almost magical fixture hanging before it.

"The man never had the time or inclination to take her himself, but some of his money was directed to her care, which is likely why her cousins ever responded to the headmistress's letter at all," the older nurse explained.

The lady made another sound of sympathy. I heard a faint step on the stairs but made no notice of it.

The pieces of wood holding up the massive windowpane were at first blocking my view. When I crept around them, I could not restrain a gasp of amazement, for the floor before me was, by the help of the sun through the glass, converted into a fantastical puddle of multicolored light. What I saw when I raised my eyes utterly surpassed it.

"And what of these cousins of hers?" I heard the man say.

"Oh, I'm sure they'll be here soon," murmured the elder nurse vaguely.

"Actually, ma'am…" The younger nurse's voice was apologetic. "I asked after them on my way in after you took the child inside, and the doormen said they were foreigners. Not of this town, that is. No one's heard any word of them yet."

The older nurse huffed in annoyance. "Well, they'd best not keep us waiting, for we must be on the stagecoach tonight!"

I, meanwhile, was unable to conceal a few soft squeals of delight, for I had stepped forward and was now standing with one foot in the patch of forest green and the other in a pool of violet. The earthy shades of brown and grey made the framework of the cave in the picture look three-dimensional, and I narrowly refrained from reaching out and touching it. I did, however, gaze down at my open hand and marvel at the colored pool of light gathered therein. In the glowing glass above me, the oversized hand which rested upon one voluminous outcrop of stone at the cave's mouth looked so soft and peaceful where it lay that I wanted to touch it.

The back of it, however, made me frown with worry. His hand looked so tanned and peaceful – much darker than my own, I noted – with natural rough edges and paler on the inner parts of his fingers. But the back of it was ugly with a deep red and purple gash. Specks of white gave perspective, inferring that the wound was a hole that went all the way through. My little mouth bunched up with worry. I cupped my hands, catching the stained sunlight which passed through this wound as if to stop his bleeding.

"…won't speak a word, not on your life!"

"She seems afraid of almost everyone she meets, and she smiles only fitfully. A strange child, I say. Needs a good whipping!"

The man in the window was only shown from the waist up and he looked like he had paused mid-stride, one hand resting upon the cave door while the other disappeared from view beside him. He was plain-looking with a big nose, fluffy hair, and very dark skin, but his expression made me stand frozen where I was with my hands clasped under my chin, gazing for all I was worth into what seemed to me the eyes of God.

The conversation from the level below no longer reached me while I lost myself in his gaze. He was not smiling, exactly, nor was he glaring down at me like the oil paintings in the orphanage office. But no matter where you stood, he seemed to be looking right at you.

His eyes were as soft and dark as the soil of a flowerbed in the months before anything had come up, but his brows lifted as if in the most intense relief. His lips were just barely parted, and you could practically hear him whisper a name – what name, none could tell, but as I stared, I received the strange, growing impression that he was about to whisper mine.

I got down on my knees and crawled deeper into the carpet of light. I giggled and rolled around in it, watching the kaleidoscope of colors dance across my own arms and shabby dress.

Soon enough I was curled up fast asleep in the warm puddle of sunlight.

Chapter Two

I stirred when I heard a pair of voices near me. Two people stood at the opposite end of the hall, speaking to each other in low voices. They didn't seem to know I was there. When I looked closer, I realized the smaller of the two was the angel-man's wife. The other wore all black with a neat little patch of white at his throat. His sideburns were long and dark and framed a pleasant smile, but there were streaks of grey in his hair and hard lines on either side of his nose.

"It is good to see you already helping with the ladies' charities, Mrs. Gladstone," he was saying. "Doing work within the parish helps one get established in a new place. How has your family been faring?"

"Quite well, thank you," she said with a smile. "It's different from being in the country, so there's a lot to get used to, especially for our daughter. She doesn't understand why she can't play in the street, even though we've told her time and again that there is much more traffic here and she could be crushed by a horse and buggy if they turn a corner and can't see her."

"Ah." He chuckled. "And what about your husband?"

She smiled thoughtfully as if something pleased her. "I'll admit, he's been the most difficult to transplant. He's used to having miles of forest or meadow around him, so it hasn't been easy for him to confine himself in a city." Then she added quickly, as if to avoid causing any offense, "But he says every time I ask that as long as he has his wife, our baby, and some good work to do, he will get along fine."

The sideburned man nodded deeply, clasping his hands behind his back. "I'm sure he's right. I'm sure you will all soon have adjusted to your new home."

She gazed straight ahead as she walked, but she was perfectly in step with him. His head was turned over his shoulder so he could look on her fully.

"Mrs. Gladstone, I've meaning to ask you, have you been in contact with Mrs. Evans and Mrs. Cunningham?"

"Indeed." She raised her eyes to meet his frankly. "They are the leaders of the ladies' committee, yes?"

Her confidence seemed to surprise him, and he straightened unconsciously as if to mirror her easy grace. "Why, yes," he said, relaxing his stride to match hers. "But perhaps there hasn't been time for them to explain all of the rules surrounding our charity operations."

The lady raised one eyebrow, looking almost amused. "Is anything wrong, Father?"

"Oh, no, no," he said hastily. "But some of the ladies

were talking about someone who has been handing out blankets in the neighborhoods of the stonemasons."

She nodded her head regally without looking his way. "It's almost November, after all. Some of the workers don't have enough fuel to keep their homes warm."

He frowned, slightly puzzled. "Well, yes, of course. It's only strange since the parish ladies make blankets to be handed out from the church, not in that side of the city." He raised his palms with a smile. "Again, it was only something I overheard and I thought I would ask if you knew that was how things are done."

She turned to fix him with a smile. "You are right that it was me, but I am under no misunderstanding about the policies of the parish. Further, I assure you I used only my own materials to make those blankets. The ones constructed from the scraps collected by the church were given to the ladies' organization. I would never use parish resources for my own projects without approval."

"Oh, I certainly didn't mean to imply that you would." He looked embarrassed, but his smile was more genuine. "I merely wanted to point out that that is not how our parish goes about its service to those in need."

Her eyebrows went up. "Do you mean to say you force the needy to seek you out instead of stepping in where the need makes itself known?"

He looked a little flustered. "We want people to know that our service comes from God, and that the parish is a safe place to look for help."

"And how are they going to know that unless

someone goes out of their way to reach them where they are? Are we not supposed to seek out and save the lost?"

Now his face showed she had him totally turned around. "Mrs. Gladstone, I respect your desire to help in any way you can. I suggest that if you have any questions about how the parish does its works of charity, Mrs. Cunningham would be happy to explain." His tone sounded final.

The lady's eyes had taken on a dark tint. "But you forbid me to do service outside of the parish?"

He lifted his chin to gaze sternly down his nose at her. "It would be best for our parish to remain *united* in its work. We wouldn't want to send the wrong message."

Now she had turned to face him incredulously. "Which would be...?"

"The chief purpose of this church is to save souls," he answered seriously. He was clearly back on well-known ground. "If we teach them that we will bring them what they want without their ever setting foot in a church, how are we to accomplish that purpose?"

"And we can't hope to control them," she countered respectfully. "There will always be the chance that they will reject the Lord even if we should get them to come here on Sundays."

The priest looked as startled as if she had slapped him. She pressed her point.

"Besides, it should be our kindness and our willingness to help which draws them to His flock, not whatever thing we give them in itself. And if we do all we can and their hearts are not touched, well then, it is up to God to retrieve them from wherever they are, is it not?"

The priest's face was a blank wall of stone. "I would appreciate it if you would support this parish with your acts of service and not strike out on your own at the risk of confusing those whom we serve. That is all."

With that, he swept out of the room, his black robes sweeping the floor with a final flick. The woman's jaw clenched, but she watched his retreating back without a word.

"Is everything all right?" The angel-man had appeared from the opposite end of the gallery, near where I was lying. I shut my eyes and pretended to be asleep, but I was too curious to keep from immediately opening them again.

"Oh, I've just had a pointed conversation with the associate pastor." The lady's eyes closed with a grimace. "Apparently, to give blankets to someone without is verboten unless you have permission from the leader of the church ladies and are handing out ruddy pamphlets to make them visit the church!"

Her husband raised his eyebrows. "Interesting. And who is this leader of the ladies'-"

"That would be Mrs. Cunningham."

"And which one is she?"

"Oh, you know her: tall, shapely, chestnut hair, wears hats that look like they're about to swoop down and eat you whole?"

The way he laughed told me he did know her. "Ah! That formidable creature."

She shushed him, glancing over her shoulder and

lowering her voice. "Look, she's a generous and industrious lady and highly respected in the church. I'm told she does everything around here, and the implied message is if you don't make a good impression, you may as well find someplace else to go to church."

"And you've quarreled with her?" His eyes popped open and he looked down at her with a mock-innocent smile. "I guess we'll have to tell Nellie we'll be moving again."

She barked a laugh, then muttered an insult before she stood on her tip-toes and gave her roguish husband a peck on his lips, which he relished. This behavior baffled me. I had never seen two people be so nice to each other for so many minutes together, and especially a pair of adults so relaxed and happy even in the middle of ordinary conversation. And for a man and a woman to be so familiar...Even I, lonely and small though I was, knew enough to be surprised to see someone kiss in a church. All of this was unknown to me, and I didn't know yet whether I liked it.

She motioned to something she could see from the railing. "Darling, those two women are anxious to leave. Do you think we could possibly watch the little girl until-"

She stopped and followed her husband's gaze to where it was softly fixed on me. His smile was as warm as the sunlight.

"What do you say?" She smiled up at him, not bothering to finish her previous sentence.

He took her hand, his eyes bright and his smile broader than it had been. "I would love to. Would you mind going to scatter the hens?"

She laughed at his terrible choice of words and gave his arm a swat, but then bent her face upward to give him another kiss on the mouth.

"I will," she said. "Are you sure you would-"

She paused, noticing my fearful wide eyes staring uncertainly at them both. The tall blond gentleman lowered himself to sit at the edge of the pools of light, keeping a respectful distance as he joined me. I looked up at the glass. The spear of sunlight was gone, leaving only a paltry gleam where the shining glory had been, but still I lay protected within the circle of light that remained.

She nodded once, then kissed him on the top of his head. He held her there for a second, apparently just enjoying having his arm around her waist for a moment. They smiled at each other. The lady massaged the back of his neck with her fingers, frowning thoughtfully. He let his head loll forward with pleasure and closed his eyes.

At last, she disentangled herself from his arms, giving him a playful wink. "Well, I'll go and inform those two nurses they can make their escape. If the Brandons arrive, be sure to introduce them and let the girl know they won't bite! She doesn't seem fond of strangers."

With that, the lady was off down the stairs. I shuddered at the way she stood so straight and tall; it reminded me of the stiff, strait-laced nurses who had hated me so much in my old home. I wasn't going to miss them one bit.

When I looked up, I recoiled in fear. The striking

gentleman sat with his extraordinary eyes fixed upon me. In my heart were mingled both terror and awe as he peered at me intensely, seeming to read my very thoughts. My lower lip started to tremble under his scrutiny. Surely he could see that I was an insolent, disagreeable little waif. I did not know what any of those words meant, but I could tell by the way that my nurses had said them – indeed, the way most of the parishioners had looked at me when I'd uttered that scream – that I was every bad thing they could think of.

To my amazement, his expression showed neither shock nor disgust at the emotions written in my little face. He frowned faintly, but not in anger. I cocked my head, trying to comprehend what turned out to be the unfamiliar savor of compassion.

He stretched out his hand to me and I flinched.

"Hello, Little One," he said softly, and immediately I decided his voice was the most beautiful sound I had ever heard.

I scooted a bit closer and sat up on my heels, gazing up into his face. His hand rested on his lap now, and he looked right back at me, allowing me to take him in, to judge him however I liked. He really was peculiar, something not of this world, but I liked him. If one had to be odd to not be shouting and frightful, then I would make it my life's goal never to be around anyone who wasn't odd.

"Now, that's a more natural look for a child," he laughed softly, reaching out and lightly tapping my dimpled cheek.

I hadn't realized until then that I was smiling, but he

later told me I had looked just like a cheerful little bird, perched on top of my feet and beaming at him for all I was worth.

At that moment, we heard a dreadful pounding of feet, and it took his staying hand to keep me from wriggling away further under the pane of stained glass. With his other hand, he hurriedly covered it back up.

Four imposing women clattered to the top of the stairs, their wide dresses swishing and sending dust bunnies scrambling into the corners. They planted themselves in front of me, looking down like eagle-eyed titans at my pitiful form. The man's hand, still holding my arm, was nice and warm, engulfing my entire forearm, but still I trembled in fear. I wiggled out of his grasp as soon as we were on our feet and looked wildly around for any escape from all those looming eyes.

A little whine like a puppy's made its way out of my mouth. But then I spotted a familiar face. At the back of the party, there was the woman who had kissed the angel-man on the mouth. Her face was soft the way his had been, and she didn't look like she wanted to spank me. In fact, she smiled at me as if I was already her friend.

I had been shy of her before, but I ran to her now. I clung to her skirt, burying my face in it. I felt rather than saw the others closing in.

"Oh, the little hussy!" boomed a complacent, feminine voice. "First she runs away, and then she begs forgiveness. Before she can be punished, I'm sure!"

"She's quite pretty," giggled another woman, "but how did she get so dirty? My goodness, can they not have noticed? And her hair! It's disgraceful. I wouldn't let *my* daughters out of the house looking so disorderly. And in the house of God!"

"She's probably been playing in the mud while they were bringing her here." The other woman spoke with such assurance that one must think she'd witnessed it herself.

I felt a soft touch on the back of my head and looked up, terrified as a field mouse in the grip of a hawk. The hand belonged to the lady to whom I had run for refuge, but soon her kind eyes grew wary and I turned to look. Before us stood a formidable beauty in dark blue taffeta.

"You must be Emmanuella," she announced. "How do you do?"

She said it as if even if it hadn't been my name, she had just made it so. I was about to decide that she was pretty, with her smooth beeswax skin and pretty little mouth, but then one of her slender black brows arched, and I realized I had been asked a question.

Everyone stared as I lowered my head and opened my mouth. I tried to speak, but just as it always had, my chest started to press inward, as if a large piece of metal had been placed on top of me and was crushing me. Not one sound came out and my stomach burned with fear.

"I've just addressed you, my dear," the woman said sternly. "It is impolite to ignore someone, especially an adult. You are Emmanuella, are you not? For heaven's sakes, speak when you are spoken to."

I lowered my head in shame. Just once, could I not respond? I forced my lips together as tears stung my eyes and I resigned myself to weeping in front of all these women. My whole body started to tremble; I could even see my knees knocking together.

I felt a soft pair of hands on my face. Through my wet eyelashes I could see nothing but a pale face in a black background. The angel-man's wife.

"Hush, dear," she crooned softly. "No one is going to hurt you."

A choked sob escaped me. Disapproving scoffs from the women around me told me my reaction was unwarranted, but when I saw my protector opening her arms to me, I hurled myself into them, wiggling as close to her as I could like an orphaned puppy. I couldn't tell why I was crying, for no one had struck me and I had never been held before, but I couldn't stop. She rocked and patted my back, making little hushing sounds.

"Well, I never," said the blue lady primly. "You can't even greet her without her making a scene. She will certainly have to learn her manners before she can be allowed to play with the other children."

Suddenly, there was the angel-man, blocking my view of them completely with the long, slender expanse of his black coat. With one accord, the church ladies all stood up a little straighter and pinned him with wary, admiring stares. My protectress pressed me closer against her, and I dared rest my head lightly against the patch of lace at her collar.

"Surely," he said in his soft, gruff voice, "surely you will excuse her, having had such a long journey through a strange land with no one to accompany her but two nurses who were clearly happy to be rid of her. We ought to welcome her with kindness, yes? As if she were one of our own infants. Or is that not Christ's way?"

There was an icy edge to his voice, and I felt the lady holding me stiffen. But when I sneaked a glance up at her, her black eyes were like fire, a smile turning up the corners of her red lips.

"Here, here," boomed a deep voice from farther down the corridor. "Indeed, '"Suffer little children, and forbid them not, to come unto me: for of such is the kingdom of heaven,' as our Savior said."

The man who was approaching was massive and round as a peach, dressed in long robes and an impressive hat, but his face was pink and his eyes were twinkling. There was no reproof in his tone when he quoted Scripture. I learned later that he was the archbishop, come to oversee matters at the cathedral while the older priest recuperated.

Everyone in the room bowed or curtsied as he drew near, and my protectress got to her feet in respect. When the blue lady's sharp eyes scorched me again, I quickly made my feet go one in front of the other to force a clumsy curtsy. But as he drew level with us, the newcomer just smiled and tousled my hair.

"And who is this bonny wee lass?" he asked the group in general. "I don't know many of the children, but I don't believe I err in thinking she is a new face."

"She is an orphan, Your Grace," said the blue lady gravely. "Her nurses brought her here to meet with the relatives who are to take her in, but we have heard nothing of them and it is almost dark. The child won't speak to us and has not ceased to make a scene since she arrived."

She looked as though she were about to pronounce further opinions upon my character, but then the angel-man cleared his throat sharply and she retreated.

"The poor thing probably *is* tired," the giggly one quickly added.

"She's probably exhausted and fighting all kinds of sickness, after a journey across the ocean in one of those cramped little vessels," another cooed. Her expression was overly sweet, suddenly solicitous for my health. I frowned darkly back at her.

"Whenever her cousins arrive, they will have to teach her some manners." The leader of the pack straightened primly. But she stopped there, once again checked by the angel-man's icy stare.

The portly man nodded. "Alas, I have heard something of these cousins, and unfortunately they will not be arriving today, nor probably even tomorrow. They've been delayed, according to their brief note, and apparently hope someone here will have the hospitality to take her in until they arrive." His lips were pressed together, and the sparkle was gone from his eyes.

"Of course, we will have to arrange for her to stay the night somewhere." The blue lady was already rallying.

"We could put her in the infirmary," suggested one woman. "They have an extra bed."

"Perhaps," said another doubtfully. "Otherwise many of us are mothers and could certainly-"

"No." The angel-man's voice cut through the conversation with the most authority, and everyone turned.

To my surprise, he turned and swept me up into his arms in one smooth motion. I gazed all about me, amazed to be up so high. He held me at the height of his chest, one of his long-fingered hands nearly covering my back. The ladies all looked small to me now, with both of us towering above them. I smiled. The angel-man's eyes sought those of the dark-headed lady, looking like a solicitous child himself.

"Yes," she said, coming to stand by his side and rest her hands upon his waistcoat. She turned to address the rest of the group. "We have a daughter who will not mind the company. She'll stay with us."

The blue lady looked back at the portly man, who nodded.

"Very well." She turned to face the angel-man's wife. The blue lady nodded deeply, as if conferring a grave assignment rather than acknowledging that the angel-man's wife had beaten her to the punch. "It will be your duty to teach her her prayers and see that her needs are met, including sound discipline. Whenever her cousins find it in their hearts to fetch her, I will send you word." Her face had softened minimally, almost fondly. "Thank you, Mrs. Gladstone, for your example of God's mercy. Ladies, take note."

The others nodded solemnly and a little guiltily. I glanced up just in time to see Mrs. Gladstone raise an eyebrow and purse her lips in the most evocative way, but she hid her expression before the ladies could see it. She didn't move until the entire flock of bustling charity and the portly man had disappeared.

Then she turned to the angel-man, looking a little amused. "Well. You certainly got over your fear of Mrs. Cunningham in a hurry."

He blushed slightly and looked away from her. "I cannot abide unkindness to a child." With that, he set off with long strides down the hallway toward the stairs.

The woman hurried to keep up with him. She doggedly remained beside him, fixing him with a pointed smile until he finally turned to look at her. They pulled to a stop. Without a word, she beamed up at him, her expression emanating joyous approval. In an instant, his soft smile had returned. Then she got up on her tip-toes to kiss him on the cheek. I was flabbergasted. Again with the kissing, and still in church!

In a heartbeat, they both turned to notice me and laughed at what must have been a stunned expression. The lady reached up and playfully pinched my cheek. Embarrassed, I buried my face in the man's coat.

"Come along," the lady said with a smile in her voice. "We've caused enough damage around here. Let's collect Helena and go home."

Chapter Three

As we descended the stairs, I lifted my face to watch the drab hallway shrinking away behind us. My gaze lingered regretfully upon the hastily covered pane of glass and the small remaining pool of light escaping from the bottom. In the dying light, it had lengthened so that it painted the opposite wall as well. Its colors only seemed all the more resonant to the senses in spite of the fading light, like the rumble of distant thunder. I rested my cheek on the angel-man's shoulder. I hoped I would see them again.

When we exited the arched entryway and came within view of the burned rectory and the cathedral's damaged wall, I ducked my head close to the angel-man's stiff collar. Something about its blackened walls made it seem like it was closing in, angry and hurt by what had happened here. *Why?* its many voices seemed to hiss, curling in invisible rings of smoke around the churchgoers and searching for some reason, or someone among them who would care to listen to its story. The sense of a sentient evil was overwhelming.

The angel-man must have felt me trembling, for he gently pressed the back of my head with one hand as if creating a protective hood over me. I wrapped my arms tighter around his neck and sighed. I had never felt such peace.

Still, the scene around me haunted my heart until after we had crossed the threshold. There, we descended a pair of stone steps and entered a small but sweet little courtyard. It was no bigger than the entryway of the side door through which my nurses had brought me and was carpeted with soft, pale grass. Skeletal roses still put forth tarnishing blooms as their thorny bodies crawled a short ways up the stone walls on every side except the church proper.

A small shed in one corner marked where the caretaker kept his tools, and on the opposite side a little aperture through which a grown man might have to turn in order to climb through led somewhere else within the outer walls that guarded the church grounds. Directly before us, high, slender spires of iron formed a large gate which was only half open to let the last stragglers pass from the sacred space into the city. Beside these landmarks, there was nothing in this little square plot except a single half-grown oak.

I had raised my head from my benefactor's shoulder to gaze around in wonder, but now my eye fixed upon a dark figure on the parapet high above. I say dark, for he was dressed completely in black, standing out in sharp contrast to the strip of white at his throat. It was the man who had confronted Faith earlier.

Even at this distance, his expression was one of

stone, all strength and discontent. His eyes followed us, or perhaps they merely seemed to watch everything that happened in that courtyard. Either way, I decided this man was both deep in thought and displeased about something on his mind. For a second, I was sure his eyes rested upon the head of the angel-man's wife, though she was turned away from him. Then he turned and disappeared.

My arms gripped too tightly on the angel-man's neck, and he turned to glance at me questioningly. With his free hand, he patted my shoulder reassuringly, tilting his head as if listening even though I was silent.

"Helena!" the dark-haired lady called, waving to a group of little girls clustered against the church wall. "Come along! It's time to go home."

For a second, it was not clear which one was Helena, for two girls stood up, but shortly one of them gathered up her things and skipped toward us. As she came closer, I could tell without a doubt that she belonged to these two benefactors, for she had her mother's hair and mouth, but I saw her father in the wide set of her eyes. She pulled to a stop at their feet and gazed soulfully up at both.

"Why do you have her?" she asked without pretext.

"This is Emmanuella. She's going to be staying with us for the night," here the lady exchanged a glance with her husband, "and perhaps a little longer. We're going to make her feel welcome, all right?"

With one accord, both of us decided we wanted to examine each other and fought to do so, she with her arms upraised in a simple gesture of command, I wiggling in her father's arms like a tot just beginning to walk. He laughed and set me down, and we stood toe-to-toe like a couple of fighters sizing each other up.

Around then, Helena must've been about six, so she towered over me, being a year and a half older. Still we stared at each other with matching frowns of concentration, each trying to get a feel for the other's personality.

It wasn't long before both of our faces cleared, for I decided Helena seemed like a friendly sort, and she later confessed she had taken an immediate admiration for my auburn hair.

"I'm Helena," she announced, proffering her right hand. "Papa named me that because Helen of Troy was the most beautiful woman in the world. I'm going to be your sister."

Her parents smiled at each other in amusement, and a small smile kindled in the corners of my mouth as I accepted the overemphatic handshake. When the adults both turned toward the gate, Helena slipped her hand into mine and towed me along beside her as naturally as if we hadn't just met.

To my surprise, this appeared to be some sort of family custom. The mother came up beside Helena and took her other hand, while the father stood beside me and took my hand, though he had to bend considerably to do so. There we were, a chain of people in the churchyard, and once again, I started to smile. Off we set, obliging the doorkeepers to reluctantly open the other half of the gate a little so that we could all fit side by side.

I stared behind us in amazement, wondering at how

naturally I seemed to enter this little family. My tiny heart glowed with newfound warmth, and I beamed the entire way to their house, gazing down at my feet when the whole party slowed down for me to navigate the loose cobblestones. It seemed they didn't have anywhere in the world to go and we were just out for a stroll. At one point, a lighthearted laugh broke free of my ironclad mouth. Both adults just smiled in surprise while Helena questioned me about what was so funny.

As we walked, the streets got steeper and steeper. We had passed many cheerily-lit houses and taverns as well as darkened shops which were closed for the night, though often the family had a light on in the apartments above where they lived. Now we were passing into the lower reaches of the city where the working classes lived.

I was young enough not to know to be afraid in such a place, though it was nearly full dark. Besides, this family, I soon found out, lived in a quiet corner of the nicer apartments, where other families lived and there were flowerboxes in the windows. All the buildings here were conjoined in long, unbroken lines, so at first I got excited thinking the Gladstones lived in a palace.

However, as we got closer, the divisions between houses became more apparent. In fact, they lived in a very small house. It had only three rooms, two comfortable little bedrooms and a larger living area comprised of the kitchen, dinner table, and sitting area.

The furniture was comfortable and plain, made of light-colored wood with the occasional handmade cushion. But here and there were signs of life, little tokens of a family's comfortable coexistence which showed themselves in the most unexpected places like flowers blooming out of cracks in the pavement. Here, a few sheets of paper with a child's coloring utensils, there, a colorful and orderly sewing box. In the corner, a blanket lay in a rumpled heap where someone had been ensconced in it, and the slant of two cushions on the sofa let me know that two people liked to sit in the middle very close to each other.

As I stood enraptured by my new surroundings, I felt a hand tenderly brush the top of my head as the mother and father put their coats and wraps away. I heard the mother murmur worriedly about my not having a proper coat when it was nearing winter. Helena clearly still had many questions about me, but she was getting sleepy and merely watched me through half-mast eyes while her father helped her take off her coat.

I looked around the main room, imagining myself having to sleep there for several days. I had no idea who my cousins were and wouldn't have recognized them if they had walked in the door, so I had no way to imagine what my future would be. All that stood before me were a series of questions, and all behind me were lonely days of ceaseless noise and sadness. I decided to make myself comfortable.

Even when the father had lit a few lamps around the house, it was dim enough to remind one it was night and to make weary little heads droop, so I made straight for the sofa. I had just wrangled my way onto the cushions and was preparing to make myself a little nest for the night when I heard a little laugh and felt someone lifting me from my place. I let go a surprised squawk, but the hands held me firmly about the waist like I was a little dog or a kitten. I kicked, not sure what was happening.

The father's warm hands passed me over to the mother, and I immediately went rigid with uncertainty.

"Tell them I'll be in to say good night in a few minutes," he said, giving her a little kiss on her forehead. Then he passed from my sight.

With the realization that I was suddenly alone, that is, without my protector the angel-man, all of my original panic came back and my heart began hammering in my chest. I started to tremble.

"Oh, it's all right, dear," the mother said soothingly. "You'll be sleeping in Nellie's room." When I continued to stare worrifully after the angel-man, she smiled. "You'll see him again soon. He's coming back to say good night."

Helena preceded us into the other bedroom with a candle, revealing a low bed with rosebuds on the comforter, plus a little bookshelf the perfect height for small hands. As the mother deposited me upright on the bed, I continued to look about me with interest. There were little animals painted all over the walls; in fact, it looked as if the room had been papered in white and then *drawn on* by hand. Some of the animals were perfect, as if a master artist had drawn them. Others, the ones down by the floor, had clearly been made by a child.

Helena went to a chest of drawers, yawning, and rifled through the second-to-bottom drawer. I was still focused on watching her when I felt the mother lift my dress over my head, then begin removing my other garments. My shoes were deposited neatly beside Helena's, lined up so perfectly that they looked somehow happy there near the end of the bed. The mother visited the chest of drawers and reached over Helena's head to withdraw a white garment.

When she returned, she told me to raise my arms and slid an oversized nightgown over me. I looked down and instantly smiled, toying with the lace at the collar and surrounding the cuffs. It was the nicest thing I'd ever worn. Unfortunately, this also meant I wasn't much help as the mother tried to get me into a pair of bloomers which was a little too tight, for I was too busy counting the buttons up and down the front of the nightdress. The mother sighed and set me on the floor, then proceeded to unpin my hair, setting some of the pins atop the dresser and, after a moment's examination, throwing a few of the others into the waste bin.

I at last seemed to awaken as her gentle hands brushed out the last of my braid. Helena was seated on her bed with the covers drawn back, her feet straight out in front of her, and watching me with some interest. I looked a question up at the mother, and she smiled.

"Helena, would you mind sharing your bed with Emmanuella for tonight?" she asked.

"I already made room," she replied, gesturing to where her doll was wedged against the wall. But her curiosity was not yet satisfied. "What if she stays longer than tonight? Will she get her own bed? Will we have to get a bigger house?"

The mother laughed. "She's just going to be staying with us until her cousins get here, and then she will go and live with them. But she may have to stay with us for more than one night."

"Oh."

Helena was clearly disappointed, though by which part of the explanation I wasn't sure. She obediently scooted over nearer to the wall and snuggled her doll. Then the mother held out her arms for me. Liking this welcoming invitation, I held my arms out for her, too, and she lifted me up onto the bed beside her daughter.

"Oops! We almost forgot socks for you."

She went to the dresser and retrieved a pair of thick woolen socks which, when put on my feet, reached up almost to my knees, leaving little knobs behind my legs where the heels were supposed to go. She and Helena thought this was wildly funny, and I was just joining in their hilarity when the angel-man appeared in the doorway.

Immediately, I hopped down from the bed and took a few steps toward him.

"Oopsie!" the mother said, and Helena echoed her. The mother scooped me up and put me back on the bed, then stood aside while the father came and bent past me to wrap his arms around his daughter.

"Good night, Nell," he said, giving her a resounding kiss on the side of her face.

"Good night, Papa," she replied cheerfully, returning the kiss with an obnoxious smacking noise.

He laughed, then slid the covers over her shoulder once she was laid back against the pillows. Then he turned to me.

"Good night, Little One," he said softly. I noticed he always lowered his voice when he spoke to me. He bent and kissed me on the forehead, then straightened and let me lie down. After a pause, he reached down and gently placed the covers over my shoulder, too. Then he knelt beside the bed.

His wife knelt beside him, and they exchanged one of those glances as they took each other's hands. Then they bowed their heads.

"Heavenly Father," the angel-man prayed, "we thank you for the blessings of these girls. Their tender hearts remind us to be gentle, just as their stubbornness reminds us to be both firm in what is right and patient in their discipline."

I heard a stifled giggle from beside me and turned to see that Helena's hands were folded and her eyes were closed. It hit me then that we were praying and I hastily folded my hands as well and closed my eyes, only to pop them right back open and stare intently at the bowed golden head and the inky black one beside it. The angel-man was smiling and had raised one eyebrow. His wife nudged him without opening her eyes, but there was a playful smile on her lips, too. Then she took a breath and continued the prayer.

"We thank you for Nellie's kind heart and the way she thought to reach out to her lonely playmate when Eliza's friends had abandoned her. We thank you also for protecting her when she fell out of the tree and did not land on the stump beside it. We know that was by your hand."

The couple's joined hands swayed back and forth with their elbows resting on the comforter, but I couldn't see whose hand was moving the other. Then the father took over again.

"Thank you, Father, for the lovely blessing that Faith is to my life, for bringing her when I least expected it and for the way her patient friendship has transformed my life."

The mother lifted his hand to her lips and kissed the back of his thumb.

The father's lips were pressed together, and his sandy eyelashes moved faintly. "She is daily the dearest comfort to my heart, and I will love her and work beside her forever."

Faith had to bite back a smile before she continued. "And *I* thank you for my beautiful family and for making us each other's safe place when everything else around us is so new and forbidding. Please help us as we navigate our new church home and learn to function within it."

The father's face had turned grave. His wife's hand released his and moved up to rest upon his shoulder with her finger and thumb framing the base of his neck.

"Please guide Theophilus as he goes to work in the rebuilding of the church. Let him have everything he needs to do his best work for your glory, protect him from harm and frustration, and inspire him with images to create."

The father turned aside to nip her hand with his lips and then went on. "We promise to love, instruct, and honor one another as your own children and to share the best of our lives." He then raised his head slightly. "Nellie?"

Helena added her prayer without hesitation in a matter-of-fact voice. "Dear God, thank you for our house, my mother and father, and for not letting the Westons' mare die while she was giving birth."

The father's eyes opened slightly. The mother nodded and whispered, "We had a letter from Daisy."

Helena spoke almost over top of them. "Please help Toby to find the kitten again, and help Eliza to find some better friends because mean ol' Rose isn't nice even to people who like her."

I heard a choking sound, but I wasn't sure from which parent. Helena swiftly wrapped up her prayer.

"And thank you for gingernuts, my new shoes, and turkey feathers. Amen."

"Amen!" the angel-man agreed, squeezing his daughter's shoulder and smiling at me. "Try and get some sleep, all right? Tomorrow will worry about itself." The incongruity of these words with Helena's prayer made me pause, and I realized he was talking to me. It was as if he knew I was thinking about the cousins.

"Good night, love." Faith bent down and tucked Helena in tight, then pressed a kiss on her forehead. "You might start adding Rose to our prayer list, as well. Just a thought," she added while her mouth was still close to Helena's head.

Then she turned to me. "Good night, my dear."

After her words to Helena, these felt distant and cold. I found myself wishing someone loved me the way the two angel-people loved Helena. But she still bent down and tucked me in just as tight as she had tucked in her own girl, and the kiss she pressed on my forehead was no less warm. I nestled into the pillow, preparing to hold the memory of their kindness close when I was once again far away.

"See you in the morning!" With that, Faith blew out the candle and all was darkness.

For several minutes, I lay still, wiped out from the day and ready to rest. But once the sounds of movement had stopped coming from the other bedroom, I felt Helena turn over to face me.

"When we sleep, there's no talking, singing, or jumping up and down," she felt compelled to tell me. Then she was quiet for a moment. "Was your name Emmanuel?"

When I didn't respond, she repeatedly poked me.

"Hey! Are you asleep?"

My indignant grunt let her know I was not. I heard movement in the other room, whispers between the two parents. It sounded like they were discussing whether to visit us once more, but one decided that we should be allowed to speak a bit tonight while we were getting to know each other.

"It was Emmanuel, wasn't it? Or E-Manila or something like that." There was a pause. "Well, we need to think of something shorter to call you. Emmanuellie is too long. And besides, you have the same name as Jesus. *That* could be confusing." With this, she turned over and sighed. "Good night."

I didn't know why, but I liked her.

Chapter Four

My first memories the next morning were of muted yellow sunlight making a rectangle on the floorboards, an unfamiliar scent clinging to every fabric, and the distant voice of the angel-man. I decided to go investigate and lifted off the covers. I slid the short distance to the floor with a little thump, then toddled to the door in my bare feet – the enormous socks had slid off in the night – without noticing whether Helena was up.

I drew back the door and peered out, hoping to see without being seen.

The lady, Faith, was even prettier than I remembered. She had her hair in one thick braid down her back and was slender and nice-looking. She was sitting across the table from the angel-man, whose name I hadn't caught, and the expanse between them was spread with papers. The angel-man was gesturing excitedly, but he paused when he realized his wife's attention had shifted to the doorway of Helena's room. His eyes also landed on me.

I quickly shut the door and turned, preparing to run and leap back into bed. I had made a terrible mistake! What if they beat me? I shouldn't have opened the door, but I was so quiet that I never thought they would-

I'd barely gone three steps when the door flew open. I whirled around, uttering a squeak of surprise and fear.

"Good morning!"

The angel-man's voice was so jovial that I smiled back before I knew what I was doing. I simultaneously backed away from him and reached up to take the warm, expansive hand he offered me, unsure whether I felt more like a spy or a cherished guest. He took my hand between a thumb and two fingers and led me out into the main living area. His wife took one look at me and burst out laughing.

"What did you do, Theo? She's just gotten up and already she looks wary and bewildered!"

Dazzled by her sunshiny grin, I let her scoop me up while Theo, as she had called him, piled up a few chair cushions in one spot.

"There!" he said proudly, and his wife lifted me ceremoniously to the top of the pile. From here, I could see all the way across the table and comfortably rest my hands in front of me.

I gazed around, much excited, as the myriad papers were cleared to one side and Faith spooned steaming porridge into a bowl. When she took her place again, Theo drizzled an amber liquid over the porridge and set it before me.

I stared into it, admiring the sharp lines of the sweet

liquid. In a few seconds, he had created a design I couldn't begin to describe. It was like a star or a sun, but with all straight lines and many little triangles hidden inside it. I barely noticed when he set the little cup of milk beside my bowl. Absentmindedly, I picked up the spoon and poked at the sticky lines he had made.

"Ah, ah!"

I looked up sharply and hurriedly set the spoon down. Both of them were looking at me, and I didn't know enough to realize they were not angry.

"We pray before we eat."

The two bowed their heads and prayed while I mutely listened. I was too tense to even notice what words they said.

When they had finished, the mother nodded encouragingly at me, but I was too afraid to move. I didn't want them to speak sharply again. I merely sat with my shoulders hunched, my head down, and both hands clasped together in my lap.

"Now that we've thanked the Lord, we can eat!"

Theo reached across the table with one long arm, trailing the tip of his sleeve in my porridge (his wife didn't manage to warn him in time), and held out the spoon to me. His smile was also encouraging. I took the spoon and tried to smile at him, then proceeded to clutch the spoon and stare again at my feet. He heaved a sigh and looked at Faith. She considered me for a moment, then got up with merely a wink at her husband.

When she sat back down, she had an apple in her hand and was pretending not to notice me. My face had grown hot under her husband's eye, so I was glad for that at least. She pushed some of the papers where she and Theo could both see them, and while they continued their work, some bills and a new design for the church if I remember correctly, she surreptitiously crunched away at her apple.

She barely sneaked a glance at me, but her plan worked. As I saw her eating, I gradually relaxed and dared to take a nibble of the porridge. It was still warm, though the others had clearly eaten before me, and when I got a little of the gold stuff on the back of my spoon, I discovered to my delight that it was very sweet. After that I ate happily and with gusto, enjoying the occasional beaming smile cast upon me by my benefactor.

A little before I was finished, Theo stood up, collecting his papers, and bent to kiss his wife. He tousled my hair on his way past and then went out the door. I turned to look uneasily at Faith, but she smiled and wiped away a drip of honey from my chin with her thumb.

"Theophilus has to go to his workshop, love," she said, beginning to clear away the other papers from the table. "He stays at home for a few hours on Monday mornings to go over the bills with me and help with any heavy work around here, but now he has to go to work. He'll be back; don't worry."

Though I didn't really know what she was talking about, I perked up and nodded. She was happy and calm and explaining it to me like she knew I was really there and cared that I knew she noticed me. I swung my feet happily as she talked about more things I didn't comprehend, like Market Street and soaking things and something about rutabagas. When she took my empty dishes away, I hopped down from my chair. Unfortunately, I was much higher up than I'd anticipated.

Faith whirled around. "Oh, no!"

Once again, I took her sudden emotion as anger and staggered to my feet, wringing my hands and backing away from her when she came toward me with both hands out.

Helena appeared in the front doorway. "Did she fall?"

I hid my hands behind my back, but Faith caught hold of my nightdress.

"She did, but she's not crying, so she might be all right. Did you scare yourself?"

I was still too panicked to understand her words, so I stood there, nodding and shaking my head over and over again.

"Here, let me see." She grasped my shoulder firmly with one hand and brushed aside my hair from my forehead with the other. She nodded. "It's not bruising. I think she must've just landed hard. Good." She pecked me on the forehead and stood up, then peered down at me. "Are you sure you're all right?"

My heartrate had finally come down, and I remembered to nod. But Helena had come to stand beside me and wore a frown.

"No, she's not. Her hands are scraped and she's about to cry," she announced helpfully.

Faith whirled back around and gently took my wrists. Sure enough, I had scraped both hands on the bare wooden floor, but I was more afraid of making a scene than anything else. Faith cooed over my wounds, running her thumb across them until she was sure the skin was only grazed and not broken. It was when she kissed them both that I realized she was not angry, only worried for me.

I frowned in a daze as she went and got a washcloth, then knelt to rinse my scraped palms. They did sting, but I had been taught not to cry if I could help it, for my tears only ever invited anger and exasperation.

"She's being very brave," Helena remarked.

Faith smiled. "Yes, she is, but I think they do hurt, don't they?"

I didn't answer, but Helena ran from the room and came back with her doll.

"Here." She tucked the doll between my arms, careful to make sure I was holding her tight enough not to drop her but wasn't touching her with my hands until Faith was done.

Even after the treatment was finished, I stood hugging the doll, watching the others with amazement. They clucked back and forth to each other about the need to clean wounds before bandaging them, then agreed that since there was no blood a bandage would not be necessary. Helena was a little copy of her mother, walking almost on her heels and changing her opinion only when Faith gently disagreed with her.

"She will have to get dressed before we go out, won't she?" Helena's voice brought me back to the present, and I noticed they were putting on hats and containing Faith's braid in a sort of wrap around her head. I looked down at myself and shuffled my bare feet uncertainly.

"Yes, she will. Would you mind helping her get dressed while I get our things ready for errands?"

Helena straightened like a proud little soldier, then towed me back into her bedroom. She opened several drawers of her dresser and methodically laid out many layers of clothing, holding them up to me and chattering away.

By the end of the whole operation, I had a short, plain dress with warm stockings and my own shoes. My bloomers, however, she had noticed were far too tight and traded out for a pair that was too big. Hurried by her mother's voice, she found a piece of string and used it to tie the bloomers up, then pulled my skirt down over the top and dragged me out into the living area.

While Faith locked the main door behind us, I looked around. The world was a different place in the morning light; instead of long blocks of darkness flanking the lumpy, sloping streets, I could now see a hodgepodge of different building materials even though the buildings were all either connected or close enough that one person could barely walk between them. Some were broken down, while others looked tidy and proud in their simplicity; Helena's family's was one of these latter ones.

"Off we go!" Faith said cheerfully. She reached out her hand for me, and I took hold, glancing back at Helena. Apparently, she had run errands often enough not to need to hold on, for she was allowed to skip and explore within a moderate radius of her mother as we made our way up the street.

At the top of the hill, we entered a street full of shops in similar repair. Here, Faith called Helena to us and did not allow her to wander as far. Several of the shops had bars over the windows or more than one lock on the door. The people here were wary and scowled as we passed, and Faith sailed through the street like a person on a mission.

Some blocks later, we made another turn and found ourselves zigzagging dizzily through several narrow alleys. I was afraid, for I could not see the sky as well, but Faith and Helena freely frolicked like they were on holiday. Few of the buildings' windows faced this way, and the two played hopscotch and gamboled down the sloping streets without a care that someone should see them.

I watched them uncertainly. I had always been discouraged from such behavior. I didn't know *why* my nurses had always been angry, but a good whipping was enough to make one walk however one was told. In my case, this meant shuffling quickly along with my head down and my hands clasped against my coat.

Just then, however, I felt a hand grasping my little forearm and was propelled forward at great speed. I glanced up in alarm to see that Faith had a hold of each of our arms and was dashing toward a great puddle at the bottom of a hill. I cried out in alarm; there was no way around it, for it spread the entire width of the alley. I tried to get my arm free, but Faith's grip was firm.

I glanced over at Helena. Her expression was one of

exhilarated concentration as she picked up speed.

"We'll never make it!" she called dramatically.

"Here we go! Get ready to jump, Emmanuella!" Faith replied, and suddenly I realized this was a game.

I ran as fast as my little legs could carry me, almost tripping over loose pieces of pavement.

"Hmm," I heard Faith say.

Just as we reached the edge of the water, which would probably have reached my knees had I stood at the middle, Faith reached down and caught us both by the waist, then vaulted gracefully across. When she set us down on the opposite side, I quickly adjusted my bloomers to make sure they would stay up, a grin of exhilaration from the leap still dancing on my lips.

"Mama! We could've made it!" Helena complained.

Faith surveyed the puddle, looking less convinced. "Sorry, love, but it was a foot farther across than usual and these are Emmanuella's only shoes. Maybe next time."

With that, she again took our hands and we rounded the corner. What lay before us was a street that looked as wide and flat as a river, with big stone buildings on either side and streams of people moving in each direction. Horses and carriages trundled down the middle as the people walked along the outer edges. Soon, powerful scents began to draw my attention, everything from the heady smells of horses and manure to those of baking bread and roasting meat.

The people here were different. They didn't quite scowl at us, but they stood taller and looked around more, every once in a while sizing Faith up with a cool nod. Helena and I were virtually always ignored. This, however, left us greater freedom to play while Faith carried out her morning tasks. When she was buying a sack of flour from one shopkeeper, Helena informed me that we were a pirate crew and that if I was good, I could be her first mate. I eagerly agreed, glancing at Faith to see if we would be scolded, but she merely warned us to stay out of the way of the carriages.

Helena, who had been told far more tales than I ever had, softly described our watery domain to me, envisioning whitecapped waves that flashed in the sun like crystals, pirate kings draped in gobs of stolen jewels, towering squalls whose hail tore through our sails and whose lightning made the black sea as bright as day. Her childlike voice opened the doors of other worlds to me, and I reveled in the freedom of it. It helped that she borrowed here and there from reality. The spires of the church became the masts of an enemy ship and the rich people's uniformed butlers were captains of the English Navy whom we had come to plunder. One of them, overhearing our play, squinted his eyes playfully at me as if keeping a weather eye out for pirates. This sent me into peals of delighted laughter and set him grinning and blushing as other people turned around to see what the fuss was about.

As our games carried on from shop to shop, pausing only briefly to help Faith carry packages or hold doors, I began to gain confidence. Once, when Helena couldn't decide what color her magnificent coat would be, I whispered that it should be purple. Surprised, she considered my suggestion and then nodded. But when I suggested peacock feathers for the plumes of her hat, she insisted they were turkey feathers. I think she didn't know what peacocks look like, or she else would've agreed with me.

Anyone else would've realized the significance of me speaking at last, but Helena, too, was only a child, and her matter-of-fact prompting and bickering encouraged me more than the intense scrutiny of an adult would have. Once or twice, I saw Faith's chin turn abruptly and a smile warm her face when she heard my little voice joining in play. After a while, her eyes only glanced in my direction to reassure herself that it was indeed my voice, but then she behaved as naturally as could be, addressing us both and assigning us each packages to carry.

The only time we nearly got into a scrape was when Helena spotted Mrs. Cunningham walking on the other side of the street. I immediately scowled in her direction with childlike forthrightness, but Helena shook her head and seized my hand.

"Quick! Straighten up!" she instructed me.

I glanced down, baffled, while she helped me dust off my shoes and smooth out any rumples in my skirt. Then she turned me to face Mrs. Cunningham and stood very straight and tall.

"Now when she gets right by us," she whispered, "cross yourself. Like this."

Just as she passed us, Mrs. Cunningham happened to look across the street. She looked mildly surprised or bewildered, but I don't know whether it was us she saw. We did, however, stand there as solemn as soldiers and cross ourselves when she passed.

Moments later, we felt a hand on top of each of our heads, and Faith's low voice came from just behind us.

"Your father was only kidding," she said thickly with repressed laughter. "Don't really do that."

"She looks like she has your pirate hat," I whispered to Helena as we watched Mrs. Cunningham's retreating form enter a shop. I was rewarded with an infectious giggle from my playmate. My own laughter sounded strange to me, rusty and unfamiliar, punctuated by strange little gasps.

We walked side by side to the next place, quiet for the moment. Faith glanced back to make sure we were following close, then brought us to a place which stank of lye and told us to wait outside. Then she disappeared into the cascade of hot steam which constantly emitted from the door.

"It looks like a ghost!" I whispered excitedly.

"It's from the vats," she said simply. "This is the laundress's."

I was momentarily disappointed, but within minutes she had concocted the story of a massive ghost ship. We sat on overturned buckets while she recounted the tale in all its haunting glory, embellishing here and there as she was inspired by new details from our surroundings. For a child it was powerfully rendered, but I somehow knew she was making it up. Still, I sat entranced. Compared to both smoggy London and this cold, grey town, it was the best place I'd ever been.

When Faith emerged, she was still in conversation with a woman wrapped from head to toe in clothes that looked like white sheets. Her skin was red and rough-looking.

"It's all right that we can take on so much of the sewing, but I'm afraid we're going to need more time than we have, for the snows will be coming soon, won't they?" Faith said.

The other lady shook her head. "Oh, no, dear, we've got a good two weeks, perhaps three at the most. We'll help you when we can."

Faith forced a smile. "Thank you. We could take some of them now-"

"I'll send Alfred with the fabrics later. There's quite a lot of them and you won't want to carry them all that way. 'Specially with two little ones beside-"

A bell clanged from the cathedral high above us, hidden behind pines at the top of the hill. Faith turned quickly to look, her face grave. She looked at her companion.

"We'd better go. Thank you," she murmured.

The other lady nodded hurriedly and went inside.

With her eyes still upon the cathedral, Faith took both of our hands. Helena and I exchanged a worried glance.

"Mama?" Helena said softly.

Without answering, Faith turned to a young man who was coming up the path with a wheelbarrow filled with laundry. "That wasn't the hour, was it?" She sounded like she knew but wanted to be told she was wrong.

He shook his head. He looked distressed. "No, ma'am."

She nodded. "I didn't think so." She took the packages from our arms and handed them to him. "Bring those to the Gladstones' when you go with the blanket materials later and I'll pay you extra. Thank you."

"Mama, what is it?" Helena tried again.

Her mother merely hugged her against her, scrunching her hand through her daughter's hair, before straightening and taking our hands again.

"Come with me, girls. We have to go see..." She trailed off without telling us what we were going to see, but it was enough to make us clasp her hands tighter and hurry along without complaint, all play forgotten.

Abandoning all she had told us earlier, Faith ran out into the street and dodged between horses and carriages. She looked lost or as if she was searching for someone. We were headed back the way we had come, and I could tell by the concerned glances of Helena that this was not routine as everything else had been.

All at once, Faith seemed to mark her quarry and hurried us across to the opposite side of the street. As we reached the shops, we saw another well-dressed lady who seemed to know her, and Faith started to slow down.

"Is it-? Was that...?" Faith couldn't seem to get the words out, but not because she was breathless.

The other lady nodded sadly. "Yes, dear. Isn't it sad?"

The other woman bowed her head. "We had a messenger not five minutes ago who's spreading the word. It's the father."

Faith didn't cover her crestfallen face as the realization sank in. Her mouth stayed open, as if she could force away the truth if she just had the right words. The other woman adjusted the parcels in her arms and reached out to give Faith a hug. Then she straightened again.

"I must go home and tell my family and neighbors. They will want to know, and we'll have to prepare for the service. Are you all right?"

Faith nodded distractedly, barely returning the press her friend gave her hand. She gazed up the hill at the cathedral. We were much closer than before, and when I looked up, its bare flank was a hulking grey mass framed against the now overcast sky. Veins of light peered out from behind the screen of clouds.

"So Father Forsetti will rise to take his place?" Faith's face had passed from sorrow into sympathy.

High above us, a dark figure paced slowly out of a door to stand at the edge of the parapet. He rested his hands upon the railing. Straight arms supported a pair of shoulders which seemed to sag under an unbearable weight. His head was bowed almost to his chest. His clothes looked extra dark where he was framed in profile against the silver brightness of the sky.

At last, the woman answered. "For a time, perhaps. It will be the archbishop's duty to find someone new to lead the parish. But in the meantime, yes, he will have to be the lead pastor of the church."

The lady took her leave. After the rustling of her skirts had faded into the distance, the street seemed oddly silent.

Chapter Five

That evening was a solemn one of fitful tears and a sense of fear which I keenly sensed but didn't comprehend. The angel-man's eyes were sad when he greeted his wife, and they just held each other for several minutes before coming inside.

Helena, too, seemed oddly distressed.

"But I thought he was our Godsend," she said plaintively. "What about now?"

Her mother's response was to go and hold her tightly for several moments.

By the time the dinner plates had been cleared, my curiosity had risen to an irritating pitch. Once I got down from my chair, more safely than I had this morning by way of a little stepstool placed there while I was busy playing, I found my way over to the angel-man where he sat in the armchair with his lanky legs spread out in front of him. His eyes were fixed on some unseen point before him.

I stood just outside his line of sight and waited for him to notice me. By this point, my brow was deeply furrowed with consternation.

His own brows lifted with a small smile when he spotted me. "Hello there."

He opened his hands toward me, and after a moment's hesitation, I came closer. He kept his hands out until I was close enough for him to reach, then picked me up and placed me on his lap. I was surprised, but the warmth through his homespun shirt and the scent of his soap quickly lulled me to lean my shoulder against his chest and look up at him with a question in my eyes.

"Has no one explained to you what's happened, Little One?"

I shook my head.

He sighed. "There was a man whom you haven't met, whose leadership made his flock flourish and his Shepherd proud. He was our friend." He let go a heavy sigh. "He was the priest of this parish, but today he died. Do you know what that means?"

I nodded. I had learned plenty about death in my short life, enough to understand that was why people were crying. I nestled my head against Theophilus's shirtfront. He bent to press a gentle kiss against the top of my head, lingering for a moment, then fussed with my hair with one finger.

"He was a good man. He truly understood how to serve like Christ."

Helena sniffled from where she sat in Faith's lap on the couch. "He was our friend and he loved us."

Faith nuzzled her daughter's hair sympathetically, then smiled. "It seems funny, you know. We haven't known him more than a couple of months, and yet our lives are completely different because of him. It makes me wonder, did we do the right thing in coming here?"

Theophilus looked up heavily. "Just because our guiding light is gone does not mean he wasn't leading us along the right path. Only that it's going to be harder for us to see without him."

Faith's mouth twisted. Theophilus picked me up and went and sat beside her, wrapping his long arms around the whole group of us. Faith wept without hiding her tears, but for some reason it didn't frighten me. I reached out and put my hand on hers, barely covering from her wrist to the bottom of her thumb. She lifted my hand and kissed the back of it without saying a word.

The funeral service was held at dawn the following morning, before people had to work. The whole world was silent except for a few murmurs as we trudged up the hill toward the church. I had never seen so much black, nor so many feathered hats.

"What is it about funerals that says to these women, 'Please, wear your gaudiest hat'?" Faith mused under her breath. "The man has *died*, for heaven's sakes."

"Speaking as a former bachelor," her husband muttered, "any church event is a hunting ground for the matchmaker, and I've never seen a church so rife with them."

We were silent as we made our way to the iron gates. Faith stopped just before the courtyard, letting the streams of people flow past. She gazed up at the fire-scarred bulwark, sorrow casting a lurid shadow over her features. Her husband held her hand, glancing from her up to the roof.

"He was with us when we found our way here, and he will be with us even when his servant is gone," he said softly.

I frowned. "I thought he died," I whispered to Helena.

"The priest is dead, but God is with us," she responded without looking.

I considered her for a long moment. She didn't look like she was rehearsing words which meant nothing to her; she looked as if she was reminding herself of a happy memory in the midst of all the sorrow.

For some reason, this brought tears to my own eyes, but not for the priest who had died or for anyone who missed him. Seeing someone who didn't feel alone even when her Godsend had just passed away made me feel even more alone, for I had never had anyone. Helena took my hand and nudged away one of my tears with one finger. Ahead of us, Faith laid her head on Theophilus's shoulder as they led the way inside.

This was the first time I had ever been inside the old sanctuary. The high wooden ceiling made me think of an upside-down ship, but the black hangings everywhere reminded me that both man and building had faced an inferno.

Everyone was silent except the occasional ruffle of taffeta or clearing of a throat. It was so crowded that some people stood outside and listened through the open doors, while the rest of us were crammed in so tight that you couldn't even get down the aisles. I could see why the younger priest had wanted a bigger place.

I had expected the service to be interminable, but

soon after it started, Theophilus lifted me onto his shoulders so I could see. Helena he balanced with her feet on the back of the pew in front of him, leaning her back against him so she wouldn't fall.

The casket was right at the front, where the very round man from two days ago stood solemnly in his tall hat. Perhaps the ladies were following suit in admiration. While he spoke, several people cried, including Faith and Theophilus. I don't remember a lot of what he said, but one particular part of his speech stood out to me. It was where he talked about the grieving of believers versus non-believers.

"Paul tells us in 1 Thessalonians that we don't grieve like those who have no hope. Death, though terrifying, is not the hopeless ending that it seems. It brings us face to face with the three things we as humans fear the most, that is, permanent endings, being alone, and the unknown.

"But for believers, not one of these dreaded three items is true. No, for us, death is only a bridge between a life of toil and a life of endless happiness; therefore, it is not an ending, or if it is, only an ending of trouble. We each face it alone, yes, but only to be brought face to face with the One who has always lived within our hearts; thus, we are never alone. And finally, while it is impossible to comprehend, nothing is unknown to God and He waits on the other side, and in that, we may have trust.

"Therefore, although our brother has suffered, he is now with God and suffers no more. We are the ones who must face the tragedy of death, and that is life without him. Until we meet again."

It seemed everyone's eyes were drawn surreptitiously to the bowed head of the associate pastor who stood silently on the opposite side of the altar, grief etched into every line of his face.

When the funeral was ended, the pallbearers lifted the casket onto their shoulders and some of the assembly followed them out. By one accord, our little family remained in the church. Many others buried their faces in black lace handkerchiefs or whispered to those nearest them. Those who accompanied the pallbearers to the grave went out the back of the church, which meant they had to cross through the worst of the burned section. Men with tools flanked the area that was safest, creating a little hallway so that nobody would step into the less stable parts.

As we waited inside for the burial to be over, Helena grew restless and had to be scolded. The noise level in the sanctuary was high enough for us to be able to talk to each other, so that helped. I was too stunned by my surroundings to want to speak and spent my time observing the others around me.

"I can't believe he's gone," one woman was saying. "He taught me my prayers as a child, married me and my husband, baptized each of our children, and said my father's funeral. I can't imagine this parish without him. Now what will become of us?"

"I'm going to miss him," another woman said simply through her tears, leaning into the arms of a friend for support.

"Will the archbishop stay with us now?" asked one young man.

An older man shook his head. "No, he will stay

while we get reestablished, but he has a much larger community to worry about. Probably Father Forsetti will have to-"

"But he's so *young*!" an older woman fussed.

"Not for a man, but for a priest," a young woman agreed.

Though most of them seemed to be speaking of the priest, many of them were also staring at Theophilus, whispering the occasional remark to those nearest them. I unconsciously stepped closer to Faith, grasping her hand for strength. She squeezed mine and rocked it back and forth, the way she had Theophilus's during prayer on that first night. Her other hand rested on top of Helena's head where it was leaned against her plain black skirt.

All at once, a chilling sound swept through the whole of the church, sending a chill racing up my spine. It was the sound of many people weeping.

Faith clutched us both closer to her and Theophilus stood guard at the end of the pew as the black-clad churchgoers returned from the outside, grass clinging to their shoes and tears staining nearly every face, grief creasing even the most stoic ones. I wrapped my arms around Faith's legs and clung to her skirt, feeling the hairs raise on the back of my neck at the sound of communal mourning.

Gradually, the people began to filter out, some of them saying a word or two to the archbishop before they went. Many gripped his hand or even embraced him with tears running down their faces. His was flaming red with his own grief.

Eventually, there was space to move around.

Theophilus turned to say something to Faith, but she was looking out across the remaining people. She touched his arm.

"There's Father Forsetti," she said softly. "I want to speak to him."

He nodded, lifting Helena onto his back. Faith hurried into the quiet throng, dodging around people toward the steps of the altar. Without thinking, I hurried after her.

By some miracle I wasn't lost in the crowd. Faith practically ran all the way up the aisle, but as soon as she reached Father Forsetti, she abruptly stopped a few feet away from him. She bowed her head, matching his grieving stance. Evidently their previous spat was utterly forgotten.

"Father Forsetti, I am so sorry," she said softly.

The priest didn't say anything for a minute, nor did he raise his head. Then he managed to say shortly, "He was ready."

Faith pursed her lips and took a step forward. "He trusted you," she said. "He would be at peace, knowing the parish is in your hands."

At this, he raised his head. His eyes sparkled like diamonds for all the tears imprisoned in them, but his look was one of deep gratitude. Faith took another hasty step forward, bringing her to a comfortable distance for the setting, and took his hand. He squeezed it appreciatively.

"We spoke of it often this past week," he said brokenly. "He tried to prepare me, but I was too stunned. I think I always believed he would be here forever. We were a good team. He was the spiritual leader, I was good at the practical side of things, and I thought-" He swallowed. "I didn't think God could spare him here," he almost whispered.

Faith nodded in agreement. "But he didn't leave us emptyhanded, either. Our parish is ready to support you and whoever comes to lead us."

With his eyes still fixed on the floor, he gripped her hand. They stood in silence for a minute. Then Faith smiled faintly.

"You know, I think he would've been satisfied with his life."

The priest's head lifted noncommittally. She persisted.

"His last act was one of service to others. He didn't leave the rectory until everyone else was out, and because of what he did, several lives were saved."

The priest heaved a sigh and raised his head a bit. "Three. The housemaid and two of his guests. Yes. He died for the people he loved most. It's an honor many priests never even think of, but of course he didn't even flinch at the chance. He died like a true shepherd."

But as he spoke, he turned away. An ugly expression passed over his face, his dark brows contracting over seething green eyes and his lips convulsed almost to the point of bearing his teeth. Even Faith seemed taken aback.

"What is it?" she managed timidly. "What's the matter?"

"No one had to die." Father Forsetti's face became almost unrecognizable, steeped in a bitterness that bordered on contempt. "This evil was allowed to pass for God's purpose, but it was still a wicked human soul which kindled the blaze."

Faith squinted, uncomprehending, then raised her voice slightly. "You think someone started the fire on purpose?" She glanced about with wide, disturbed eyes before turning back to him.

The priest straightened, and the veil of sorrow seemed to slip off him like dried sand. He hid his hands inside his black robes and smiled darkly down his nose at Faith. "Thank you for coming, Mrs. Gladstone."

With that, he whirled around and was gone out the side door of the altar with a swish of fabric.

Faith stood staring for a moment after he was gone, but as soon as she came to herself again, she hurried to collect the group of us and hustle out the door.

Of course the instant we were home she told Theophilus everything.

Theophilus stood with his hands tucked under his arms, his expression serious. "Do you think he's right?"

Faith flung her hands up as she paced. "I don't know. He didn't mention any of his reasons for thinking it was arson, but he seemed so sure-" She paused, then stopped pacing. "I have a bad feeling about this, Theo."

Her husband frowned and came closer. He wrapped his arms around her. "Which means?"

She turned dark, troubled eyes to look up at him. "I don't know whether he's right. But I don't like where this may be heading."

The next day, the weather had turned cold and there

was still no sign of my errant cousins. On the day of the funeral, Faith had even sought out the fearsome Mrs. Cunningham, but still no word. She was, however, informed of a great need for more blankets and requested to work as quickly as she could.

The rest of the week followed much as the previous days had, minus any funerals or abandoned orphans. Two days after the funeral, we got a letter from my cousins saying that they would be another week late because they had some errands to run and didn't want to disappoint a friend they had said they would visit. Theophilus muttered some dirty words about them and got an even dirtier look from his wife, then spent the next half hour playing with me on the floor. I think he was mad at them for my sake.

Helena and I often got into trouble for chattering late into the night after the parents had put us to bed. We created an imaginary world out of the furniture in our room and decided to keep it a secret unless we had both agreed to tell.

I missed our pirate days, so at my pleading, Helena agreed to let us return to sea. But, she said, now we were part of the royal Navy and this was the captain's cabin. I consented and fell asleep every night imagining the tossing of waves and rocking of the ship. Sometimes I dreamed that my cousins didn't exist and we would stay like this forever.

One week slid into two, and another message arrived, this one more cryptic than the last. It did ask for my clothing measurements, though it gave no indication of where to send them. Each return address had been different. The handwriting remained the same rounded script ground deeply into the paper.

"At least they made *some* effort to prepare for what they're taking on," Theophilus remarked to Faith on the day they got it, secondhand from Mrs. Cunningham.

Faith shook her head slowly. "They're coming to adopt a little girl and all they want to know is her size? They don't even know who's been taking care of her."

Before long, the old archbishop had reached the end of his residence in Riversedge. Even the other children were glum, for he'd been kind to them, briefly playing games with us whenever he passed through the courtyard. A thick, grey dampness seemed to settle upon the spirits of the congregation, for after his departure, it was all too obvious that their old priest was missing. Faith described this period of acclimation as "the second wave of grief," when everyone mourned again.

Father Forsetti conducted the first service after the archbishop's departure. He left everyone murmuring that it hadn't felt like a real Sunday, not without one of the white-haired old fellows, but I liked his preaching. His was a fiery style, full of passion and calls for repentance. Most people sat solemnly, a little startled by his vigor, and then quietly left to savor the vinegar left in their mouths by his words. Even Theophilus and Faith were divided over his methods, but they soon let it pass. In the next few weeks, they said, other priests would visit until the archbishop chose one to be our new pastor.

Then the chaos of the blankets began.

By the time Helena and I awoke one morning

shortly after Theophilus had left, the entire house had been transformed into a forest of fabrics in all different patterns and colors. Faith's sewing was spread all over the big table with chalk and pins and all sorts of colors of threads spilling out of her sewing box. Even Theophilus's chair had a pile of fabrics on it.

Faith, who had already been up and working for a few hours, feebly attempted to calm our excitement and to get us corralled for breakfast, but no such luck. Helena was determined to explore everything, and I wasn't going to be left out. While poor Faith prepared our porridge, the two of us prowled about the living room and even the parents' bedroom, ducking under sheets where they hung from everything, admiring the patterns, petting the fabrics, and giggling in delight. It was such a small change, but to our tiny world it was thrilling.

Finally, Faith got us seated on the sofa with one of her aprons spread across both of our laps since the table was occupied. Armed with bowls of porridge and attached as we were, we were admirably contained while she arranged her work and retrieved any stray pins. Then she settled herself across from us and laid down the rules.

When Jesus talked about "the poor," he was describing people who couldn't fulfill their own needs for themselves. The rebuilding of the church had brought in a lot of people who needed work but maybe didn't have enough blankets or fuel to keep themselves and their families warm. Since winter was coming, a lot of those people would need a little help, and so we were going to do as Jesus asked and make them some blankets.

For that, she would need our full cooperation and maybe even some help. She seemed prepared for a fight, but this was met by more cheers of excitement. To witness the transformation was one thing; to be able to participate was ecstasy.

Laughing, she thanked us for our help and released us from the apron to put our dishes in the kitchen. Then she made us carefully wash our hands and roll up our sleeves and said we were ready to learn what to do to help make blankets.

First, she showed us the blanket she was already making. She let us stand on the kitchen chairs so we could both see and pointed out how while some scraps of fabric were no good in themselves, they would be strong enough to be layered or stuffed with other materials to make quilts or at least warm blankets.

When Helena asked which blanket she was going to do next, Faith sighed despondently and sank into a chair.

"When I asked the church ladies to help me find big pieces of fabric that weren't needed anywhere else, they really did, but I had no idea..." She sighed again, then motioned helplessly around at the forest of textiles.

"Looks like they did *too* well," Helena said confidentially.

Faith smiled and ruffled her daughter's hair. "Maybe. Or maybe I need a better system." She stood up. "Why don't you girls come with me and we'll look at what we have? Then we can see where the best pieces are and make a list of anything we still need.

Bring me any bits that are thick enough by themselves to just hem. Oh! And remember to keep your eye out for any fabrics that *you* like, Emmanuella. I asked if I could make a blanket for you, and the ladies agreed we shouldn't send you on your journey empty-handed."

We leapt into our work. While Faith picked slowly through a tidy stack on the armchair, Helena and I attacked the monstrosity piled in the corner. There were so many bulky pieces of fabric that the pile was taller than me, and for a minute I could do nothing but giggle at the wildly patterned mountain.

While Helena picked up one piece, unfolding it entirely and commentating even though she didn't really know what we were looking for, I began to unearth some of the ones buried at the bottom. I suppose I was looking for a treasure of some sort.

What I found was a roll of nasty-colored orange wool. With a frown, I began to re-bury it when Faith spotted me. She laughed and came to crouch behind me.

"What, don't like that one very much?"

I scowled and shook my head at her.

"Wait, let me see. It looks like it might be good material."

I paused, then resumed burying. Faith laughed again in genuine amusement. Helena, who had come over to see what all the fuss was about, put her hands on her hips and considered the roll for a moment before she pronounced her opinion.

"Mother, that is the ugliest piece of fabric I have *ever* seen," she declared.

"Oh, stop it, you both," Faith protested. "It doesn't

have to be pretty to keep someone warm-"

"UGLY! UGLY! UGLY!" we both shouted, hopping merrily about the room. Truth be told, we were more excited to have a reason to jump than disgusted by the wool.

Faith had to pause where she was attempting to unearth the maligned fabric and hold her face in one hand, laughing. "You two are terrible! Just come here and look at this – it might not be that bad."

We plopped on the edges of her skirt that were pooled on either side of her. Now that she had it out on her lap, it looked even uglier than ever. I didn't know why someone would've chosen to make such an awful color; I had seen dog droppings that were a similar shade. When Faith turned to me expectantly, I wrinkled my nose, got up, and walked away. Faith howled with laughter.

"Mama," Helena said, as seriously as if she were about to confess some sin, "it's ugly. Mama, don't give that to the poor people. They'll think we're mad at them."

We all laughed while Helena repeated her pronouncement.

When Faith had recovered, she considered the fabric as she ran her hand over it. "It is, kind of," she admitted. "What are we going to do with it?"

"BURN IT!" Helena shouted, raising her fists like a champion athlete. I began to jump with her.

"No, we are not going to burn perfectly good-"

There was a knock at the door. Faith set the fabric aside and went to answer it. "Good morning, Angeline."

"Hello, dear! I was just coming to drop these off and see if you needed any help with the blankets." An adorable round-faced, blonde-haired lady made her way inside. She caught sight of the hideous wool and barked a laugh. "Is this the stuff Mildred sent over? She said she was sending a bit whose color had been ruined by mistake."

"Is that what happened?" Faith chortled, picking it up by an edge.

"Yes! She said her husband had set it in some yellow and then her daughter dumped in a bottle of red because she wanted to make it pink."

"IT'S UGLY!" repeated Helena.

"When Emmanuella found it, she immediately tried to hide it again," Faith added, accompanied by everyone's laughter. "And when I pulled it out to see what she thought of it, she just walked away!"

Angeline joined in our merriment, and to my surprise, she bent to give me a little hug around my shoulders.

"It sounds like she has good taste!" she agreed.

I smiled. I liked her, and she already seemed to like me.

"Her name is Emmy."

Everyone turned to look at Helena. She was standing with her hands behind her back and her feet spread apart. Her father sometimes stood like that.

"Emmanuella is too big for her. She needs a shorter name. We should call her Emmy."

Both women looked at each other. Then Faith looked down at me.

"Would you like to be called Emmy?" she asked.

I tilted my head to one side. No one had ever called me Emmy before. I wasn't sure how I liked it. But when I looked across at Helena and remembered how her papa called her Nellie, I began to smile. When I looked up into Faith's pretty, pale face with its dark eyelashes, I wondered if she would want to name me, too.

"Would you like that?" she asked again softly.

I paused for a moment, then looked up at her. "Yes."

She smiled and hugged me, warm and tight like I was really hers. "Emmy it is, then."

Soon, Angeline and Helena had joined in the hug. Then we were scattered once again to sort through the fabrics. Most were not as hideous as the orange wool, and some of them were as soft as Helena's nightdresses. It was from these that I chose the fabric for my own blanket, and had to be scolded in order to stop repeatedly burying my face in it. It was a soft pink and smelled like someone's home.

Angeline had brought a picnic lunch, which we shared on the living room floor in the only clear space that would fit us. We had sorted through enough of the fabrics for Faith to begin laying them out and seeing which pieces went well together. Unfortunately, it was soon after this that Helena and I discovered to our delight that many of the blankets now smelled like an unfamiliar soap and went around sniffing them until we were lightheaded.

When the women unrolled the contested wool, they found to their dismay that it was much larger than they had thought. Then it was discovered that it had thinned and had holes in places, and we resolved to cut it into pieces to use for insulation instead of keeping it where it could be seen. They both looked relieved, but none were as relieved as Helena.

"Yes!" she yelled. "Cover it up like a dirty secret!"

Faith gave a pained look as she threw her apron over Helena's head. "I think it's high time you stopped quoting your father when other people are around!"

Angeline stayed almost until dark (it was getting dark uncommonly early as the fall drew on into winter), but then she had to go home and make dinner for her family. Faith flopped on the sofa for a rest while the two of us ran to Helena's room and jumped on the bed. An hour later, we reconvened for a snack of apples and renewed efforts at sorting.

We were still at it when Theophilus threw open the door.

"Daddy!" Helena ran over and leapt into his open arms.

He scooped her up and held her up by his shoulder. "Where is my other little girl?" he called.

Unexpected tears stung my eyes as I ran to him, calling out, "Here I am! Oh, here I am!"

He would have lifted me, but my face was buried against his leg and he had to settle for embracing me awkwardly with one hand. When he released us, his and Faith's eyes both looked moist. She came to him and kissed him.

"I don't know why I said that," he murmured wonderingly. "It just felt-"

"Oh, I know!" Faith was squeezing his hands. She shook her head sadly. "What are we going to do when those cousins come for her?"

He pulled her close and muttered something in her ear about pitchforks which made her laugh, but I was quiet. Truth be told, I didn't know what I would do, either.

Chapter Six

That Sunday, everybody was dressed their very best. The ladies wore the prettiest pinks and purples I had ever seen and wore hats which must have either forced them to sit farther apart or else offered shade to the person on either side of them. Once, a lady was passing the altar when her ribbon brushed a nearby candle and caught fire. Embarrassed and clearly unsure whether to say something to her and cause a fuss, Father Forsetti ended up quenching the flame in his hand and sat there turning scarlet while the oblivious woman found her seat.

The man that preached was very dry. He used a lot of words I didn't know and talked about a few different kinds of grace and the various levels of sin. Helena whispered to me that even she hadn't known there were so many. Once, Theophilus's head dipped forward as he began to doze until Faith almost imperceptibly flicked him on his hand and woke him up. Eventually, I gave up listening and watched a bug climb up the back of the pew in front of us and clean its wings at the top.

The following Sunday, even more people showed up with even more precarious hats and beautiful gowns. The same man preached again, this time speaking passionately against something another church was doing. He said that by rejecting church leadership, they were removing themselves from the Body of Christ. The way he spoke made me anxious, but Helena clearly did not share my concerns, for she fell asleep with her head on my shoulder.

As we made our way out into the church courtyard, thankful to see something as cheerful as the pale November sunshine, Father Forsetti made his way over to us. This time he was smiling, but he still walked with his hands clasped behind his back.

"The Lord be with you, Mr. and Mrs. Gladstone," he said, then added, nodding to each of us, "Helena, Emmanuella."

The parents both smiled politely and nodded, but Helena spoke up.

"Her name is Emmy," she staunchly informed him.

One of his eyebrows went up and he smiled faintly. "Very well." He turned to Faith and Theophilus. "And how do we find you on this beautiful though bleak Sunday morning?"

Faith nodded. "Very well, Father, thank you."

The priest turned to Theophilus. I was surprised by the angel-man's expression, for it was uncommonly guarded and solemn and he kept his eyes fixed on the back of one hand as it wrung the other. Father Forsetti made as if to speak, then changed his mind. His eyes were wide with admiration and he had difficulty returning them to Faith, the apparent spokesperson.

"And what have you thought of Monsignor Lowndes?" he asked. "He comes highly recommended and is, as you probably know already, an accomplished scholar. It's been a great privilege to have him here, and if all goes well, he may be assigned as our new pastor!"

Faith nodded, but her expression was almost a wince as she bit her lips.

Father Forsetti cocked his head. "You do not approve? That very much surprises me."

The Gladstones merely glanced at each other before Theophilus once again turned his face away. The priest laughed and made a beckoning motion with his hand.

"Please, share with me your thoughts. It may be either that your objection can be explained away, or that you may have noticed something I haven't. Come." When neither moved, a genuine grin of amusement set the area around his eyes to wrinkling. He motioned once again. "Truly," he added encouragingly.

A sheepish smile twisted the corner of Faith's mouth and lifted one eyebrow. Theophilus stared fixedly at the toes of his shiny black boots.

"Well, to tell the truth, Father," she ventured softly, "we didn't like him very much at all."

His eyebrows were raised in amusement. "I'd gathered that."

"It's not as if we know him personally," she said quickly, "and perhaps if we did our impressions would be different, but-"

The priest nodded for her to continue. He was no longer smiling, but the earnest look in his eyes told us he was indeed listening.

Faith sighed, gathering herself. "It wasn't necessarily something he said or that he didn't say, rather..." She pursed her lips again, thinking. "But one can read a lot about a person's faith from their words, can't one?"

Father Forsetti looked astonished. "You have concerns about his faith?" he asked incredulously. "Mrs. Gladstone, this man has had the privilege of studying at-"

"Yes," Faith said firmly. "As you've said, he is a very learned scholar, and that much was clear. But it seems to me that perhaps his emphasis of the church's own rules have obscured his view of the Gospel. What I mean to say," she added before Father Forsetti could interrupt, "is not that the church rules themselves are wrong or that we shouldn't follow them-"

Theophilus touched her arm gently, but his eyes were on Helena. "Nellie, what was it you said to me about his preaching just before we left the sanctuary?"

Helena peered nervously up at the priest but then drew close to her father. "He made it sound like obeying the rules and doing things in the church were the best goal we could have. Like there wasn't anyone else but the people who were already here."

Father Forsetti nodded, looking like he understood. "I see." He smiled. "I don't think you need to worry about Monsignor Lowndes not working to grow the parish. His zeal may become confusing when it's buried in church teachings which are beyond most people-"

Faith stiffened almost imperceptibly.

"-but I assure you that when it is applied within a parish, great things have been known to happen." He smiled again. "Any other concerns?"

Now the look Faith and Theophilus exchanged was worried. The priest's smile faded. His quizzical expression looked faintly dissatisfied.

"Then your concerns about the man's faith remain unresolved?" he said.

His tone had changed, seemed colder. I slipped farther behind Faith's skirts, alarmed by the tension in the air.

Faith took a deep breath before responding. "What I see is the man before me, not what others think of him. My impressions gave me cause for concern, and that has not been driven out by reassurances that others feel differently. I mean no disrespect."

Father Forsetti nodded gravely. "I am sure you don't." He peered past us for a moment. "I will look into this matter. I strongly suspect that your fears are unfounded, but-" This time we heard someone calling him. "Excuse me," he said at last, hastening back into the church.

As we made our way down the path, Faith looked up at Theophilus. "Do you think I was wrong?" she asked softly.

"Nope," Helena said firmly. We all turned to look at her. "The feeling in there was like dust so thick I couldn't breathe."

Faith nodded reflectively. "When I go to church, I think of the flock being fed by the Shepherd's words, and the priest as helping us understand His teaching. But this time…" She shook her head. "I think I'd have to eat before I arrived, if you know what I mean."

Theophilus laughed. He looked much more relaxed now that we weren't pinned by anyone's watching eyes. I gave a little skip, happy to see him looking normal again.

"I agree with both of you," he said. "What that man needs is a little more fresh air."

"Theophilus!" Faith glanced nervously over her shoulder, but the church was hidden by the rows of shops we had passed.

He looked at her seriously. "Like you, I don't have any problem with scouring the Scriptures and looking for what we may have missed, or with deciphering where we should stand on tough issues based on what He's told us about others." He took Helena's hands and swung her in front of him. "What I do have a problem with is studying it like any other subject, as if what God wants of us is hidden in some secret code."

Faith nodded, appearing relieved. "It's not a list of rules or a logic puzzle."

He nodded emphatically. "It's a relationship, and if we want the answers we need to be drawing closer to Him. I don't really know if what Monsignor Lowndes was arguing was right or not, but what I do know is that you can drive yourself crazy chasing those questions – not unimportant exactly, but extraneous. He's said what He wants of us: 'Act justly, love mercy, walk humbly with your God.' I don't think He would be as concerned with us knowing all of the right answers so much as staying close to Him."

Faith smiled. "Which you can't do if you're only reading Scripture and church writings like they're a logic puzzle that it's up to you to figure out."

"Jesus already did the legwork," Theophilus agreed. "His nearest followers were not the ones who had the best teachers or studied hardest, but the ones who came right up to him in the simplest faith." He smiled approvingly down at the top of Helena's head.

For a moment, everyone was quiet. Then Helena spoke up from where she walked between her parents, holding onto one of each of their hands.

"I wonder if the monsignor knows Jesus."

Faith frowned and exchanged a look with Theophilus, but neither spoke.

The next Friday, quite a commotion bubbled through town. Everyone kept talking about a fabulous window and how they felt they could stare at it for hours. They said some people even wept. I could not for the life of me understand what was so interesting about a window. Didn't the beauty of a window merely consist of what was on the other side?

While I was getting on my shoes, I kept asking Helena where we were going.

"I told you, to the church to see the new window! Now hurry up."

The old sanctuary was now blocked off, leaving room for renovations. The new sanctuary had been completed and if all was ready, we would gather there on Sunday.

But the main event at the moment was that new window. The one I had seen before was in the second floor gallery and, I later found out, was meant to be kept a secret until the entire cathedral was finished.

The new window, evidently from the tight press of people, was in a much-used corridor that faced west. This corridor was in the oldest part of the church, but it would not only connect both the new and the old sanctuaries, but provide a backbone for renovations in its grandly simple style. Made of stone, it had not burned with much of the rest.

Admittedly, I was not in a good mood as we waited to see. I fussed and poked at Helena until Faith was forced to scold me. I sniffled quietly to myself after this but submitted.

At last, we entered the back corridor, and again I heaved a prodigious sigh. What was everyone on about?

Without a word, Theophilus scooped Helena and me up, one on each solidly built shoulder. As he drew closer, those around us stared at him in wonder and a little discomfort and backed respectfully out of his way. He smiled and nodded uncomfortably at them all, but his eyes told me he was terrified. Then all attention was returned to the masterpiece before us.

For a long moment, no one spoke. Theophilus grinned back and forth between the glass, his wife, and me. As for me, I stared openmouthed without stirring for a solid five minutes, as obnoxiously riveted as those around me.

The scene before us was a portrayal of the Last Supper, but it was not like any I had ever seen before. Since the window was much smaller and the scene more crowded, the details were far less pronounced than in the window I had seen in the upper gallery, but still it was evocative.

Thirteen dark-skinned men (I heard Helena counting them) reclined on floor cushions around a square, short table. The angle of the picture made you feel as if you were seated at the table, with three or four people on each of the four sides. You viewed the table kind of at a diagonal, seeing only the hands and table settings of the people to your left. Jesus sat opposite these invisible ones between two Apostles. Everyone appeared aghast with horror.

Below it was carved into the wooden frame: "*One of you will betray me.*"

Helena and I stared in wonder as long as we could. I couldn't speak, but she had plenty to say. Her parents often smiled and gently shushed her when her excited voice began to rise above the crowd. Thoughts which had never occurred to me before began to stir in my heart.

A raucous voice cut through the reverent murmurs and made me jump. "Well, that seems an odd thing for it to say!" an older woman in gorgeous furs squawked indignantly. An equally handsome man beside her made an effort to quiet her, but she turned to address him loudly. "This image is a portrayal of the most important act in our faith and instead of referencing the Body of Christ he chooses an insignificant quote about His betrayal?" Now the woman's husband had a warning grasp on her arm, but she spoke all the louder, addressing those in the near vicinity. "Why, it's nearly sacrilege!"

Helena bristled and swiveled to face this woman, drawing her little self up as high as she could, augmented by her seat upon her father's shoulder. She looked like she was prepared to give the lady what-for, but Theophilus merely laughed. He knelt, placing us on either side of him, and pressed one finger to his smiling mouth, nodding to one and then the other of us.

Gradually, Helena's cheeks, which were flaming with indignation, faded to a normal color, and she nodded. I glanced from one to the other, not understanding what was going on, but then Faith took my hand and we all made for the outer doors. When we reached the first steps, Theophilus swooped down and scooped us both up again, carrying one on each hip.

"Daddy, why didn't you answer that lady when she said those things about your window? I thought it was beautiful," Helena pouted. Then she frowned uncertainly. "And what does 'sacrilege' mean?"

Theophilus's wide grin puzzled me. "She's just expressing her opinions."

Helena frowned. "Well, most people would get a spanking for talking like that. Especially when the artist is around. It could hurt someone's feelings!"

I frowned up from where my head rested on his shoulder. "But what *is* sacrilege?"

As often happened when I spoke, Faith and Theophilus both turned happy looks in my direction. This time, though, it was followed by a glance at each other. Faith's expression was one of concern.

When we reached the end of the walk but before we had exited the gates, Theophilus stopped and set us both atop the stone wall surrounding the garden. This way, he could more easily look us both in the eye. We leaned in, soberly expectant.

"Now, ladies, this is important for you to understand: When I made this window, I had no intention of scorning the Eucharist or of showing disrespect for Christ or his people. I merely represented that scene as it appears in my mind: Jesus at the hardest turning point of his ministry. Do you remember what happened that night?" Helena started to answer but he gently stopped her with a motion. He turned to me. "Emmy, do you know?"

"J-Jesus gets betrayed. He dies," I said quietly. I didn't like to dwell on this morbid subject.

Theophilus nodded. "That's right. But it wasn't just one person, Judas, who betrayed him, was it? It was a much harder night."

Helena's eyes, too, were troubled. "All of his friends left him," she said softly. "They ran away when the soldiers came for him, and then lied about being his friend when they were scared."

He nodded again and stroked our hair. "Yes, my loves." He smiled affectionately. "But then what?"

Helena took a deep breath. "But then he dies and our sins are forgiven and he comes back to life in three days and goes up to heaven and sends us his Spirit to live with us." She took another breath. "And he's coming back."

Theophilus smiled gently. "Well said, Nellie. Yes, and that's the core of our faith right there. If you have nothing else, you have that, and it's enough. Some of the rest of it starts to get confusing, and that's where people really start fighting with each other, even among believers."

He shook his head. "But there are two main reasons I wanted to show that scene the way I did. One, I think the Eucharist is a well-documented and much-remembered part of life in this parish, so they don't need any more reinforcement from me. I counted, and there are six separate references to Holy Communion in the church's artwork already, ten if you count the newest parts that only some know about yet.

"The second reason was that I wanted everyone to pause and remember what Jesus went through. It wasn't just physical pain that he went through, nor even the torment of separation from God when he took our sins upon himself. He was betrayed or abandoned by everyone he knew." Theophilus's eyes were heavy with sorrow, and I had the sense that he knew something of what Jesus had experienced.

He wrapped his arms around us, lifted us, and began to walk again. "My hope is that whenever someone enters this church feeling lost, alone, betrayed, or falsely accused, they will look up at this window and remember that even if they have to go through it, Jesus did, too." His voice was barely above a whisper when he added, "And he will be with them through every step."

There was a long pause. Then Helena piped up over Theophilus's shoulder. "Mama, why are you crying?"

Faith shook her head. "It's nothing, baby. Why don't you and Emmy race to the baker's storefront and back?"

Without a word, Theophilus set us down. As we darted off, he turned to wrap his arms around his wife.

She buried her face against his chest and he rested his chin on top of her dark head. His eyes were thoughtful as they traced the majestic bulk of the church above us on the hill.

When we reached the storefront, I pulled Helena to a stop. "Why is she crying?" My voice had dropped to a hoarse murmur.

She nodded knowingly and wrapped me in a hug. Given our age difference, my head only reached as high as her chest. "They need to talk alone. That's what they mean when they send us off like this."

I frowned. "But why is Theophilus sad?"

She pursed her lips. "Something happened to him when he and Mama were engaged, but they won't tell me what it is. They said they'll tell me when I'm older. I'll let you know as soon as I find out."

With that, she poised to take off back up the hill toward the adults again, but I stopped her. "But what if I'm not here by then? What if my cousins come to take me away, and I'm not here to know what happened to your papa?"

For some reason, I was upset. My chest heaved and I stood with my fists clenched by my sides and tears in my eyes. Helena studied me coolly for a long moment.

"We'll hide you," she pronounced firmly at last. "When your cousins come for you, we'll tell them you ran away, and then you can stay with us forever."

Once more, she tried to run off, but I clung to her skirt. The tears which I had suppressed until then were now running down my face.

"Do you-" *Promise.* My voice died away before I could finish the phrase, but I forced myself to try again. "Do you promise? You won't let them take me away, will you?"

By now I had buried my face against Helena and was sobbing heartily while she stared at me in astonished alarm.

The parents must have noticed something was wrong, for moments later I heard their hasty footsteps clatter up to us on the pavement. I hunched my back, trying to hide my face from them. Helena had taken hold of me and was wavering between pushing me away and giving me a hug.

"What's wrong?" Faith asked breathlessly. "Did she hurt herself?" Her hands tugged on my shoulders, but I firmly resisted. "Emmanuella, let me see."

"You have to promise!"

Helena squeezed me tightly, then gently pushed me away. "Emmy! Emmy, let Mama look at you."

Theophilus had gone on his knees beside us. "What's she upset about?" His voice was steady and calm.

Helena's little brow was furrowed uncertainly as she turned pleading eyes on him. "She's afraid her cousins will come for her and she'll never know what happened when you and Mama were younger," she explained.

I heard a sorrowful intake of breath. Then I felt a giant, warm hand on my back.

"Emmy," Theophilus said softly.

His voice was as rich and sweet as the honey that he'd put on my porridge that first morning. I sobbed harder, frightened by my own emotions and not even sure why I was crying.

"Emmy, do you not want to go with your cousins?" he asked.

"No!"

"She obviously doesn't," Helena added helpfully. Faith took her by the hand and pulled her against her.

With my shield gone, I was forced to stand toe-to-knee with Theophilus, but I wouldn't look up. I stared down at my shoes, wringing my hands and crying.

"Do you know them? Emmy, look at me. Has someone told you they'd be unkind to you?"

I let him lift my chin up, but the tears were coming so thick that I couldn't even clearly see him, and I let my head drop as soon as he released me.

"Emmy, tell me what's wrong." He waited, letting me wear myself out until my sniffles became less frequent.

"I don't wanna go," I said softly. "I wanna stay with Helena and be sisters forever."

"You *can* always be sisters," Faith said earnestly, touching the top of my head. "You'll always be friends if you want to be. You can write to each other. We will-"

Theophilus hushed her. He suddenly pulled me against him, mushing my face against his waistcoat, his voice muffled in my hair. "We will always love you, sweetheart, and you will always have a home with us." He let me back from him a little. "But what if your cousins love you, too? They might be as much of a family-"

"Or maybe they just want the money," Helena retorted.

The parents whirled on her, expressions furious. She

looked fearful, but still she stood tall. "That's what Emmy told me they wanted. Tell them, Emmy!"

Both slowly turned back toward me.

"Surely that's not true," Faith said soothingly. "No one would-"

"Sure, they would!" Helena protested. "She says her nurses used to talk about it all the time, didn't they? Tell them about the man who came to see your headmistress."

The parents looked at me inquiringly, sadness written in each face. I was not crying now, but my soulful gaze told them everything they needed to know. There was no hiding it.

Feeling very small, I told them what I had heard.

Theophilus's sandy brows were deeply furrowed. "And your cousins. What have you heard about them?"

"That they're brother and sister." I shook my head. That was all I knew.

Before anyone could speak, Faith suddenly took my hand. "We'll talk about this later, Theophilus. Girls, it's time to go home. Don't worry about any of this until tomorrow."

Young and full of hope, I believed her. I was quiet and docile all evening and didn't even complain when they sent us to bed early, though Helena threw a fit.

When we were tucked into bed, she scooted over close to me and whispered, "*I* think they want to keep you."

Nestled up beside Helena with her doll protectively between us, I fell asleep.

Hours passed; I did not sense how many. After the

high emotions of the evening, my sleep was deep and restful.

All at once, however, I was wrenched from the embrace of slumber and thrust into a world of darkness by a shout.

"FIRE!"

Helena and I both jumped, immediately awake. That voice had been right outside our window.

The parents exchanged a few urgent words, followed by loud scuffling. Then I heard Theophilus's boots rush into the living room and out the front door.

Moments later, our door banged open to reveal Faith in her nightdress. Her hair was in a loose braid. "Girls? Are you awake?"

"Yes, Mama." Helena's usually strident voice quavered with fear.

Faith strode to the bed and wrapped her arms around us. "Your father is going to go see where the fire is and if there's anything he can do to help. I'm going to stay in here with you girls, all right? Lie back down."

The rest of the night felt like a single tense hour. The entire time, Faith sat with her legs stretched out in front of her on the edge of our bed, as though shielding us with her body. She alternated between rubbing each of our backs and running her fingers through our hair. Whenever one of us stirred, she soothed us back to sleep, or at least until we were quiet. She didn't realize I was awake for most of the night because unlike Helena, I didn't speak.

All the while, Faith's pale face was bathed in a patch of moonlight where she had opened the window a crack in order to see out. Though her hands were soft and comforting, her face revealed an alertness which was enough to unveil the fear she kept inside. Every so often, lots of feet would clatter past, either out on the street or right by our window, waking Helena. Worried voices murmured to each other by turns, and sometimes someone even shouted. At these moments, Faith hurriedly shut the window and murmured or sang to us to cover the noise. Long before morning came, vigorous energy was thrumming through me, preparing me to rise and face whatever terror had come about in the night.

Chapter Seven

The watery yellow dawn came on so gradually that it still felt like night when the front door softly opened. Faith sprang off the bed and flew into the main area, letting the door of our room bang open behind her. Helena sat upright, whimpering a frightened call for her mother. I stroked the back of her hand until she was calm, then clambered out of the bed and followed where Faith had gone.

It was clear they didn't see me in the darkness. Faith stood there in her nightdress, clinging to Theophilus. His shirt and pants – for he had been fully dressed – were blackened in places and his eyes were swollen and bloodshot. He gripped his wife's elbows with sooty hands.

"It was in the Benches," he said. The Benches were a choppy area of the lower reaches of the city where Faith had told us never to play, noisy taverns where ladies waited outside in flamboyant gowns with rips at the bottom. "They say one of the women started the fire by dropping her candle when she'd had too much to drink-"

"Is that not the case?" She was too quick not to catch the change in his tone.

He shook his head. "I don't believe so," he said quietly.

"Is everyone out?"

"No." Theophilus glanced over his shoulder, then back down at his wife. His eyes looked glassy, tinged with horror or disgust. "No, the staircase collapsed and we'll have to get in from the other side. I came back to get my bottle of aloe for the burn victims. I thought I had some here."

Faith nodded and hurried to a cupboard. "So the fire isn't out yet?" She handed him a greenish bottle half-full of fluid.

He restlessly shook his head. "We couldn't get it. There was too much-" He stopped, lowering misting eyes. "We'll have to let it burn."

A shouting voice made them both start. Theophilus dashed away from the open door for several moments. Then he reappeared, his boots landing on the front stoop with a resounding smack.

He shook his head, his mouth grim. "The tenements have caught." He glanced over his wife's shoulder, considering the piles of fabric everywhere.

She removed his hands from her shoulders. "I have some old nightdresses." She whirled around and hurried into and back out of their bedroom, holding a pile of clothes. She smiled ironically at her husband's blank stare. "It's night. Not everyone's going to be, um, dressed for the weather."

He let out something between a gasp and a laugh.

"You're a good woman." He kissed her soundly on the cheek and took the pile from her. Then he hurried back to the door.

"Do you need any help?"

He turned, cradling her jaw between a forefinger and thumb, and kissed her mouth. "Take care of the girls."

Then he was off. Faith watched him gravely, then summoned another woman from next door. They huddled by the door, talking until the dawn had turned pink.

By midday, much of the Benches had been reduced to ashes. Shops in the area had remained closed to help contain the flames, mostly out of self-interest; the buildings here were so closely packed together that for the inferno to gain another step was to say goodbye to someone else's home and business. People didn't have anything good to say about either the block or the people who frequented it, but nobody wanted another such catastrophe anywhere, and even those of the lowest morals were tended by the neighbors for their burns.

Even though the area was many streets away from our little niche, Theophilus was out all day to help. Faith's smile was proud when she told others he had chosen to help when they remarked quizzically that his workshop was in the opposite direction.

She kept Helena and me close, however, for the victims of the fire were led past our street to seek shelter elsewhere, and it was still true that many were not people whom one would trust near one's children even for a moment. We played close to the house while

Faith hung laundry from the clothesline, her eye always slantways on us. By evening, we had grown accustomed to the sound of the cough which Faith told us was from breathing in so much smoke.

It was near sunset when Theophilus kicked the front door open and trudged inside. His once-tidy clothes and golden hair were an ugly grey and he stank of burnt wood, ale, and smoke. Without even a glance at us, he sprawled full-length on the sofa with his arms and legs poking off the ends and immediately seemed to fall asleep.

Faith nodded faintly, collecting Helena to help her with supper. I, however, approached the sooty, fallen form of the angel-man and stood mere feet away from his head, now much closer to my own level and at the perfect height to examine.

His stained white back rose and fell fitfully, occasionally jolted by quiet coughing. Faith softly called to me to leave him be, but I peered closely at his face; it was hidden under his spilled hair, ashen gold free of its ponytail. I bent with my hands on my knees to get a better look at him. It was funny; in some ways he looked the same, but somehow the fire had changed him. He was dirty now, subdued, prostrate. And yet to me he seemed all the more human.

Faith called me again, wiping her hands on her apron. She began to walk toward me, but when she saw I wasn't going to wake him, she paused. Drawing still closer, I reached up and gently rubbed a swatch of hair. Soot came away on my hand, and I wiped it off on my apron with a scowl. Then I petted the colorful stains which Faith hadn't been able to completely get out of his sleeves. His arms were strong, but they would never hurt anyone.

"Emmy, come here," Faith said softly. "Daddy's tired; let him sleep."

Sometimes I pretended that my frequent inability to speak also rendered me deaf and used this excuse to do as I pleased. I did that now, turning my attention to Theophilus's hands. His arms were crossed at the wrists and shielding his downcast face. I looked up at him again, but still he remained quiescent, and I found myself smiling. His openness made him less intimidating than most on an ordinary day, but this was even better. I giggled; resting as he was, he didn't seem so different from me, and I felt my fears slip away.

His long-fingered hands were stained the darkest, with bits of black under the nails. There was a cut along one forefinger, running almost the length of it. I reached up and lightly touched his hand. When it moved limply, I took both hands and opened them palm-up, examining them.

A grunt alerted us that Theophilus was awake. His head jerked up, and he stared down at me in surprise.

Faith smiled apologetically. "I'm sorry, love. I was going to have her come over here, but then she was so quiet and I didn't think she would-"

"It's all right." He pulled himself up to a sitting position, leaning his elbows on his knees and letting his head dangle forward with weariness. After a moment, he sat up to look at me again.

To both our surprise, I had toddled right up to him (I would always keep my distance until beckoned, and then had to be physically pulled any closer than a few yards) and stood between his feet.

"What are you about, little girl?" he asked playfully.

His eyes stared vacantly, looking as if they'd been painted. I found myself giggling. For the first time, I was standing very close to someone without feeling one bit afraid. A smile tweaked the end of his mouth.

"What?" This time it was a genuine question.

Without a word, I beamed up at him. Then I stood up on my toes, gave him a shy little kiss on the cheek, then turned and went back into the kitchen.

From that night on, I'm told I was a different child. If Theophilus sat down, I wanted to climb onto his lap. Only he could read to me, and if he left before dawn, then I was up too, either to eat breakfast or merely to sit beside him until he left and I returned to bed. Helena was baffled by this behavior; much as she loved her father, nothing would make her rise earlier than necessary except the promise of a special errand or sweet.

This did not mean I was distant from Faith; now when she brushed my hair, I would sit quietly in her lap and while she ran her hands through it, marveling at what she called its "autumn glow." If she ran errands, I was right beside her, holding her hand and appearing to actively take part in whatever transaction she made. Helena even became jealous and returned more often from play, demanding to participate.

One day, Theophilus came home to find me sitting in a sullen heap outside the kitchen, enfolded in a big towel with only a few damp curls and a face of consternation peering out.

"What happened to you?" he asked in amusement when he bent down.

"Bath," I informed him.

Theophilus's grin was infectious. "It happens to the best of us," he said confidentially.

Up until this point, I had only allowed Faith to sponge me off, barely letting her clean my face and neck before I got away and hid from her. Helena had taken many baths while I was here, but I had been too stubborn for anyone to convince me of the safety or sanity of the practice.

Later, when Faith casually reminded Theophilus that he needed to take a bath, instead of complying as usual, he stole a towel from her and swatted her with it, then ran away. The next half hour was bedlam as he danced away from and teased her while she laughed and tried to catch him. At last, he caught her in the towel and playfully dunked her in the suds. Helena and I howled with laughter.

That Sunday, we viewed another of Theophilus's windows for the first time. This one delighted everyone, even the sourest of parishioners. Theophilus's task, he said, had been to portray as many of Jesus's miracles as possible in a single window, which had been quite a feat! For this one, he'd chosen to fill the tall, slender frame just inside the sanctuary so that he would have lots of room. Each pane depicted a different part of the story, but all of its occupants were looking to the foreground, at Jesus. There he sat, lifting a woman's weeping face toward him. She was kneeling in front of him, but her eyes lit with hope and astonishment as she stared back into the eyes of Love.

Faith and Helena couldn't seem to stop grinning over one of the little children with Jesus. She was small, barely dressed in a dirty and ragged dress. The only thing that was beautiful about her was the expression of bliss on her face. That, and her auburn hair. She stood on Jesus's lap with one of His arms wrapped around her, and though she clung to his clothes with one hand for balance, she was reaching toward a butterfly and turned away from Him to examine it. Where her hair blew in the wind, I was told there was a letter "E," but I couldn't find it.

Beside Him sat another child in the grass, appearing equally oblivious to Him. She sat with her back toward Jesus's feet with her legs spread out in front of her, intent on what she was doing. But if you looked closely, as Theophilus pointed out, she was making daisy chains with dandelions, and Jesus had one on His wrist where He was reaching out to the woman on her knees. Hidden in this little girl's sleeve was the letter "H."

Behind Jesus, the towering window contained images of countless other biblical figures, all turned toward Him in wonder. Lazarus stood in the mouth of his tomb, apparently wrestling out of his burial wrappings with a grin on his face. The woman beside the well clutched the clay jar to her chest in openmouthed disbelief. Some people held out their hands to each other with delight, while one soldier was dropping his sword to the ground. Others didn't even look at Jesus from where they sat on the ground, hungrily tearing into bread and fish.

Above them, it was harder to see until Theophilus lifted me onto his shoulders. There was a crowd of parents hugging their children; these, he said, represented those whose children had been healed from sicknesses or demons or had even been brought back from the dead. I didn't like it because it made Faith cry.

Just behind them were a group of well-dressed people in bright colors. They held fat scrolls and other religious objects I recognized. They were looking at Jesus, but with a menacing or even mocking expression. Two of them whispered to each other behind their hands, reminding me of some of the ladies in church with their fans. Several were looking at the children in disgust. Many of them were the Pharisees, Helena told me. Faith's eyes were wide as she whispered with Theophilus about this, and even he looked both excited and uneasy. "Bold" was the only word I could catch, and one which she kept saying over and over.

Our happiness from that night was cruelly quashed the next morning by news: there had been two more fires, this time in the well-to-do neighborhoods on the other side of town. Three people were dead, and the houses had been destroyed. Two families who had never known want were thinking of entering the poorhouse until they could find someplace else to stay. People said the families not only grieved the loss of family and shelter and possessions, but were embarrassed for their loss. Faith said they were ashamed of their new circumstances.

Services for the dead were held the next day. When

the death bells tolled, now a familiar sound, the cathedral was suitably backdropped by a serene pink and blue sunset marred by inky black clouds where the remains still smoldered.

The following Sunday, services were followed by a town meeting. People were warned against leaving candles and fireplaces unattended, and children were enjoined to help their parents keep fireplaces swept clean. But throughout the discussion, Father Forsetti stood at the back, not saying a word. His lips were pursed so tightly they were as pale as his cheeks, and his stern eyes often found Faith's across the room. When they did, her knuckles turned white where she gripped the back of the pew in front of us.

The ensuing weeks showed the world opening to me in a new way. My hands grew steady enough to help in the kitchen; before, they had shaken every time someone spoke to me until I was sure to drop whatever was handed to me. Helena was not the only one to lead our games, and sometimes my voice echoed through the house as we acted out a dramatic scene. Little was said about my cousins during this time except in jest, for nobody liked to speak of my leaving. Gradually, the unfortunate pair became the butt of every joke, to my wicked delight.

My confidence and comfort in the bond between myself and each of the others grew until I could play tricks on Theophilus, quarrel heartily with Helena, and bargain with Faith when she insisted it was bedtime. I didn't hide anymore when I'd done something naughty; I would bow my head or sniffle if scolded, but I was no longer afraid they wouldn't love me after what I had done. Once, I even endured a spanking after having stolen a sweet, but after my punishment, I was able to approach them without fear and start again.

Not even the church ladies could cow me as I walked proudly between Faith and Theophilus, holding one or both of their hands unless Helena tired of running ahead and wedged between us. I was still wary of the other children and often preferred to play on my own, with Helena dashing back and forth to spend time with me between intervals of the bigger group's games.

One day, however, we had more to fear than even Mrs. Cunningham. Faith, Helena, and I made the first of many trips to the church with a gaggle of other ladies who had come to sort the blankets into the neighborhoods and families to whom they would be sent. Each time, our house was emptied of blankets only to be refilled with materials and donations of winter clothes. Everything was spread out on long tables so we could stack them together with the proper label and prepare them for their departure.

A few other children had come, but I'm afraid that once we found each other, we weren't much help. Mostly we hopped over the piles of blankets or hid behind pillars to scare each other. I didn't realize until years later that the women had traded off so someone was always on guard to keep us out of trouble. Sometimes, one of the women would get us organized for a task, but more often it was just best to let us play.

By the time we'd finished, it had been four hours and the sun was getting low. Nobody wanted to be out after dark, so children and workbaskets were swiftly gathered up, and a mass exodus was made for the door.

"Come on, girls," Faith said to us, taking our hands and turning before we'd reached the big main gates. "Let's go out this way."

"Mrs. Gladstone."

Helena and I jumped and we all jerked to a stop. Father Forsetti had materialized out of the stonework and was fixing our mother with his most glinting stare.

"A word with you, if you please." It didn't sound like a request.

We looked up at Faith, clinging to her hands in fear. But she seemed to grow taller, lifting her chin and pulling back her shoulders. She drew her shawl regally against her upper arms and turned to gaze at him coolly.

"Certainly, Father."

The answering glint in her eyes seemed to take him aback momentarily, and he backed a few steps away for her to settle us first. I'd never heard her voice so ice cold. My chin started to quiver. But when she turned toward us, her smile was as calm and kind as ever. She bent so she was at eye level.

"Look after your sister," she told Helena. Then to me: "Stay with Nellie, and no tricks. I'll be back soon and then we'll go home." She touched each of our faces lightly, then turned and walked a short distance into the shadow. Father Forsetti waited for her to draw even with him, then followed.

Helena and I looked at each other wordlessly. Then she, being the eldest, dutifully led me a little farther away and set up hopscotch for us. We played in peace for a little while, and Helena watched me as vigilantly as a little mother hen.

But it wasn't long before Faith and the priest's voices began to rise. I waited until it was Helena's turn to hop through the long course she had set up, then slunk silently away.

I came upon their meeting place shortly, staying tucked behind one stone buttress so I could hear. Their voices were so angry that it took me several seconds to gather the courage to look over. When I did, I saw Faith standing calm and erect. She faced forward even while the priest prowled in circles about her, his normally genial face streaked with scarlet.

"So you decided to defy not only your priest, but Mrs. Cunningham, a respected lady in the church and one of your own friends?" he was saying angrily.

Faith answered, smooth and cool as cream. "I beg to differ."

"Really."

He came to a stop just in front of her, glaring down from where he stood head and shoulders above her. She still didn't make eye contact, but stared straight forward.

"No, Father. As far as *your* parish is concerned, I did what was asked-"

"But when refused what you really wanted, you decided to find someone else whom you could bend to your will!"

Poised as he was, he reminded me of a picture I saw once of a bull preparing to charge a matador. But once again, instead of shrinking back or noting how big he looked beside her, Faith seemed to rise up. Her face looked as if it were level with his even a foot below it.

"I have not betrayed you or this parish by asking for another church's help, Father. So let's just state things the way they really are."

Already he looked taken aback by her boldness, but it was not only anger which lit his expression. A kind of astonishment threatened to give way to admiration. She reminded me of a queen, beautiful and strong and not about to give an inch if it didn't suit her. In fact, instead of beating a meek retreat, she took a step toward him. Confusion and alarm entered his features, but he held his ground.

"When confronted about my possible misuse of church community resources, I obeyed; I did not give those blankets to even the poorest neighbors on my doorstep." Her eyes flashed dangerously. "But when I asked permission to help those who needed it most and my plea was denied, both by you and your parish-"

Father Forsetti went white with rage, and her voice warbled momentarily. Then it grew into a thunderous declaration.

"I availed myself of the help of another part of the Body of Christ." He started to speak, but she cut him off, brandishing a scolding finger. "And if you're going to criticize them for belonging to another denomination, just remember that it was them who cared for the neediest people in town, not this parish!"

"I don't have a problem with your wanting to give aid to the poor," he shouted, "but with your flagrant and repeated insubordination to the church! I'm beginning to think that it's not out of Christian charity that you defy me-" here, Faith was the one to turn scarlet, "but a hatred of authority! Tell me, do you believe you could correct God Himself?"

"Which of us claims to speak for God?" she asked softly, seething. "You answer *to* Him, not *for* Him!"

Father Forsetti recoiled. "Then you deny the authority which was passed on to us by *Christ Himself*?"

"Your appointment by him does not guarantee your obedience to him." Her voice had turned to a murmur, pleading with intensity. "I do not wish to defy you. But you backed me into a corner when-"

He barked an incredulous laugh. "I what?"

"Yes, you did. When you resolved to only help those who swore their allegiance not only to Christ but to your church-"

"Mrs. Gladstone!"

"-when you found it more important to cling to the barriers between your churches than to obey the commands of Christ-"

"Stop this-!"

"-and to see those who were most in need of your help-" She paused to gulp a breath. Now her voice warbled continuously, for tears of rage and something else trembled at her lashes. "I had to make a choice. A choice I will continue to make as long as you force me to choose between the commands of Christ and yours."

"Mrs. Gladstone, you are on very dangerous ground," he snarled lowly. "You are questioning an authority much higher than you realize."

"And this is what I can't stand!" she snapped, making him flinch. A look of concern passed briefly over his face. "You believe because you are a teacher of the faith that in order to reach Christ others must pass through you. You stand *between* them and Christ-"

"Mrs. Gladstone!" His voice was like a thunderclap. "You must remember that you are a layperson and a woman, and that your place is one of submission, to your husband and-"

I saw the whites of Faith's eyes mere inches from his face as she spat the words through her teeth. "*You* are *not* my husband!"

She would not bear any more. She grasped her skirts, whirled away from him, and strode across the courtyard, neither looking back nor acknowledging his remorseful calls.

When she turned the corner, I could not hide my shock, nor the fact that I had been listening. She froze, and I burst into tears. I was sobbing so hard that I could not even read her expression to see whether it was one of anger or remorse. Even her calm, cooing voice could not still my unhappiness, though I had no idea why I was weeping.

Chapter Eight

In minutes, she had gathered me up and carried me on her shoulder to where an astonished Helena still waited for us, and ushered her disquieted little brood home. She sat us down and explained something about adults having conversations with people they disagree with, but my disturbed heart let it through like a sieve.

When Theophilus came home, things were little better. Throughout dinner, even Helena was shocked into silence, and he could get nothing out of me. Faith clearly didn't want to further disturb us and tried to settle everyone down, but to no avail. Eventually, the two of them had to step away into their bedroom to speak among themselves. Helena and I played in subdued quiet until bedtime.

I had been in bed for over an hour and Helena had long been asleep when I heard them speaking. I looked over; our bedroom door was open, and theirs was cracked slightly. Since the house was silent, I could pick up their conversation as I hadn't when we'd been playing. I went to the door of our bedroom, then to theirs.

"Why are you still awake?" Theophilus was saying to Faith. "Come to bed, love!"

"I can't stop thinking about my fight with the father," she said. Her tone was foreign to me, quiet and expressionless.

She shook her head and buried her face in her hand. She was seated on the foot of the bed while her husband was waiting for her under the quilt. As she spoke, he frowned and crawled forward until he was seated beside her with his legs hanging off the side of the bed. He wrapped one arm around her.

Faith didn't look at him. "I keep thinking I ought to apologize, and yet I can't bring to mind a single word I regret having said." She laughed emotionlessly. "But still I am scared sick of what message I've sent to our daughters today!"

Theophilus cocked his head. "What message is that?"

She stood and shuffled a few feet away from him. "To question the authority of the church." She sighed and shook her head. "I'm responsible for their souls, you know."

Her husband rested his elbows on his knees, a faint frown of concentration on his face. "Not by yourself, you're not. And at what point did you do something which would endanger their souls?"

She wrung her hands. "I've showed them to strike at the authority of a priest, and to question his motives and the decisions he's made with the church which was entrusted to him! To refuse to submit to their church leadership!" She hung her head again. "This is exactly what I do *not* want them to believe about the pastors of their own churches when they're adults! That to tear the community apart over a small issue is acceptable or even worthwhile."

Theophilus got up from the bed and took hold of her arms, stopping her pacing. "We both know that that's not what you did, nor the reason why you did it. You called out problem attitudes we've been talking about since we got here, ones which are not uncommon in other churches, too." He shook her gently, trying to make her look at him. "Faith, your example to the girls has done nothing but make me proud. You're overwhelmed and it's time to put it off for the night. Please, come to bed."

But she shook her head, trying to push away his arms. Her eyes were wild with fear, caught by the moonlight. "I cannot sleep! Not after what I've done."

Without being rough, the angel-man refused to let her get the better of him. He caught her wrists with one hand and gathered her against him, bending to rest his chin on her head. It wasn't long before she ceased fighting.

When she looked up again, her eyes glistened with tears. "Theo, what if they're right about everything? What if I just spent several minutes yelling what was a slap in the face to Christ?" Her voice lowered with horror. "And what if they excommunicate me? Theo, what if it's true? That whole 'keys to the kingdom' thing they say, about being able to shut people out of the flock if they-"

"Faith!" he cut her off sharply. "That's enough!" His

arms tightened around her as if he were fending off her nightmares. "They wouldn't excommunicate you over something so small, and you know they can't take away your salvation." When she didn't answer, he shook her slightly. "You know that, Faith! Is that what this is about?"

A strangled hiccup let him know he was right. He frowned, his anger clearly directed at the specters which kept his wife from sleep and not at the woman herself. He squeezed her even tighter as if to bring her out of the waking dream.

Then he sighed. He bent down and picked her up as if she were a child. He placed her on the foot of the bed and knelt facing her. He took her hands in both of his. Her eyes had lost their tormented isolation, but still she watched him with burdened sadness.

He sighed impatiently. "And this is what I hate, this fear-mongering that happens in so many churches! Everyone should be fighting for what's right, and while it's true that we can't always be fighting each other and expect His church to remain intact, it's just a matter of fact that we're all going to have to accept correction sometimes, whether we like it or not, and sometimes we have to hear it from the people we least expect. I don't believe that's wrong, Faith. I think that's life."

Faith hiccupped a laugh and smiled at him incredulously. "But did I have the right to take on the entire church hierarchy?"

Theophilus shook his head, his mouth pursed in distaste. "That's not what you did, though, and you know that, right? You were merely correcting him-"

"Which I had no right to do, being not only a layperson in his church but a woman." She stood and turned away from him.

Immediately, he caught the hidden implication and his back went straight as a ramrod. "Did he say that to you?"

She didn't answer. He got to his feet and impulsively reached for his robe.

"That's it. It's time for him to go toe to toe with a layperson who's a man, if that's what will-"

"Theophilus, don't!" Faith hurriedly caught his hand, then resumed her seat as if to keep him anchored.

Her husband whirled to face her with a wild but earnest look on his face. "If he wants to waylay a God-fearing woman in front of her children, then berate her for obeying God's commands better than he has, only to pull rank and throw every form of authority in her face, then perhaps he would prefer it if said husband were to take a jaunt over there and disturb *his* sleep in solidarity with this God-fearing wife. Layperson, indeed! Of all the ways to respond to just criticism-"

"Theophilus, no!" He was strong enough that in clinging to his wrist to restrain him she'd been dragged to the floor and now stumbled over to him, giggling, and arrested him in both arms. "Theophilus, stop. There is no need for you to take this any further. We both have lessons to learn. I should've just gone to Mrs. Cunningham again when she refused me."

"Of course you should have!" He pulled a face. "I, too, enjoy kicking the dens of poisonous reptiles."

Faith buried her face in his shirt to smother her

laughter. "Stop it! Don't. Even if we've enough reason to dispute them, we haven't got the right to insult them. Now, stop."

Though he smiled, his tone was serious. "If you're ready to let this go, then I yield. If not, I still say Father Forsetti ought to join in this night of sleepless worrying. Let *him* ask himself if-"

"Shh!" Faith's face was once again taut with fear.

Theophilus frowned, pressing her into her seat on the bed. "The Faith who left the house this morning knew her salvation was safe in God and feared no one else that I know of. Now, what's happened to that Faith?"

She took the hand that was caressing her face and gave a long sigh. "I'm just afraid after all I've said. I mean-" She floundered for an explanation which would satisfy her husband. Then she said simply, "But what if I'm wrong?"

He cocked an eyebrow. "It's always good to entertain that possibility, but you shouldn't have to wonder if you're saved just because you made a priest wonder if he was right!"

The remark did its work. One could see the tension release below her skin, and she slowly nodded. Her eyes and smile showed her gratitude.

Visibly relieved himself, Theophilus pulled her to her feet. "Enough now. Come. Let me comfort you and then we'll get some sleep." Then he added, "And no more pushing me away when you're afraid; we're in this together and it scares me when you make like you believe yourself alone." He tugged at her hand until she met his eyes, which glistened like the wide, dewy eyes of a child. His voice caught a little, though his tone was playful. "That's the one thing we agreed that neither of us would ever be."

They wrapped their arms around each other. Her eyes drifted blissfully closed as he pressed his lips to the side of her face, then trailed gently down her jaw and buried his face in her neck.

A natural instinct told me it was time to beat my retreat, and I turned away. My feet pounded across the hallway, through our doorway, and hopped into bed just in time. I heard Theophilus's soft, heavy steps enter and pause at our doorway. I didn't move.

Then his hand stroked my hair. "Emmy, are you awake?"

I turned over and sat up. It was a cold night and the lack of blankets had probably aided in giving me away. I watched him hesitantly and waited for an explosion, but none came.

He bent down and kissed me on the forehead. "Everything's all right, Little One. Your mommy needed to talk things out with me, but she's fine now. Go to sleep. There's nothing more for you to worry about."

He drew the blankets over my shoulder, then pecked each of us on the head again before he left. I didn't even look up to see him close the door; with the faith of a child, I happily accepted his explanation and fell into the arms of immediate peace.

Thus, when Theophilus left earlier than usual and returned before daybreak, I thought little of it, even though I caught the words, "couldn't get to the shop, too much damage." He and Faith spoke together in low voices for a long time. Eventually I fell back asleep.

When the whole family ate breakfast together, I didn't worry. When Helena and I were permitted to play instead of joining Faith for chores, I rejoiced in the opportunity and began setting up the sofa to be our ship. I was excited to teach Helena how to sail; I had never yet told her about my time at sea and couldn't wait to tell her what it was really like. She was sure to be impressed.

The parents remained in their room or at the kitchen table all morning, with occasional moments where one of them ran out to speak to someone at the door or run a swift errand. Whenever they did that, the other of them would sit with us, watching the door. Once we heard someone softly crying. Helena bade me stay and went to look into their room. I was glad she went, for I was too afraid.

She was gone only a few minutes, but when she came back, she seemed less like a child and more like Faith. My assertive playmate melted away into a soft-spoken caretaker, letting me lead our play and guiding me away from our parents and the front door. When it was time for lunch, she prepared it as best she could for both of us, and I ate happily, enjoying the notion that we were playing house.

Sometime after noon, Theophilus and Faith appeared in the doorway to their room. Faith's eyes were red and swollen, and Theophilus's face was taut and ashen. At the front door, he turned and gave her a quick kiss, then held her hands for a moment, speaking without words into her eyes. Then he drew her to him one last time, pressed his lips against the side of her head, and released her.

When he came toward us, Helena got to her feet and started to move toward him, then stopped. Her feet seemed stuck to the floor. He frowned, arms half open for a hug, and started to inquire. Then she burst into tears.

Theophilus seemed to reach her in a single step and swept her up into his arms, pressing her face against his shoulder with one big hand. Hidden in his dark woolen jacket, she sobbed. The questions she asked him were too garbled to understand, but he crooned back to her in fatherly tones without answering any of them.

When he turned to me, I still sat where I was, shell-shocked. My doll dangled forgotten and half-dressed in one hand. The sight of Helena's tears had frightened me. All day she had been so brave, and between her kindness and her father's words last night, I had believed that nothing could be very wrong; even Faith's tears were not enough to scare me with this banner of protection over me. But now all that was shattered. I stared at him in horror. My own lower lip began to wobble as I wondered uncertainly whether I should be crying, too.

He had set Helena down and let her go to her mother's arms. Now he held out his hands for me. My own hands shook a bit as I dropped our homemade playthings and scrambled toward him.

"What's wrong, Papa?" I asked in a small voice right beside his ear.

"Nothing, baby," he told me, squeezing me tight.

He tried to tickle me, but under the circumstances I wouldn't laugh. Twirling me a bit the way I liked, he placed me in Faith's arms and brushed his hand across her cheek. His eyes were younger again, like a child hoping for a playmate. She gazed back, her sweet brown eyes wet with tears but open to communication. He kissed her again.

"I'll go and see the shop," he said heavily. "I might be back later than-"

"Just don't go if it's too dangerous," Faith burst out.

He waved her complaints aside. "Enough," he said firmly. "Ben says they've cleared enough of the debris that we can reach it. I have to know whether we've got anything left."

In response to her welling eyes, he motioned very slightly with his chin at Helena and me. Her eyes said something to him that I couldn't catch. He reached out and wrapped his arms around all of us: Faith against his chest, me perched in her arms with my face near hers, and Helena standing at his feet. For a moment, we just stood like that, our arms around each other and our hands resting on anyone we couldn't actually reach. I patted Faith's face and she even laughed a little.

Then she turned and walked away with us back into their bedroom. I was curious, for she didn't often take us in there. I didn't hear the front door close behind me.

Faith perched each of us on the end of her bed, then took the quilt and wrapped it around our shoulders. It wasn't especially cold, but this seemed to calm her. Her eyes were worried and sad. Then she took the edge of the quilt and went to sit beside us, but there was a knock at the front door.

She threw her portion of the quilt in our laps and hurried to answer. I shifted as though to get down and go after her, but Helena motioned for me to stay put. Scowling, I raised my eyes to watch the door. She scooted closer to me to try and see as well, but I pretended not to notice and didn't move over for her.

Standing framed in our simple doorway was Mrs. Cunningham in all her navy, ruffled glory. A towering black hat sat on top of her head, spraying its plumes this way and that, and her beady little eyes peered dangerously out from under it at us. Though she had not yet been invited in, her gaze pierced all the way to the back room.

Helena leapt up to impulsively shut the door to the parents' room, cutting off her view of us. I jumped down, still wrapped in the quilt so that it trailed luxuriously behind me like a queen's robes, and pressed my ear up against the door. Helena was doing the same.

"Good afternoon, Mrs. Gladstone. I trust that news has reached you of the fire among the borrows of the workmen."

"It has indeed, Mrs. Cunningham." Faith sounded tired and small, like a child. "Theophil- My husband has just gone to see whether his workplace has survived."

One could almost hear Mrs. Cunningham's eyebrows raise in surprise. "Oh, indeed!" she said. "Is that where he works? I would have thought we would find his shop in a more-"

"Yes, well, he has gone to help and might not be back until late. Until then, me and the girls are here."

There was a long pause.

"I see," said Mrs. Cunningham. "Well, perhaps it *hasn't* yet reached your ears that the police have found these fires to be arson?"

Faith gasped. "All of them?"

Mrs. Cunningham sounded smug. "As usual, the father's predictions have proved correct. He had to keep after them, but eventually they had the good sense to-"

"But how do they know?" Faith sounded distressed. Her feet began to clack back and forth across the wooden floors. "Can they be certain?"

"My dear," the older lady said in surprise, "of course they can be. One by one, they've shown that in each case the fire was set somewhere that nobody would have brought a candle or a lantern, and that the area smelt of kerosene."

Another pause.

"Who would do this?" Faith asked quietly. The sofa creaked as she sank back into her seat.

"Well, someone well beyond the reach of reason, of course!" Mrs. Cunningham remarked. "Only a person whose mind has come completely unhinged could commit such an evil act."

Faith sighed. "I wish that that were true."

"Come again?" The lady clearly didn't like being corrected, and her voice sounded like a rap on the desk of a naughty student. "And what do you know of such matters? Such a young person should not-"

Faith's voice took on a sudden strength. "I have seen

evil," she said passionately. "And I have seen hatred. It doesn't have to be reasonable for it to originate, nor based upon more than shared emotion for it to grow."

"Indeed!" Mrs. Cunningham sounded genuinely incensed. "Well, if you know who has been setting these fires, I wish you would enlighten us, as *versed* as you are in the art of detecting intentions!"

Faith remained silent.

"I do know that Father Forsetti has his theories," Mrs. Cunningham went on, "and that he is being rather tight-lipped about them. I've implored him to share his wisdom with the parish, but he refuses – says he doesn't want to make any false accusations." She harrumphed. "I've told him that his instincts have not yet been wrong and that it would be better to have made a mistake and have to sort it out later than to have let a murderer go free but-" She clicked her tongue disapprovingly. "He has always been so willing to believe the best in people, and sometimes that lets the worst of them get the best of him!"

Faith sounded skeptical. "Has he been swindled in the past?"

Helena made a face at me; Mrs. Cunningham's bristling was nearly audible. I didn't bother to listen to the latest tongue-lashing. Instead, I let my gaze rove. I'd been in the parents' bedroom before, usually for making blankets, but I'd never gotten a chance to really examine it. Despite Helena's hushed protests, I wandered away from the door and began to prowl about the room.

The first thing I noticed was a big oval of plaster hanging above the head of their bed, right in the center. In the center was a tiny handprint, with a larger one on its right and an enormous one to its left. My heart ached hollowly. Who would hang the imprint of my little hand on their wall? Who would care if it grew big and rough or had bruises and arthritis when I was old? I turned away.

Hanging directly beneath it was a wreath of dried white flowers bent into the shape of a heart. The walls on either side of the bed were busy with life: a profusion of plantlife mingled both dried and fresh, clumsy practice stitches accompanied delicate needlepoint, and childish paintings and expert sketches hung side by side. A pair of substantial drawers, easily attributed to their owners by the neatness of the one and the chaotic explosion of men's socks out of the other, stood at the foot of the bed.

There ended what was pretty in the room, I thought. All over the walls on Theophilus's side of the bed were shelf upon shelf of weird little trinkets. Most of them appeared mechanical, but the rest were incomprehensible to me. A funny little plant I was sure was a weed stood in its tiny little pot, painfully crooked and impossibly thin but still thriving in spite of its shadowy corner. I frowned. Viewed with rosy childhood lenses or without, the angel-man was stranger than most.

Over in the corner, a dressing table with a big oval mirror held no bejeweled combs, elegant hand mirror, or perfume bottles. Instead, it was draped almost comically with seven or eight white shirts. Men's shirts, and all identical except for the wide variety of brightly-colored stains upon the sleeves or odd tears in the hems. Between them and wherever she could fit them, tiny bottles of varying chemicals for stain removal sat corked and carefully labeled in Faith's handwriting. A string of the shirts with stains more or less removed hung from a set of pegs above the table.

Next to the door of the closet, a dark woven basket brimming with exquisite white lace housed a curious collection of children's stuffed toys, worn adult clothes, and a breathtaking doll with a china face. I stared at her for a minute; she was angelic in a gilded church kind of way, but the tall, lanky man with the shy face and deep voice who made stained glass and hid behind his family when spoken to was more of an angel to me. Perhaps this was why in the massive, ornately-decorated sanctuaries I always felt lonely and out of place. But when I was with Helena and Theophilus and Faith, I felt that we belonged together – that is, we *didn't* belong, none of us, but we did so together.

As I stared up at the simple wooden cross above me, I was tormented by conflicting emotions. I'd heard everyone around me talk about Him, but who *was* God? Would He even like me? A few people did, but I was beginning to find that many people didn't like *them*.

Did He spend all His days in the little golden hut in the back of the cathedral like the archbishop once told me? Did He live in a big stone house with beautiful stained glass windows and walls scorched by flames? Had He ever visited the places that burned, either in the slums or where the wealthy lived? And could He hear the cries of a child, orphaned, lost, and alone, while she sailed the seven seas from one unhappy caregiver to another who didn't care enough to collect her from the house of a stranger?

And what was He like – did He stare down his nose at me like Mrs. Cunningham did, waiting for something to correct, or more appropriately, for one single thing I did right?

Or was He like the angel-man – funny-looking and outcast, always doing and saying things people didn't understand but evoking a sort of reverence in those around Him which even they didn't understand? Did He make the most highly respected people uncomfortable while He turned kind eyes upon the dirty form of a disagreeable little orphan? Did He see this little whelp – whose relatives only wanted her for the money which would follow her from yet another oblivious relative – and smile?

Was He a Roman, or a Luthern, or a Press-bear-tear-yin? Or did He bother making sure people called Him the right thing while He was putting out fires, sewing up blankets, consoling people who were grieving, and playing – yes, playing – with the children?

Suddenly I didn't think He was either a king on a throne or a peasant doing carpentry. If one day we saw Him, He would probably be so familiar-looking that no one would ever recognize Him.

As I gazed up at that cross, my eyes blurred with tears. But if He was my Angel-Man, where had He been when I was so alone in London that I sometimes forgot my own name? Did He see when I was a lost little piece of meat being pecked to death by Christian vultures? Had He been in the streets when someone had set fire after fire – watched as the beloved monsignor breathed his last breath – stood silently while Mrs. Cunningham ripped into precious Faith in the other room?

But He didn't answer that – not directly, exactly. Instead, it was as if I felt someone gently pressing my head down to look at something before me. As I did so, I instinctively lifted my hand to look at the palm. Immediately, a memory of the light streaming red through the stained glass into my hands returned to me, and for the first time, I felt my heart go to Christ.

He would not tell me why I had these scars, but He would willingly show me His. If His love could reach me through the hands of Faith when I was under attack or the protection of Theophilus while the fires raged, then His love was enough for me. The hands that had bled for me were extended not just to the lonely orphan child, but to a family of outcasts, a grieving and conflicted priest, an angry parish, and even the broken soul who had set the town ablaze.

Even, I thought resignedly, to a nasty church lady who seemed to have taken root in our living room.

Chapter Nine

I turned to see Helena frowning at me from where she still stood with her ear to the door. Feeling remiss, I hurried to huddle beside her. The conversation outside had escalated in volume and intensity.

"So let me get this straight." Faith's voice was almost as forceful as when one of us had been naughty, but this time it was tinged with trepidation. "You are saying that you believe someone in the city has not only been setting these fires, but intentionally targeting our church."

Mrs. Cunningham was clearly relishing having gotten the upper hand. "Well, it stands to reason, my dear. All of the fires were started the same way. Each one except for the one in the Benches was a direct attack on several members of the parish, and the first required access to a certain key. But of course it can't have been a parishioner; no true Christian would commit such a heinous crime." Her ominous tone deepened. "But whoever did needed the means to do so. The reason might have been religious in nature, so-"

"But has Father Forsetti told you this?" Faith ground out. She was growing frantic. "Does he really believe that someone we know is an arsonist, that someone intended to kill that sweet old priest, and along denominational lines?"

Mrs. Cunningham's syrupy voice made me imagine her face looking just as unbearable. A swish of skirts told me she stood up. "Hatred of the Church has never been uncommon, Mrs. Gladstone. We must always be on our guard against attacks from the outside. I've told Father Forsetti he would be wise to look for the roots of the problem," Mrs. Cunningham went on, "so he's been examining everyone's motives and history in the parish, family by family, looking for someone with connections outside the parish. Surely he will soon be able to spot any troublemakers."

The rustle of voluminous skirts began to make its way toward the door. "Hopefully he will find something before there's another fire. He's been wondering, you know, why the fires always come after a new stained glass window is unveiled."

She clearly expected a response, but Faith had gone oddly silent.

"I can't imagine who would hate us enough to set fire to places in our town," Mrs. Cunningham tried again. "I know most everyone who has grown up here. But unfortunately there's been such an influx of foreigners lately!" She clicked her tongue. "Really, since you live among so many of them, you ought to be careful. No doubt it's one of the workers nobody knows who-"

"I don't think we should be making accusations," Faith said suddenly.

"Very well, but don't forget I said this was private!" Her airy laugh made me want to punch something, so I pinched Helena. Her voice went soft and confidential. "We don't want to tip anyone off, do we? Now just remember what I said; not even your husband! Why, they say it's us who like to talk, but then they gossip just as much…"

Her voice got fainter and fainter as she made her way out into the street, presumably with appropriate salutations to Faith.

We watched each other's faces for just one moment, and then the clack of Faith's heels approached the door and she threw it open.

"Come on, girls," she told us in a hushed tone. "Get your things on to go up to the church. Never mind how you look; just bring something to occupy yourselves for a little while. Your father won't be home for at least a few hours yet, so I wouldn't feel right leaving you here."

We wordlessly got our things together. Faith seemed almost absent from us, while she was usually conscious of our every move. Helena took her hand, but she didn't even squeeze it and look down and smile; she just held it tightly in her own and hauled us up the hill at a pace that was too fast for my tiny legs.

She had barely abandoned us in a safe little corridor of the cathedral to play when she spotted her quarry.

"Father Forsetti!"

She ran after him swiftly enough to startle us, picking up her skirts to reveal the black, flashing heels of her boots. He turned in surprise, but darkness descended over his face when he saw her.

"Mrs. Gladstone," he said. Those two words were heavy with meaning. He held open the door through which he had been about to pass. "Would you come and walk with me? We can speak on the way."

The instant the door closed behind them, I marched after them, but Helena's hand stayed me. I looked up at her questioningly.

"Mama says we mustn't eavesdrop," she said seriously.

I frowned, then pulled away from her. She caught me again and yanked me back, surprised at my defiance.

"Mama *says*-" she began again, but this time I stopped and looked at her.

"Mama's in trouble," I said lowly.

Helena frowned, uncomprehending. "Mama can handle herself. We ought to stay here so she can find us when it's over."

I had no answer for that, but I was determined to follow Faith. I trod firmly up to the heavy door they'd passed through.

"Emmy, don't!" Helena called after me. Her feet pitter-pattered across the unyielding blocks of stone. "That's naughty! It'll get us spanked."

All at once, a gleam of mischief overtook me. I turned back to her and leveled this one question: "What shall you do? Tell Mama?"

Helena, an only child up to this point in her life, was deeply puzzled. I left her to ponder the conundrum that she would have to disobey her mama's orders as well if she wanted to tell on me now and forced open the heavy door by pressing my feet against the frame. It gave way to a completely black hallway thick with silence.

I was daunted, but I had to outrun Helena in case she ceased her pondering, so onward I went as fast as I could. The only thing I could see was a gray shape far ahead of me. It appeared disproportionately small, but reason told me it was light at the end of the corridor.

I banged my shin on something on the way there and didn't notice the warm blood trickling down until I had turned the corner. Father Forsetti's grave tenor voice carried along the halls to me with Faith's bounding shrilly after it. Though she wasn't raising her voice, I could detect, as children do, the note of agitation, and it set my heart to thundering and my stomach to tying in knots.

I hurried along the adjoining corridor, peering into rooms as I passed them. Many were smaller chapels or prayer rooms with lit candles and solemn, downcast statues of various saints. Most of them were empty.

At last, ahead of me I spotted the silhouettes of Faith and Father Forsetti turning another corner. I ran after them, straining my ears to catch their words.

"Father, a reliable source said you suspect someone is targeting the parish. Please tell me what this means."

At last, I had reached their corridor. They were in a large, well-lit library with shelves reaching well above their heads. Father Forsetti paced solemnly to where a globe sat beside several layers of paper on a heavy wooden table. He did not look up at Faith.

"What I may or may not have said to others in private is not something I wish to discuss with you, Mrs. Gladstone." He turned the globe idly with his finger, his other hand clenched behind his back.

Faith took another step closer, then came to a rigid stop. Father Forsetti glanced up, startled by the strength of her emotions.

"A danger to the parish my children attend," she said tightly, "certainly is. I need to know-"

Father Forsetti sighed. "Mrs. Gladstone, the police are looking into the fires, and I am making my own inquiries. God willing, it won't be long before we find the culprit and put a stop to this destruction."

"Father-"

"I understand that you and every other person in the parish wants to protect his or her loved ones." He sighed again. "And I believe that to trace the source of the disaster is what will best serve that end. Please, pay no more heed to rumors."

Faith gazed at him for a long moment while he fingered through one of the books on his table, his mouth moving as if he were reading the words. I thought he was praying. She turned to go, then stopped.

"With all due respect, what kinds of inquiries have you been making?"

Father Forsetti smiled. "If it were anyone else, Mrs. Gladstone, I would find some way to comfort you without answering your question, but since it is you, I know I will get no peace until I give an honest answer." He looked almost playful.

Faith continued to watch him closely. His smile

widened a little.

"You're a quick-witted woman," he went on casually. "Certainly you, too, have noticed the pattern. Perhaps you've had suspicions of your own."

"Pattern?" Faith murmured carefully.

He turned toward her fully and rested the backs of his legs against the tabletop. He folded his arms and raised his eyebrows.

"There is no need for games, madam," he said. "I know beyond a shadow of a doubt you've noted it, as well, even if no one else has."

Faith remained silent. He frowned. Taking a deep breath and squaring his shoulders, Father Forsetti turned and moved toward Faith. His soft black shoes made no sound on the broad grey flagstones beneath him.

"Something has frightened you, Mrs. Gladstone," he said, watching her closely. "And not the fires, I think."

"What do you mean?" Her voice was dangerously blank.

He clasped both hands low behind him. "You've kept your head through all of this even with a husband and two little girls at home, and the fires have been moving away from your neighborhood." He smiled a little. "You hardly seem the type to lose your nerve now. Something else has frightened you."

At last, she gathered her breath, slowly, as though it was difficult. "I have indeed noticed patterns," she said, her voice wavering, "but they could be nothing. This is why I hesitate to connect them; I'd hate to see anyone place blame without knowing the truth for certain."

Father Forsetti nodded. "It was for the same reason that I didn't reveal any names to those in whom I confided my suspicions. But you can rest assured that I will not go out of my way to arrest someone without being fairly assured of their guilt."

Faith's back heaved faintly as though she were letting go a deep breath.

"However," he went on, "if all my years of experience have taught me one thing about human nature, it's that patterns tend to repeat themselves before they escalate."

"What do you mean?"

Father Forsetti's jaw tightened grimly. "I mean that those who commit evil on a grand scale tend to start smaller first," he replied lowly. "Nobody goes right from being an ordinary man to a murderer in a day, and I suspect the same holds true for arsonists. There is more than one among us with a history of violence, or at least of rather odd behavior, and that's where I'm hoping to overturn something in my inquiries."

"But that's only the past." Faith sounded almost frantic. "People can change. People can be wrong…"

"Oh, certainly!" Father Forsetti didn't seem to catch the seriousness of her words. "But when looking for a criminal, it often pays to look among criminals, even former criminals. Fortunately, most places are good about keeping records of that kind of thing."

"But sometimes those records are wrong!"

He turned to look a question at her. Then he made a placating motion toward her. "I don't mean to say that I would suspect someone based on their past alone.

But it just might give me a place to start."

"But-"

"Mrs. Gladstone, surely you would permit me to trust the word of the police!"

She remained silent.

His lip curled unpleasantly and he emitted a low laugh. "That's right. You have a strong aversion to placing trust in any kind of authority." When she didn't move, he went on. "I hope your daughter does not adopt this cynical attitude. Surely her mother's skepticism and distrust of the church oughtn't be enough to prevent her from joining the community of faith."

"You don't know anything about us," Faith ground out.

Father Forsetti's expression darkened. "More and more now you seem angry with me," he said.

His feet began to trace a wide circle around her. She struggled to keep her voice calm.

"*I* have never gone out of my way to stir up trouble."

"Do you mean to imply that I have?" The anger, to this point adroitly concealed, was spilling forth in both his expression and tone. He stopped near her left shoulder, staring at her until she dared turn to face him. "Madam, I have done nothing except to protect my church. It is you who are quick to stir up trouble and cause divisions." His eyes narrowed. "It makes one wonder what you hope to achieve, Mrs. Gladstone."

"If anything has aided in causing divisions, sir," she replied, her back heaving steadily, "it is your tendency to regard everyone and everything that isn't done exactly your way with fear or outright hostility."

He tried to speak, but she raised a finger to cut him off.

"I think what you fear isn't that someone will start misleading the flock which is under your care; it is that you are beginning to lose control. Yet why should you fear a lack of control when control was never your calling?"

Father Forsetti's expression registered shock, but no words came out of his mouth.

"I understand the desire to keep the ones in your care away from sin and harm; I have two daughters of my own. But to equate disagreement with you and true evil is pushing the limits of your calling."

"Be silent!" he roared. "Perhaps your husband has not attempted to curb your violent temper and poisonous tongue, but as your pastor, I shall!"

The two stood facing each other, chests heaving with fury. Faith's face had blanched white while his flamed red. She stood at an angle with one hand behind her as if she didn't know whether to retreat or to square up and fight him.

The pastor decided for her. He took one step towards her, then another. "What about me so invites your hatred?" he demanded. "Why must you be always at my back, questioning my decisions, refusing my orders, stirring up my parish? I cannot understand your disdain for God's appointed shepherds, madam, but now it would seem your hatred has extended to justice itself!"

She jerked her face to one side as if he had slapped

her. This inflamed him further, but he regained control of himself within a split second before he spoke. It was both dazzling and terrifying, like lightning captured in a bottle.

"I will not discuss this with you any further." His voice was tight and restrained, but his grimace was almost like a smile. "Certainly, you've given me plenty to think about, Mrs. Gladstone. It is time I returned to watch over my flock, and you to watch over your family. Good day."

When Faith turned the corner to find me listening, she dropped to her knees, flung her arms around me, and burst into sobs.

Chapter Ten

I'd expected to be scolded for eavesdropping. I had even anticipated the spanking I'd gotten for separating from Helena and thought that would be the worst of the punishment. Now, however, something far worse was clearly afoot, and my child mind was not mature enough to discern what it was, nor to understand that it was not my fault and that no one viewed it as such.

I cowered in the corner of our bedroom while Helena played sullenly on the bed; she had not spoken much to me since the incident at the church. I'd expected her to follow me when I went after Faith; instead, she had dithered in the hallway, crying first because we'd left our assigned place and then because we hadn't stayed together. Her punishment had been much lighter.

Inside the other bedroom, a terrible storm raged.

"We volunteer, we make friends, I get assigned to an honorable task, and within months it's all for nothing!" A thud made me jump; Theophilus must've dropped despondently into a chair.

"We haven't made friends," Faith fretted. "We've only made acquaintances, and most of them receive us about the same as-"

"This is why I asked us to keep quiet when we got here!" Theophilus shouted.

I whimpered; I had never before heard him raise his voice higher than a warning thunderclap when Helena was reaching over a hot pan.

"We could've started a new life here. We could've been safe, but no..." His anger was far less terrible than this note of despair.

"It was my fault," Faith admitted heavily. "I don't blend in well among the other women. I never have."

"No, you stand out wherever you go!" Theophilus's boots boomed back and forth, back and forth on the hollow-sounding wood floor. This was yet another sign he was distressed; he usually took his boots off in the doorway and left them to dry so that he wouldn't muddy up the clean floors.

Faith's voice was faint, close to tears. "Darling, I'm so sorry."

"That's what your problem is, that you don't think!" he went on. "Back when it was just you, you had certain luxuries. We could stand out in a crowd. But now-" Faith tried to interject, but he cut her off, "now Helena's future hangs in the balance. If she gets thrown out of the church, it won't just be this parish, and then she will be branded for life by *this*."

A strange hiccup I suspected did not come from Theophilus. "I did what I had to do." Faith sounded crushed.

"What you had to- Faith!" her husband raged.

"Whatever in your life made you think you *had* to pick a fight with a priest, *had* to make yourself stand out among the ladies' committee, *had* to make our differences known to the entire parish?" He sounded frantic. "*Why* couldn't you just keep quiet and pretend to agree with everything they said? Now we're known as dissenters when they're looking for an arsonist connecting with the parish and..." There was a long pause, punctuated by sniffling.

"Darling," she said at last, steadier now, "I know you don't approve of what I did as far as drawing attention to myself. But I had to." He started to speak, but she raised her voice. "Based on what Mrs. Cunningham said, I had to find out whether he'd looked into us. I *had* to know-"

"*That* is not what- You know that's not the problem here! It's the fact that you stirred him up right after talking about the fires. If you would've stayed silent-"

"I cannot stand by, no matter how dangerous it is, knowing that a father of the church is making himself or his teachings an obstacle to people's faith in Christ. He is separating Jesus from them, Theophilus! He's making these little local rules into a fence over which they don't believe anyone can leap! How could you ask me to sit in silence when-"

"I don't care!" he roared. "I don't care because I don't care about any of them! When it comes down to it, all I care about is you! You, me, Helena, and now Emmy. The rest of them can go to blazes."

"Theophilus-" she tried to temper him.

"No. No, Faith!" Again, his boots thundered back and forth. "I once cared about every person I met.

Each one was a treasure to me, beautiful and important, and thus, so was all of humanity. But that part of me is *dead*, Faith." Tears were gathering, and from the sound of it, spilling down his face to his ever-rumpled collar. "It sickened when the town began to recklessly throw out suspicions, it choked when I was accused, and when they built a scaffold for someone they didn't even know, whose intentions they never made any effort to understand, it *died*. It died on that scaffold like I was supposed to."

For a moment, there was no sound but Faith crying. Eventually, I could hear Theophilus weeping bitterly, too.

"Why can't you just help us hide and let them all destroy each other?" he finished, exhausted. "Why can't we just stay safe in our own little alcove while..."

At last, Faith recovered herself. "Because," she said firmly, tears thick in her throat, "they are all still each people."

Theophilus grunted, started pacing again. She raised her voice over him.

"And whether you like it or not, I'm not going to stand by and let anyone, one person or many, turn against someone who is vulnerable. I cannot let a church hierarchy place itself as a barrier between the Christian and Christ, just like I can't let a crowd of frightened families kill an innocent man. It's always been risky to tell the truth-"

She stopped when Theophilus harrumphed again. When she spoke again, her voice was soft and burning.

"You used to be so brave."

"I used to believe that goodness would be rewarded!

But now I see, though I still believe that we will receive a reward *in the end*, that in this world, the ones who have power will use it, and if we will not bow before them, we must at least-" He hesitated, seeking the right phrase. "Keep out of sight," he ended desperately.

"You know I cannot do that. And I know that if you were truly thinking, if you were being yourself, you would not want that philosophy to be the way our daughters live their lives, as if they were victims instead of warriors!"

Something told me Theophilus was holding her by the arms. They had somehow reconnected and sounded once again like the couple I knew, though broken and afraid.

"But," she continued, sounding like a little child, "I still trust you above all else. Theophilus, if there was something I said that you think wasn't correct-"

"You didn't do anything wrong!" he exploded. "That's the sickest part of it all – you don't have to be guilty, you just have to be different." He sighed. "The trouble is, you've never ceased to be the woman I married: brave, ardent, a true believer in the deepest sense. But I've changed. Now I'm afraid. I've lost whatever I had that made me brave once."

Their sobs were muffled as they held each other.

At that moment, I looked up. Helena was holding her dolls close, her tears dripping onto their skirts. With both her parents crying, she looked pale and stricken.

I barely moved, merely shifted my arms as an invitation, and she sailed off the bed and flung her arms around me. Soon, we were holding each other and crying, too.

Our fear summoned the parents like a beacon. The door to our room softly opened and they both stepped inside. Each of them picked one of us up, rocking and hushing us as if they'd never fought with anyone in their lives. My fear, as usual, rendered me silent, but Helena's inarticulate questions were from both of us. We allowed ourselves to be comforted by their embrace, but I saw Faith and Theophilus silently communicating above us with their eyes.

"What's going on?" Helena finally pleaded.

Of one accord, Faith and Theophilus sank to the floor, placing us side by side between them. We all sat cross-legged and considered each other: pink cheeks streaked with red, pale brows, swollen eyelids rimmed with lashes glued together with saltwater, lips pressed together in an attempt to be calm. Every so often a caress went from one to the other; Helena squeezed my hand, Theophilus tilted his head just so at Faith, she patted Helena's knee.

Finally, the parents looked at each other and sighed.

"Girls, there's something you need to know, something we need to tell you," Theophilus said heavily.

Faith looked up sharply but didn't check him.

"Why?" Helena prompted.

He lowered his face and looked so like a downcast angel that I reached out and patted his jaw, which was as high as I could reach. He looked dully surprised, pressed his fingers to the back of my hand and kissed it. Then he turned pleading eyes on Faith.

She nodded and took over for the moment. "As you both know, our town is in a broken place. Someone has done a very grave thing. Because of the fires someone has set on purpose, many people's homes were destroyed, and a few people died. Everyone's trying to find out who did this." She took a shuddering breath. "Therefore, Father Forsetti has taken it upon himself to find out the history of most of the parishioners." She nodded, anticipating Helena's next question. "Yes, they believe that a person close to someone in the parish did it. Currently, it sounds like there is no one they suspect within the church, but-"

Her expression was utterly crestfallen, and at last her husband relented. He drew her into his arms and let her rest her head upon his breast as if she were a child.

"It's not your fault," he murmured firmly. "God knows, I know it's not your fault."

"We know about Mommy's fight with the father," Helena put in helpfully. "Is he going to think we're setting the fires because he's mad at us?"

Both of them smiled a little.

"No, baby, it's a little bit more than that," Faith replied. Then she looked at Theophilus, and they began.

They told us a story of two people who were virtually unknown in their village. People didn't know what passion lived in their hearts or didn't care enough to look for it, so they were forced to find it in each other. Their love grew, while the town began to subtly model them after its own image and eventually to try to split them apart, without ever having known they were together.

When the danger came, and what dangers they would not tell us specifically, the townspeople were quick to accuse. Their fear made them suspicious and everyone was a target. When the man had tried to do something to help the village, his motives were misunderstood.

Then they began to talk about something called a fair trial, which was where my mind started to wander. But my attention came back when they told us the man was sentenced to death.

"They didn't know what to think, so they decided to think what was easiest." Faith's eyes were blacker than ever. "It was someone that no one knew well, or no one would own up to knowing, so it was easier than finding the truth."

"Did she help them find out the truth?" Helena's brows were lowered with concern over wide, wet eyes.

"She did her best," Faith offered, "but when people who are frightened gather together behind one idea…"

Theophilus shook his head as he took over. "If she had confessed to loving this man or that she had helped him, she might have been put to death, too."

Helena looked stricken. I was shocked that this family would tell their daughter such a dreadful tale. For that matter, why were they telling me? I frowned a question at Theophilus, but he remained stone-faced.

"And so," Faith said carefully, "the young woman had no choice but to leave the people with whom she'd grown up, the family that she loved, and to run away with this man to save both their lives."

For a moment Faith was quiet. Then Helena sniffled

loudly, wanting to be held.

When Faith opened her arms for us, her touch was soft and familiar again, and we eagerly scrambled into her lap. She curled an arm around each of us and began to rock back and forth. Her hair was down, and I nestled against the silky black tresses that cascaded from her shoulders to her waist. Then we turned our trusting eyes to hers. In the background, I saw Theophilus turn his eyes away with a sadness that cut to my little soul.

"That was a sad story!" Helena whimpered. "What happened to them then?"

Faith took a deep, shaky breath that made me look up at her. "They got married in secret and ran as far away as they could. Then, when their money ran out, they had to find a place to settle. So they stopped in a village, where the man learned a new trade, and soon they had a little daughter."

"That's so sad," Helena repeated. "Didn't they miss their mamas and papas?"

Faith hid her face in our hair. "All the time," she said thickly.

"But what they did, they did for each other." Theophilus's smile on Faith's bowed head was as tender as a caress. "They saved each other's lives, again and again. If they could've kept safe with their families, they would have."

"Now tell me, girls." Faith's head came up with sudden courage. "What do you think of these people's actions? What would you think of them if you knew them?"

Theophilus turned sheet-white and his expression

was unreadable. Faith was flushed, but she gazed intently at us, nodding her head slightly as if encouraging us.

"I would be their friend," Helena declared. "I would've told those townspeople that they were crazy and proven them wrong." She paused. "And if that didn't work, I would convince them to take their families along when they ran away."

The look Faith and Theophilus exchanged was one of intense, smiling relief. When they looked at me expectantly, I suddenly knew.

"Emmy?" The angel-man was looking at me, and it felt like it did when he had for the first time. It was as if he had shown me all of his darkness and peculiarities and was asking me whether he could be my angel-man still.

"What do you think?" he asked softly.

I glanced from one to the other, taking in the full weight of what they had told us, as fully as I could. My eyes filled with sudden tears. "I would've gone with you," I said softly. "I would stay with you."

Theophilus's giant hands scooped me up and pressed me to his shoulder, wordless for several seconds. I heard a hiccup from Faith behind me, and a sharp intake of breath as the truth hit Helena.

"God bless you, Little One," he at last said thickly. He placed me on his lap facing him. Once again, he beamed down on me like a benevolent ray of sun. "Your trust and faithful friendship matters more to us than anything. Anything. For you, the village could've betrayed us twice and we would count ourselves worthy."

He glanced at Faith, and she offered him a watery smile back. Then his smile faded and he turned so that both Helena and I could look at him.

"We've told you this so you know before everyone else does."

Helena's eyes widened and her mouth twisted in alarm, but he met her gaze steadily.

"They know that someone has been setting the fires, and they're going to be searching for criminals among the parish. That means they will probably find out what our village said about us and they might think we set the fires, too."

"But you didn't do it!" Helena's face was scrunched up stubbornly. "Tell them!"

Theophilus shook his head. "I learned years ago not to try to change the tides," he said. "They will believe whatever they please, and there's nothing we can do about it. But I'm asking you to believe me when I tell you: we didn't set the fires, nor did we do what they said we did in the old village."

"I know that!" Helena frowned indignantly.

Faith smiled and stroked Helena's hair, then turned to face Theophilus. "So what do we do now?"

He sat back and rested his weight upon his palms where they braced him up from behind, then tipped his head to one side. "It seems we've worn out our welcome in this town."

He peered experimentally at Faith. She nodded thoughtfully.

"Where do you think we would go?" she asked.

Helena sat upright. "Wait. Are we going to run away? Just like you did in the story?"

The parents exchanged a worried glance.

"It seems that way," Faith said cautiously.

"But what will we do with Emmy?" Helena asked. "Her cousins are going to come looking for her and we will be away."

Both parents turned their attention to me. Even though I knew and loved them so well, the sudden attention made my stomach drop.

"I guess this is it," murmured Theophilus.

"But Theo!" Faith exclaimed. "Then they could have us for kidnapping!"

Theophilus threw up his hands. "From whom? What with the one patchy letter and handful of telegrams we've gotten from them, I believe they'd have a harder time proving these cousins exist than that a little one we've cared for and come to love as our own is really our kidnapping victim!"

Faith clapped a hand over her face and made the scoffing sound she made whenever Theophilus had said something terrible.

He shrugged. "She doesn't know them. She wouldn't even know them on sight, nor would they be likely to recognize her. She'll be in good hands, and for all I care, they can have the inheritance or whatever it is!"

Faith shook her head. "No, Theo! I love her as much as you do, but-"

"But what?" he shot back. "We're a family now, and-"

"But it's not safe! We're on the lam, we'd have little we could take with us, and then she'd be tarred with the same brush! What kind of life is that to offer a little girl?"

Theophilus's blue eyes were stubborn and desperate. "And what about Helena?"

There was a pause when Faith didn't dare answer this immediately.

"She's going to be up against the exact same challenges. We've got to do this, Faith. There's no more time for us here." He wove from side to side, could see that she was caving. "We've done it before and we can do it again," he reminded her softly.

Faith watched him silently for several moments as though reading invisible words written upon his face.

"God will be with us," he pleaded. "We're a family now, lovely. We can't just back out on each other when we feel like it. It's not the Gladstone way."

Faith took a deep breath. Her eyes were hard with tears that refused to fall. "But is it really loving to put her in danger?"

Theophilus smiled as he drew her close, pressed his lips softly against her furrowed brow. "Living's dangerous."

Faith turned loving eyes upon me. So sweet was her expression that I wanted to run to her, to hold up my hands for a hug and a kiss. But she only nodded faintly. "It has to be her choice," she whispered.

Theophilus bent down on his hands and knees before me, though he was still taller than me even in this position since I was sitting. "Well, Emmanuella, now is your chance. We can leave you with someone for your cousins to find you, or you can come with us."

I bounced up and down. "Oh, with you! With you!"

Helena had already wrapped her arms around me.

Theophilus lifted a hand and shook his head. "Hold up, my loves. We have to make this decision carefully."

He waited until Helena released me, then motioned for me to sit closer to him. I obediently scooted forward until I was seated cross-legged near his knees. Seated upon his heels, he once again towered above me.

"Now, Emmy, this isn't going to be an easy choice to make." His voice was gentle but serious. "If you go with your cousins, they're going to have more money to take care of you, but I can't guess what they're like as people. We've never met them before. And neither have you, correct?"

I nodded. I had heard the whispers; they only wanted me the way a girl wants a doll when she already has many – a sort of inclination which is as fickle as the wind. They might get tired of me.

Faith's eyes went from one to the other of us. Her knuckles were white where she gripped Helena's hand.

Theophilus's brows lowered as if what he had to say next pained him. "If you came with us, it would not be an easy life. All of this," he glanced up and around himself at their sweet little house, "would have to be left behind. We would leave with only what we could carry."

Helena glanced anxiously at Faith, who nodded solemnly at her and pressed a kiss against her hair.

Crowded orphanages. Noisy nurseries full of half-frazzled nurses. Thin, stained hand-me-downs and cheap pinafores. Barely enough porridge to spare…

"It would be a little scary either way," Theophilus continued. "If you went with us, we would have to walk for miles upon miles as fast as we could, probably at night for the first while. There could be very little to eat until we reach the next town, and it would be dangerous if we were caught.

"On the other hand, you would stay with one of the church ladies who would take good care of you until your cousins got here. When they came, you would go with them to wherever they live. They will have your grandfather's help in providing for you, so it will be a comfortable place, wherever it is."

I'd never known a comfortable life. I'd thought that was what the Gladstones had. But would we still be happy without what we had here?

He smiled tiredly. "It's your choice, Little One. No matter what you choose, we will be happy for you. God knows we'll still love you as if you were our own."

I gazed up at the angel-man and smiled. To me, he looked just like the man in the windows he had made, with his sad eyes and endearing smile, deep wounds in his heart if not in his hands, and the sun shining right through him enough to warm everyone he touched. And both had shined upon me when I had nothing and no one wanted me. In the images, he'd never had much, but if that light was shining on me, it was enough.

I spoke, but my voice was too quiet for anyone to hear. Faith and Helena leaned in while Theophilus bent his ear to my lips.

It came out as a whisper. "I would like to stay with

you, please."

His pursed lips betrayed consternation. "But we won't be staying here, Emmy. You realize that, right?"

I bent forward again. "Then I would like to leave with you. Please."

Theophilus's face was so full of hope that he didn't dare speak. When he turned to Faith, she was beaming. Her tears overflowed, and she practically pounced on me.

"Then welcome to the family, my dear," she said.

Theophilus wrapped his big arms around all of us, and we sat there for a minute, all of us holding each other, a brand-new family.

But the moment he released us, he strode with purpose into the parents' room. The escape had begun.

Chapter Eleven

"Only take what you can carry," Faith instructed us as she helped me and Helena to our feet.

For a moment, the two of us stood just inside Helena's room – our room – staring blankly about us. Only what we could carry? What would that mean? Being the children that we were, we immediately set out to find our dolls and their favorite clothes, both grossly overestimating how much we could carry, let alone how far we would be able to maintain that weight.

But within minutes, Faith returned with a pair of canvas bags, the kind she used for her crocheting. We both stared at the bags in our hands, stretching them to their full dimensions of about a foot in each direction.

"It's so small," Helena remarked. She glanced at the dresser. "How will I ever carry all my clothes?"

Faith smiled as she repeated, "Take only as much as you can carry."

As it turned out, what we could carry was about one change of clothes each, plus a hairbrush to share and an extra pair of stockings. Helena clung tearfully to her doll, afraid she would be forbidden to take it, but once she promised to carry it in her arms the whole time without help, she was permitted to bring her beloved companion. Theophilus even took her second-favorite dress she'd made for it and wedged it into his own bag. The rest of her things she was obliged to leave behind.

We were prepared within roughly an hour and a half. All of us wore our nightclothes under a set of traveling clothes, the darkest colors Faith could find. She pulled itchy wool hats down over our ears and tugged my hands into some of Helena's old mittens. Theophilus pulled on a long leather coat with a bit that draped across the backs of his shoulders. Helena and I agreed it made him look like some mysterious hero from a fairytale.

"Or else the villain," she added with approval.

By the time we had doused all the candles, my head was spinning. We were really leaving! This was the most firm place I'd ever known, but now I was leaving it behind with all its warmth and memories. I had never missed a place before, but I had a feeling I was going to miss this one.

Theophilus brought along a lantern but didn't light it. We couldn't draw attention to ourselves, he warned us, but we must stay close and do our best not to trip on the cobblestones. We would keep to the edges of the street where we would be concealed in the shadows or at least obscured by the dark background of the buildings.

When we stepped outside, I was immediately greeted by a tweak on the nose by the frigid night air. I breathed out and watched the curls of fog swimming into the air and rising above me. Theophilus knelt quickly to do up our scarves and tug them up over our faces. Then Faith pulled the door shut behind us with a soft, deep thud.

We started walking, Faith holding tight to my hand while Helena walked with her father, but eventually Theophilus pulled us all aside and whispered to us.

"When we reach the end of the neighborhood," he warned lowly, "we will be passing a couple of taverns. The lights will be burning and there will be plenty of witnesses. If we want to be inconspicuous, we can't have two little children walking at night. Not visibly."

Faith's mouth was set in a tense line. "What do you suggest?"

His solution, it turned out, was for him to open the front of his long coat and walk with Helena tucked under one side and me under the other. We stuck close and held his coat in, and Faith said it really did just look like one man walking unless you looked closely at the feet.

A few more blocks of broken cobblestone disappeared behind us. The bigger tavern was loud, full of music and whistles and shouting, with cooking smells and steam rising from every opening. Some men lingered by the door smoking, while the occasional woman sashayed by with a sly-sounding remark directed at them. Only once did we have a scare, when one of the men called out a brutish invitation to Faith. Theophilus pretended to be her father, making her take his arm and repulsing the men with a sharp retort.

The next tavern was quieter, but according to Theophilus, it was even more dangerous to us. The tavern-keeper always had his eye out for the lonely traveler and there was a greater chance we might be seen and, due to the smaller prevalence of drunkenness, remembered. We tucked against the opposite buildings and rushed past, our eyes ever on the homelike glow. Never before had I felt a need to fear the light.

We had soon passed beyond the roads that Helena and I knew and were headed for the opposite side of the city. Had we followed the road leading out on our side, it would have taken us through paths far too dangerous for a man to travel alone at night, let alone a family of four.

Helena soon got tired, but she dared not do more than whimper for fear she would have to leave her doll behind. Theophilus started to scold her sharply when he had told her not to make a sound, but when he saw her plight, he immediately knelt before her and removed one of the strings tying her bag shut. He maneuvered the other until it accomplished the job of two, and then made a harness out of the other. She was soon walking with her doll strapped to her front, holding her father's hand and smiling up at him like he'd hung the moon.

For my part, I was too scared and cold to be tired, or to realize I was. I was often lifted over puddles or carried short distances to help me catch up, but still we made decent progress. Faith kept glancing up at the moon, which was rising beautifully in the dark purple dome above us. It was not quite full, and one of the church spires bit into its silver disk, reminding us of the hulking black mass which watched silently from the top of the hill.

We were now closer to the cathedral than to our house, for in order to make our escape, we had to creep just below its base, one row of houses before it. It felt the way it must feel to creep beside the paws of the reposing sphinx Papa says resides in the sands of Egypt. The nearer we came to it, the more pained Faith's expression as she threw one more anxious glance over her shoulder at the immense stone bulwark. Once, she even blinked away tears and crossed herself.

At last, just when Helena pleaded that she didn't want to go any farther, we had reached the crest of another hill. Theophilus silently pointed; a few yards beyond us, the road suddenly went from black to a dull red. It was where the cobblestones ended and the dirt roads of the country began. We had made it.

Faith started forward, but I had turned to look behind us. She stopped and turned with me. Soon, the others were there, too.

Before us, or behind us, rather, spread the picturesque mural of the stone city of Riversedge, its streets sprawling away from the cathedral at its center like the limbs of a sleeping giant. From so high above, it looked peaceful, with smoke wafting out of the chimneys and even its roughest neighborhoods neatly laid out in rows. The cathedral looked from this angle like a beneficent father overlooking the beds of his sleeping infants, strong and contented with his lot.

"It's so big," Helena whispered.

Theophilus rubbed her shoulder fondly. "Too big for me," he said with some satisfaction. "And soon we'll leave it behind us."

Something drifted silently into my vision, and I crossed my eyes to see it better. I blinked and wrinkled my nose as the fat snowflake landed, then instantly melted into a cold, itchy drop which I wiped away with my mitten. I was surprised; it seemed early for snow, but then again, Faith had said earlier that tomorrow was the first of December.

"Theophilus, what is that?"

The warning tenor of Faith's voice made my stomach muscles tighten. We all followed with our eyes to where she pointed.

At first, I couldn't figure out what she saw. For a moment, all I saw was the peaceful grey landscape of the city which had so briefly been our home. Then I saw the spark.

"Theophilus, they're burning the cathedral!" she cried in horror.

No, I thought. *They couldn't be. Nobody is that wicked...*

But then the tiny orange pinprick near the feet of the sleeping sphinx twisted, writhed, began to stretch and grow.

"Impossible," Theophilus muttered, squinting into the darkness. "That whole building is made out of stone! Unless..."

"The scaffolding!" Helena said. She and I had learned this big word from Theophilus when he was supervising the hanging of his windows. The workmen had been perched at different levels of the wooden framework.

Theophilus's eyes widened. "It's everywhere in there, even inside the old wing."

"And the workers' houses are made of thatch – they're made out of thatch! *Oh!*"

Faith covered her mouth with both hands as the little tufts that were the workers' roofs caught. The glowing red monster suddenly bloomed into a mass the size of one of the taverns as it climbed atop the first roof. It seemed to engulf much of the little miniature village in one angry burst. Helena screamed.

Faith gripped her husband's hand. "We have to alert someone!"

But by then, someone was already awake. A dense row of shadowed figures swarmed out of the buildings around the cathedral. Shouts echoed off the cobblestones, and more people flew from doorways to see what the fuss was about, then hurried to the water pumps with buckets, calling for their families to awaken.

"That seemed…" Theophilus exchanged a curious look with Faith. "Fast."

At least a hundred people were already streaming about the cathedral, shouting to each other and tossing buckets of water on the flames or beating at them with dampened sheets and coats. Women stood in the doorways of houses, prepared to tend to the wounded or man the pumps if necessary.

Then, all at once, one voice rang out high above the rest, a single, prolonged call. A rush of water poured from the lower balconies of the church onto the flames, dousing part of the scaffolding and beating back portions of the thatch roofs.

Faith's eyes were fixed on a figure standing on the parapet above. "He must've prepared."

The light from the fire had dimmed considerably, but once our eyes adjusted to the new shades of smoky orange, we all spotted the black-dressed figure. Other figures disappeared, only to return moments later and overturn massive cauldrons on the flames at his command.

Helena bounced up and down, cheering. "Hurray, Father Forsetti!"

Faith was grinning broadly, a nice change on a face that had been constantly taut of late. She clasped her hands together and pressed them to her mouth, occasionally whispering a prayer of thanks. Theophilus wrapped his arm around her, watching in solemn silence.

For several minutes, we kept watch from above, but the tides were clearly turning in the town's favor. Then a deep breath from Theophilus signaled it was time to go.

We started to turn, but Faith leapt onto an outcrop which overlooked the neighborhoods nearest us, some fifteen blocks from the cathedral.

"Theo." Her voice was low and urgent. "What is that?"

He swiftly went to stand beside her and peered into the darkened regions of Riversedge. "It's probably nothing. Must be a lantern or something." But he paused for a long second. "The ruckus from the church could've woken them up."

Helena and I clustered on either side of them to

look. Far below, another yellow patch of light flickered in the blackened streets. For a moment, it held still, and then it blossomed into two: one large and growing rapidly, the other a small dancing orb that sped away from the spot.

"Oh, no!" Faith gasped. "Another one!"

The fire continued to spread, engulfing first one thatch roof, then the one next to it.

"Where is everyone?" Faith whispered.

A few black figures appeared in the moonlight, barking exclamations and dashing for the wells. But it was clear that nobody *here* was prepared. One person ran to each of the neighboring houses and frantically pounded on doors. The response was sluggish, surprised from their sleep.

"Theophilus, we need to get down there." Both their eyes were wide and rolling like those of horses, the terrified whites catching the moonlight. "We have to go help!"

The strangest look had come over Theophilus's face. His mouth moved slowly, as if he were muttering silently, thinking it over.

"Papa!" Helena yanked on his sleeve, thinking he hadn't heard.

But the look in his eyes told me he had heard; he was making a choice. He glanced down at Helena, then at me. He stroked our foreheads fondly with his thumbs, then turned a grateful look on his wife. "Let's go," he simply said.

Faith tugged at his arm. "Theophilus, don't," she growled lowly.

"A few days more and they would've been ready to

hang us all, adult and child alike," he responded in a voice as cold and hard as iron. "We never really did belong to them. Let's get out while we still have the chance."

Faith's face was a mask of fear and fury. "Theophilus, please!" No answer. She shook his arm as if trying to wake him from paralysis. "They are someone's children! Come!"

For a second, it looked as if he hadn't heard. But then at last, he slowly turned his face away from the fires. Feeling spread back into his face, transforming him from stone back into a man, a warmhearted husband and father. Something ugly, like fear and hatred mixed together, drained slowly from his expression.

With his eyes still trained on Faith's, he threw off his pack and coat, pulled her against him, and pressed a hard kiss against her mouth. Then he vanished into the darkened city below.

No sooner had he gone than we heard a chorus of screams. Faith pulled off her own pack and took our faces in her hands, her eyes darting from one to the other of us. Then she pecked us each on the forehead.

"Girls, quickly! Leave your things here and let's go and help Papa. May God protect us all!"

There was no time to be scared as we were swallowed by the shadow of the city and embraced in darkness. The streets here were the roughest, so we had to scramble over piles of unknown materials and stub our toes on pieces of broken stone. Ironically, I ran here with more freedom. The dangers of falling were far from my mind. After some time, it was as though we were deep underwater, paddling without moving anywhere, suspended in dark fluid.

The first thing I knew was a wall of heat that almost knocked me off my feet. I let out something between a cry and a whimper and threw up my arm to protect my face.

"Come on, dear!" Faith called. "Please don't be afraid."

I felt her take my hand. My feet obeyed, but it was several seconds before I could open my eyes. After the inky darkness, this place seemed overwhelmed with light. Truthfully, it was exceedingly dim, but the closeness of the blaze made everything an unbearably intense orange.

"Quickly." Faith was speaking close to my ear, smashing Helena against me so that we could both hear. "Run down the street away from the fires and knock on doors. Knock as loud as you can, and scream 'FIRE!' at the top of your lungs. When you've got to the end of the street, alert the houses on the corners and start back. And do not lose sight of each other!"

She gave us a little shove. I was still dazed from the heat, so Helena grabbed my hand. We had run only a few yards before I pulled us to a stop.

"Emmy, you go to the houses on that side of the street." Helena pointed. "I will be over here." She gestured to the opposite side, but I shook my head. I was inconsolable. She pulled me to her, desperate eyes darting over the street on either side of us. "Emmy, it's going to be okay. They need us to help. Please don't cry. You can see me, see? I'll be right over there."

One last sticky hug, and she pulled away from me. I

wiped my eyes on the front of my dress and forced my legs to bend, carrying me up onto the first stoop.

"FIRE!" I screamed and pounded, then glanced back at Helena.

"Louder!" she called. "We need to wake them up!"

I began to beat with both fists. The door suddenly opened. I shouted my word again, then ran to the next one and started beating on its door.

Faith, meanwhile, had dashed into someone's little garden and was priming the pump furiously. The sound of their water source was enough to wake them up, and soon they were shouting commands over each other. I wanted to cover my ears against the cacophony, but my job needed two fists.

As more people began to fill the street, Faith began to organize them, arming them with cookpots, buckets, and anything else she had gotten the neighbors to provide.

"FORM A LINE!" she screamed over and over until her voice was scratchy.

Gradually, the call to action had shaken the frost of fear from my bones, and Helena and I made rapid progress. The noise of the waterlines aided in our mission, and soon we gave up having to wake people and instead asked for more buckets and pails. People who didn't live in the same house both gripped the same handle and forced the oldest pumps to run; one young woman wrenched one garment after another from her clothesline and began wetting the fabric for people to tie over their faces to protect them. Chaotic shouts gave way to a single message: Get their pastor to ring the bells.

Some men were debating who should go, but Helena immediately volunteered. She disappeared as fast as her legs could carry her, with people shouting directions to the Presbyterian church after her. At first, I was afraid because we were separated, but I knew she was doing something that would've made the angel-man proud.

"Help! Help!"

I gazed around me at the people throwing water on the places where their roofs met, bringing out bedsheets and rushing into the flames.

Suddenly, I heard my mama's voice. "Emmanuella!"

She was indistinguishable from the others, coated in ash, but still I listened for her. There she was, coming toward me. How fast her dress had been ruined!

She said something else, but the roar of the flames was too great for me to hear. She was motioning to me as if to give some instruction while she coughed convulsively into her other fist. She gestured wildly, but then someone came between us and she was lost to my sight.

And then I was all alone. Alone in the middle of a bellowing, throbbing mass of people scared for their lives and barely noticing where they stepped.

Broken cobblestones.

Scuffed shoes, splashed with clumsily passed buckets of water.

Flashes of light that made me cover my eyes and whimper.

It was hot. It was so hot, but in winter. I was sweating!

I turned in circles, seeing my surroundings as if for the first time. My arms shook and I struggled to get my coat off. The sleeves of my dress clung to my arms with deep wrinkles pressed into them, drenched with my sweat from standing so close to the fire.

I shivered, but I was hot. There was no place to put my coat. People jostled past me so I was afraid they would step on me. I started to cry.

"Emmanuella." Her call was weak and raspy, but I couldn't find her in the crowd. "Emmy, dear, look at me, please." How tired she sounded. "It's all right. It's all right."

Lulled by the sound of my mama's voice, my heart started to slow down. I lolled my head from side to side to search for her face. My coat dropped to the pavement beside me.

"Deep breaths, baby. Don't be afraid. I'm coming."

A new sound was breaking through the noise, and my poor pounding head was relieved by this change, though the voices around me had escalated in pitch and volume. It was a slow, massive creaking sound; I could imagine a great old oak like the one in the play yard at the orphanage. It was swaying in the wind, but only the branches had ever come down...

"EMMY, LOOK OUT!"

I turned, not toward my mother's voice, but to where the creaking sound was coming from.

"Oh! There she goes."

CRACK!

The men backed away from the nearest building, and we watched as a big chunk of the roof, its peak, came crashing down.

Such a cacophony of crashes, breakage, and screams! I still see it falling in my dreams.

"Emmy!"

The sound scared me so much that it jolted me out of my reality, both realities: the one with the safe happy home with Faith and Theophilus and Helena and the one where all the world was burning, turning the same awful shade as that orange fabric we'd hated.

I turned on my heel and ran. It was by the grace of God that I didn't accidentally run into the flames; I didn't know where I was going, but all I know is I sought the darkness.

Behind me, I found out later, Faith's hand closed around nothing, just a little too late. She says the most terrifying second of her life was as she watched my little back dashing up into a darkened alley, and they had to hold her because she lost her senses a little bit.

I don't remember the running. I had some bad scrapes on my shins and a bump on my head that made me think of a smooth, round river rock for two weeks, but I don't remember feeling the pain. I just fled from the horrible orange flames and all of that noise.

I remember I stopped when I was cold. Then I just trudged to the hilltop in front of me. I had nowhere else to go, and I had left the town below me. It was the hilltop from which we had abandoned our escape and gone to help beat the flames. But now I was there all alone, and no one was there to help me or tell me it was all right.

I wrapped my arms around myself, suddenly shaking. The air up here was clear of the smoke; the wind was carrying it off to my right, toward the cathedral. When I was with my family, I could see the whole city from up here; now I could only see a glass mockery of my old home, writhing in massive heat waves and illumined by eerie orange and yellow flames. A black phantom of smoke surged upward like a triumphant fiend from the roofs of all the homes and advanced, roaring, toward the towering heights of the cathedral beyond.

"Emmanuella."

My papa, the angel-man, was hauling himself up the hill toward me. His dragging steps told me he was exhausted, and the cinders on his clothes had been somewhat washed away by a sheen of sweat.

He approached me, holding out his hand. But I didn't take it; I was too afraid. I had been shocked back into silence.

With a sigh, he lifted me and held me pressed to his chest. He smelled of fear, wood smoke, and rancid ash. We gazed out over the burning city of Riversedge.

"Such hatred," he barely whispered, pressing trembling lips to the side of my head. In a moment of unchildlike wisdom, I sensed that he was drawing strength from my presence.

"Come on," he said. His normally gravelly voice was raspy, like it was catching on ragged pieces of scorched fabric flapping in the winter breeze. "Let's get you back to your mother."

I didn't react as he turned away. I relaxed into the up and down of being carried, familiar with the cadence of his high, loping gait.

Suddenly, he stopped. His face was turned back

over his shoulder, and his bloodshot pale eyes were darting over the scene below, keen as knives. I knew that look; I had seen it before whenever he was making some scientific creation or explaining a concept to us.

He set me down and walked to the edge, towing me by the hand. The city was one smoldering mass to me, but his eyes clearly measured every distance, delved into every shadow, considered every spot of glowing orange inferno.

He took another step forward and poised like a hunting dog. I tried to see where his eyes were pointed and found only sweeping destruction, but- There! A new spot of yellow, a single dot in the midst of the sleeping remainder of Riversedge, and it was growing.

"Not again!" Theophilus growled. "Not another one."

Chapter Twelve

Once again, what had been a bright little speck grew into a waving, dancing demon, swallowing one house after another. But Theophilus was not looking at the houses.

At the edge of the hill on the steep side, his feet dug precariously into the loose, crumbling soil, allowing him to draw as close as he dared, and still he leaned out farther. His eyes were squinted with an eagerness which frightened me, for it was not the look of the happy scientist; it was the look of the hunter.

He straightened abruptly, and I knew he had found his mark. He seemed to have forgotten my presence, yet a staying hand remained extended beside and behind him as though to keep me back from the very dangers he courted.

"Emmanuella, go to your mother."

His tone brooked no argument, but I still desired above all else to stay close to him. Something in his heroic stance, ash-stained sweat glistening beneath the cold moon, made me fear I would never see him again.

I took his hand, then glanced once more at the place he was looking. I was unaware that that glance would save me.

He glanced back to see if I obeyed. A double-take revealed his surprise to see me still there, gazing up at him with silent pleading. He raised one eyebrow, the universal parent expression that said, "You're not fooling me for a second; I will have to reinforce my commands with actions or you will have your own way."

He scooped me up and hurried back the way we had come. When we reached a crossroads, he surprised me by taking an alley perpendicular to the one I'd followed both to and from the hilltop. We cut through several little courtyards and blighted brown gardens enclosed within knee-high fences.

When we emerged from the darkness of these little houses, we were on the street where we had been fighting the fire. I gazed up and down the street, taking in spindly skeletons of what had been thatch roofed homes, their remaining beams looking pitifully like the broken bones of a bird, crushed by something much bigger.

The fire was mostly out where I had been, and here the flames had at least been beaten back until they were contained. The line of people extending from each of the water pumps was longer than the Communion lines at church; people that didn't look like they were born of the same social world stood side by side, handing buckets of water forward and empty ones back, the very same hopeful, terrified, giddy energy lighting their expressions as the monster was subdued.

Many people had not been so lucky. Pieces of furniture, trunks, or other little objects were pushed to the middle of the street, but in an unfortunate number of cases, this pittance was all that remained of a once happy home. Wives buried their faces against husbands' shoulders; uncharacteristically somber children pressed themselves against the legs of parents, round eyes taking in the graphic spectacle.

Besides the continuous system of water buckets, almost all traffic into or out of any of the houses had ceased. Several unmoving shapes formed a sort of barrier between the blazing houses and the refuge of the street; dirty sheets covered each one. Barely heard above the cackle of flames and crunch of collapse was the sound of weeping.

"Oh, Theophilus!" Faith's shrill, broken voice was barely recognizable as she picked her way between several of the sheet-covered forms and shards of detritus. Her skirt was hiked up above her knees and pinned there so as not to encumber her, but still she staggered on the pavement.

Theophilus shook his head as if to stop her from coming closer. She paused, her expression cautious and searching. He cupped his hands to his mouth as if he was going to yell, then restrained a cough and thought better of it. Stooping, he gripped me by the waist with both hands and raised me above his head like a trophy. He waved me from side to side until he saw Faith's shoulders sag with relief. Then he put me down.

"Go to your mother." He spoke sternly in my ear

and pointed me to face her, then gave me a little push from behind which I feebly tried to resist.

I turned and watched him go. Faith, who had hurried up beside me, also watched in bewilderment as he sprinted past several people who had tried to attract his attention and bounded to the other end of the street. Then he hung a left and disappeared into the peaceful darkness.

The pitter-patter of running feet made us turn around.

"Helena!"

Faith sighed in relief at the sight of the little figure bravely racing towards us. My big sister was almost unrecognizable in the coating of ash except for her triumphant grin. Faith gathered her near, cupping her face and covering its grimy forehead with kisses.

I turned back to where Theophilus had gone, and in a moment, I had made my decision: *Wherever the angel-man goes, I go.*

I took off down the street and had made it a considerable distance before I heard Faith shrieking after me to come back. But small children are faster than they look, and my little legs carried a being who was for the first time overcome with the determination not to be left behind.

The street was almost completely dark; one could forget it was the fires set by an arsonist which brightened the alleys behind me. I knew only where Theophilus had turned; the rest I left up to instincts, God, and chance.

All at once, I felt someone near. My toes kicked against shiny black shoes; a shout of surprise rang out above my head; several voices warily responded; then I heard my name. Someone gripped my arm.

"Emmanuella?"

It was Father Forsetti. After Faith's more interesting meetings with him, my heart immediately struck up a tempo of alarm, but as he held my shoulders and bent down to my level, I felt that this time he was one of the good guys.

"Who is it?" said one of the voices behind him.

I then became aware of a small squadron of men who accompanied the priest, some mounted on horses. I was so small and it was so dark that many of them couldn't see me.

"It's a good thing you crossed with me and not one of the horses!" he said, glancing up and down my tiny frame. Then he frowned, looking this way and that, trying to pierce the darkness. "Where is your family? Are you out here all alone?"

Of course I could not answer; my silence had returned like a lead blanket when the building had collapsed behind me. The father sighed. Then he tried again.

"Emmy – it is Emmy, isn't it?"

I nodded, somewhat more at ease. He'd remembered Helena's instructions.

"Where are your guardians – are they back that way?"

He pointed behind me and I started to nod, then shook my head. Stepping free of his hold, I pointed in the direction Theophilus had gone, but up at the rooftops as a childish way to imply distance. The place where he'd been looking was quite a ways off.

"Who has gone that way? Your mother?"

I shook my head.

"Your father?" He nodded, digesting the information. "Then-"

"Emmy!" Faith and Helena had just caught up with us. Again, there was a dismayed murmur behind Father Forsetti as the two figures materialized out of the dark.

Faith caught me by my dress and hauled me toward her, but the question in her face was for Father Forsetti.

"Do you know where your husband has gone?" he asked simply.

Her chest rose and fell faster, but she could not muster the strength to fight. She shook her head.

Then he surprised us. "Can you tell us, Emmy?"

Everyone looked surprised when I nodded. Notwithstanding my silence, Faith peppered me with yes or no questions and then sketched a rough outline of the city in the dirt.

"Show me where Papa went," she encouraged me.

I stared down at the map. I could just tell them which way he'd gone or point to the general area, but I didn't think that would be enough information. They had to know the reason. If only I could speak!

Quickly, I knelt and began to draw a pair of jagged shapes. Candle flames, I knew, were rounded and smooth, but the flames I had seen today were ragged and reached out like tree branches.

"Are those the-"

Then I drew another one where Theophilus had seen it.

"A third fire," Faith breathed.

She whirled toward Father Forsetti in alarm, but I urgently tugged on her sleeve until she looked down. She immediately calmed herself with effort.

"Is that where Papa went? Did he go to the third fire?" She pointed at it and watched my face carefully.

I started to nod, then shook my head. I looked gravely into her eyes, willing her to understand me.

"No?" Father Forsetti and his crew exchanged a bewildered look. A murmur stirred through some of the ones farther back.

"Where did he go, then?"

I pointed, digging my finger in just to the right of the third fire. Faith frowned. Father Forsetti started to ask a question. Without pausing, I etched a little stick figure, then another just a fraction of an inch to its right. After a moment's thought, I placed a bit of jagged flame into the second figure's hand. Then I stopped and looked up.

Faith frowned. "Why has he gone there if not to-" She froze. "The arsonist."

"He's found him?" Father Forsetti looked as concerned as Faith did. "How did he know?"

I tapped the third fire.

"Maybe he saw him set the fire," the priest murmured. Then he turned to the men. "Come on! The little girl says there's a third fire and that the arsonist may have been spotted. It seems that it's on the far side of the Episcopal neighborhood; the smoke should guide us from there and we can chase him down."

"Wait." Faith caught his arm as he turned to leave.

He bridled with impatience. "Father," she persisted, "I know you want to go right after him, and I hope you do, but listen: if we send people out chasing him when we only know where he's been, we will only exhaust our resources and the culprit is likely to get away. WAIT!"

Father Forsetti was through with her; to his credit, it really had been a trying night. Even so, I trotted after him and wrapped myself around one of his legs, putting my full weight on his ankle until he stopped. The glance that he threw me, though stern, was less impatient than his interaction with my mother had been.

"Father." Her voice broke. "I know you don't like me, and I don't care whether you do. But I want you to think about this so you make the best decision-"

"Mrs. Gladstone, I am tired-"

With yet another burst of strength she hadn't appeared to possess, she straightened. "You can risk your life in any way you please, but my husband is out there by himself, and if you're going to help him, you will not do it willy-nilly and with only half a plan. I forbid it."

To everyone's amazement, the funniest little smile twisted the pastor's features. Then he folded his arms, back still turned, and waited.

"We ought to gather the people and form a line, as wide as we can – since we're almost finished with the waterlines it should be easy – and sweep the area as far as-"

Father Forsetti turned toward her, a new look on his face. "And make sure we don't lose him while we flush him out," he finished.

A sharp exhalation deflated Faith's squared posture and she nodded, relieved.

Father Forsetti turned and called new orders, and the line began to form. Everyone from his party was able to spread quite a distance, with the exception of a handful of riders he sent ahead just in case speed was enough to corner the arsonist. Even Helena and Faith and I took our place in the line.

Then others were gathered from the neighborhood where the fire was nearly extinguished, and soon we couldn't see either end. The repetition of instructions in every pitch of voice became a mere clamor in the back of my mind. Two of the mounted men rode to either end of the line. Minutes later, we heard first one whistle, then another, then another, echoing back and forth across the stone avenue. Father Forsetti shouted a command.

Then, like a well-trained force of something greater than startled townsfolk of every class and creed, we began to advance. It was the ends who began to move first, and then the rest of us followed, forming a wide, thin smile belting across the town. We did not join hands, for we were obliged to separate to go around buildings, but for every one, someone went inside and made inquiries, then called out that it was clear and rejoined us on the other side.

In order to keep up, Helena and I remained at a jog, with Faith gripping each of our hands tightly. For the most part, the group was silent except a sound somewhere between horse hooves and rain, created by the pattering of hundreds of variously-shod feet moving the same direction.

This was when the hours began to drag on. It was slow going even at a jog, and the exertion was not easy on any of us, especially the small ones. Faith was unable to carry us and keep up, so she gave us thirty-second pauses to hang back, then join the group. Sometimes the rejoining process was worse than the chase. Father Forsetti had acquired a horse and ran back and forth along the line, calling encouragement.

The Episcopal district greeted us with screams and the crackle of flames. Wearily, Father Forsetti split off women, children, and every third man to stay and help fight the flames while the rest went on to seek out the perpetrator. My pleas to go after my papa were flatly turned down, much to my impotent, childish fury.

"Faith."

We all turned in surprise to see Father Forsetti was the one whose hand gripped our mama's shoulder. She initially drew back in alarm, but he wearily shook his head. He said something a few times, but his voice had grown so hoarse that she had to bend very close. At last, we both caught it.

"I must join the hunt. Will you organize the rest?"

Faith stared at him dumbly for a moment. His bloodshot green eyes were traumatized but sincere. He drew her near him again.

"I know I can trust you to do this. Please."

She stared at him a moment longer, then nodded and pulled away.

Once again, we filled, hauled, and passed buckets of water until our hands were cut open and we therefore tossed small amounts of blood onto the fire. At one point, Faith stood working the pump, shouting words I could no longer distinguish, while Helena and I brought the filled buckets to the firsts of the line.

The fire here had been growing for too long. An entire block was up in smoke. The neighbors had hesitated uncertainly; when their help arrived, it was only to drag people from their smoldering homes, some just in time, others a bit too late. At this point, I witnessed more adults' pain than I had ever seen before, in the form of burns that cut to the blood or claimed limbs.

The screams had already begun to melt together with sounds of the fire, dampening their effect even on a small child. Other things riveted the attention of my heart, if not my eyes, for I had never seen so many sheet-covered, still forms all at once. This neighborhood was quickly becoming a graveyard.

As the hours passed on, I had the distinct impression of what hell must be like: all around me was the brilliant, ghastly orange which sometimes spat sparks or rained charred parts of buildings. The heat was such that Helena passed out once and had to be carried away and given water. She wasn't the only one; the less lucky of these revived only to commence a violent fit of shivering, some delirious.

At last, the dreaded truth was passed down the line in throaty whispers and ragged gasps: Leave it. We've saved what we can; the rest is lost.

The process of retreat was one which took far longer than expected. The chaos of the fires made it hard to hear, and the soot made it almost impossible for anyone to be identified. At last, those whose voices had been preserved and whose coughs weren't too bad were sent up and down the street, shouting the message over and over.

The fires at least contained, people began to slowly trickle back down the streets toward their own homes. There was nothing to be said; those who had lost everything clung to their loved ones or grieved bitterly; the dead were taken up and carried away to the various churches. It was a tragic sight when someone's remains could not be identified and their church home had to be merely guessed at.

Many of us, however, could not seem to tear ourselves away. Even when there was nothing left to do but watch it burn, dozens chose to cluster together with our backs to the unburned houses and do just that.

Beneath the flames stirred minimal conversation. Some grieved; others sought misplaced loved ones with hushed urgency. Most didn't deign to comment. Eventually, Angeline located us and she and Faith clung to each other in wordless solidarity. Helena and I held tightly to both of each other's dirty, sweaty hands. Every so often, another piece of one of the roofs would come down, and when we started, Faith would stroke our heads to calm us.

I was bone-weary, and yet I could not rest. Every inch of my body remained stoically at attention, as though ready to flee from another falling beam or to hear the fatal cry of "Fire!" and mobilize once more. I could only sway unsteadily on my feet when I wasn't crouched beside my sister, taking in millions of images that passing years would never erase.

A cold grey light gradually penetrated the thick hanks of smoke which still rose angrily into the air, and I realized it was dawn. Most of the townspeople dispersed at this point, murmuring grim predictions as to the success of the manhunt. Faith's eyes had remained alert, her ears ever listening as if even over the roar of buildings burning she would hear if her husband called for her help.

Helena, still weak from her brush with heat exhaustion, whimpered that she wanted to go home. We were all so exhausted that it seemed as though every movement made our bones creak. In the night, the soot which smeared our clothes and faces had had the appearance of war-paint; now, in the pale light of day, we looked more like grey specters risen from the grave.

Faith hesitated, looking around for Angeline, but she had already gone. She looked down at us, assessing. I knew she wouldn't go home without Theophilus, and I didn't want to, either. Weren't our packs still on the hill? We'd never intended to go home after this.

"Come," she said, reaching out her arms for Helena. "We will go up to the cathedral to see if anyone has any news. Emmy, can you still walk?"

I didn't see any reason why I shouldn't, and so we set off, Helena in Faith's arms, me plodding along silently beside her.

It was an unearthly walk. The streets looked same as they had yesterday and the day before, and yet every so often a similarly unearthly-looking figure would appear, often headed the same way. A few halfheartedly genial remarks were exchanged, but worry kept most of them quiet. I silently wondered whether I would be able to speak again if I tried.

I awoke from the hypnosis of walking when Faith suddenly stopped. I looked up. Up ahead and between a couple of shops, a tightly condensed crowd with their backs to us. The road was clear to the cathedral.

Faith was frowning. "I wonder what…"

All at once, a ripple went through the crowd, and several erupted in screams.

"THERE HE IS!"

Chapter Thirteen

"In the alley-"

"After him, go!"

After this pronouncement, the commotion escalated instantaneously so that one could no longer distinguish words amid the chorus of horses' hooves, pounding feet, and angry screams. The message, however, was clear: the arsonist himself had been spotted.

"How do they know it's him?" Helena pondered aloud.

"Someone spotted him trying to set a fourth fire," one shopkeeper answered from where he stood sweeping his front step. "He took off, but they went after him, and the lot have gotten him boxed within a few city blocks."

Faith clasped us both in alarm, shifting on her feet as though debating whether to run and where. It only took a moment to decide; adjusting Helena against one shoulder and gripping me by the hand, she took off toward the cathedral at a run.

We had almost reached the grim iron front doors when a scream made Faith stumble and pause. She whirled to see, just in time. A flash of color shot inside another door farther down. The great door slammed behind him, and a multitude of angry pursuers slammed into it, then pounded with their fists.

"He's gone inside!"

"He's in the cathedral!"

Faith hauled us back as if from a venomous snake, but I planted my feet, determined to see.

For a moment, the church doorway remained a chaotic mass of limbs and angry shoving, but then one man's arms appeared above the rest and he shouted instructions.

Before he could finish, another figure broke free and bolted from the group. Even through the caked layers of sweat and soot, his golden hair was still just visible.

Theophilus.

Faith caught her breath, and her fingernails dug unconsciously into my wrist. Liberated from the throngs, the angel-man dashed into the courtyard, followed by the eyes of several curious onlookers. A small shed stood against the craggy outer wall; with a single leap and one monkeylike swing from the edge of its roof, he ascended this and, standing on its peak, leapt to grip the bottom of a windowsill. Soon, a flood of men was on his heels, clambering up after him. In moments, he had disappeared inside.

"Around to the back! Around to the back!" one man shouted, motioning with his arm. It took me a moment to recognize the weary Father Forsetti, his voice and aspect were so changed by a night spent by the fires of the town.

But his eyes! I will never forget the look in his eyes. All the life that had left them when his pastor and best friend had succumbed to his wounds rushed back and seemed to glow, green and dangerous. Inhuman strength possessed him as he bounded to the front of the throng, every movement as graceful and deadly as that of a lion.

A surge of motion followed him, while another group took off in the opposite direction, and soon we could see they were posting men on all sides. Faith turned as if to go, surely for our sake since her heart had just leapt nimbly out of our sight, but other townspeople, especially women and children, had gathered to see. There was nowhere for us to go, so closely packed was the crowd.

Meanwhile, townsmen continued to pour in from all directions. Some had spent the night as part of the search party; others had not. They rushed into the cathedral, a river of righteous anger that seethed at every door, making deceptively slow progress up the steps. A few appointed ones sharply reminded the group that a few had to stay outside to guard the doors in case he escaped.

As the cluster of onlookers grew, we were pushed closer and closer to the stone outer walls. Faith eyed the windows anxiously, trying for a glimpse of anything of what was happening inside.

She didn't have to wait long; it was probably only minutes, but to all of us gathered down below the sphinxlike figure of the cathedral, it felt like an eternity.

The first shape we saw was Theophilus.

"Is that him? Is that the bastard?"

Faith looked around with a horror which not even the night of battling flames had elicited, but her mouth formed no words. She clutched us so hard against her that it hurt.

Above us, Theophilus was pulling himself out through a tiny, round window as agilely as an acrobat. There was no stonework on which he could stand; the window was near a peak in the roof, some twelve feet above the nearest outer ledge big enough to stand on.

He didn't look at all afraid, though; he hung practically upside down as he slid his long legs out, gripping the frame of the window with his long fingers. When he unfolded, he placed hands and feet on the skinny bars of the remaining wooden scaffolding that climbed the outside of this part of the cathedral above the parapets. Fortunately, this section had not been badly burned. He paused there for an instant, peering through the massive but spindly structure as though looking for something.

"There! I see him!" someone's voice called from a distance.

Everyone turned to see an extended arm ending in a pointing finger. In a single motion, all of our heads swiveled to a spot at the base of the scaffolding. A figure cowered in its shadows, making its way quickly along the parapet but having to duck through the wooden framework.

The crowd was becoming rowdy again, but with less gusto; it was finally clear nobody knew who was who or if either of these men was the one we sought. Every so often somebody shouted a question or attempted to answer, but still mass confusion reigned and nobody on the ground was able to do anything but grind their teeth in a rage that had nowhere to go.

Three more men appeared on the parapet at the end opposite the crouched figure. Murmurs rose; these three held torches and one had a hatchet in his hand. They stood on their toes and peered around corners and up into the scaffolding. Their view across the parapet was blocked by a flapping sheet of canvas. Someone called to them, pointing out both Theophilus and the cowering stranger. The three consulted briefly before one sprinted back inside. Moments later, a stream of other men arrived, collecting until it was blocked against the bottom of the scaffolding and no more could exit the doorway.

Theophilus craned his neck from his distant perch. He was too high to hear any of the crowd's instructions, but after observing the other men on the parapet for a minute, he began deftly climbing toward the other end. He dropped onto a platform from which the workmen must have recently hung another of his windows; from here, he peered over the side toward the lone man hidden in the lower sections of scaffolding.

The stranger started violently when he realized he'd been spotted. In a flash, he disappeared from our view.

Theophilus, however, had seen him. He hopped down through story after story of scaffolding, sometimes leaping sideways like a lemur. Helena and I laughed with delight at his antics, but Faith still gripped our hands so hard that both her fingers and ours turned red at the tips.

A commotion drew our attention back to the men at the other side of the stone walkway. They were passing a message out of the cathedral: "Can't reach the other side. He's blocked the door."

In seconds, there were four or five men struggling into the layers of scaffolding, having to move first up and then over in order to bypass several sections blocked by heavier supports. Their movements were much slower than Theophilus's, though many were fit from their daily labors. It made me wonder how the angel-man had come to be so nimble.

Faith cried out. A murmur of alarm rippled through the people near us. My head shot up; in my pondering, I had missed the split-second of movement. I scanned the parapet frantically. Where was Theophilus?

There! A flash of black among the scaffolding drew my attention and directed it toward another spot of movement where two men tussled – Theophilus and the loner he had frightened.

The black figure spirited in and out of the shadows, making its way toward the two fighters. Every so often, even he had to stop and hold on tight; Theophilus and his opponent were balanced upon a wooden platform, but even so, the structure shifted and shuddered as they struck heavy blows. It was solid enough for careful workers, but it had never been made to withstand combat. The other climbers stopped moving and clung to the supports nearest them, crying out in fear and glancing above them.

All at once, the fighting paused as one arm surfaced above the thrashing pile of limbs, clutching a hunk of stone from the wall. I gazed at the sleeve. Theophilus was wearing white; this one was dark blue.

Faith screamed as the handful of rock came down. A hollow thud made Helena's head jerk and the contents of my stomach nearly leap to escape, but the chunk of stone had merely connected with the wooden platform. Theophilus's pink face was visible just beyond it, eyes no doubt focused on the near miss.

The other man raised his arm again, pausing to maintain his seat atop Theophilus.

"STOP!" A familiar voice ricocheted off of the walls.

The stranger was startled for just a second, but it was enough. Theophilus punted him off of him with a powerful thrust of the knee. Then he scrambled onto the stranger's back, gripping his shoulder with one hand and hooking his arm through the man's other elbow and yanking it up. His victim yelped and squirmed beneath him, but Theophilus's stance was that of a wildcat and his knee was immovable where it dug into the man's back.

The figure in black whom I had seen was calling to them, and in his voice was a warning. But their struggling didn't stop, nor did the stranger cease to fight to regain power over Theophilus.

"Stop, I said!"

It was Father Forsetti. He was precariously balanced with his feet on two slender boards several feet apart, and the scaffolding was shaking under him. Faith covered her mouth with one hand. There was hope in her inkwell eyes, and Helena and I clasped each other's hands, willing it all to be all right.

An inhuman cry rent the cold morning air, making

many backs arch with revulsion. The figure under Theophilus, though about a foot shorter and significantly smaller than him, reared up with unnatural strength, the ungodly strength Theophilus says electrifies people in moments of fear.

"Don't-" Father Forsetti started to speak, but he wobbled on his shaking perch and threw his hands out to steady himself.

The stranger writhed savagely, twisting Theophilus's limbs wherever he had dared to grab hold. It was clear that Theophilus would not be unseated.

Then the man reached up and slammed Theophilus's golden head against the stone wall with a wicked thrust of his hand. Theophilus sagged and feebly touched his forehead. The other man wiggled out from under him and leapt.

The crowd let go a unanimous sigh as the man landed on the platform below Theophilus and righted himself, but barely. He clung to the outermost supports of the scaffolding, hanging out so that his shadow lay almost at our feet. Father Forsetti was shouting something, apparently to the fugitive, but the man's attention appeared to be everywhere else. Even a few stories below him, we could see him violently shaking. His stance was like that of a nervous cat which has been scared up a tree and believes its pursuer to still be near.

In fact, it was. The crowd below him had by now ascertained from the other pursuers that this man was the arsonist we all sought. Several innocent lives dripped from his shaking fingers among the beads of his sweat, and nobody would catch him if he were to fall, even from this height. Or perhaps it would be worse if they did.

He turned his head over his shoulder as if registering Father Forsetti for the first time.

"…to turn yourself in and…"

Father Forsetti's voice was fitfully snatched away by the breeze, but we heard enough to catch his drift. Theophilus was righting himself on the platform above the arsonist and trying to map out his next attack. Father Forsetti lifted a warning hand to stay him. Theophilus paced; his intentions to obey the father were doubtful. The other men in the scaffolding, however, began to back off.

"…forgiveness that God offers…even in prison…"

The stranger's shoulders were hunched with his head and neck tucked in at a weird angle like an animal's, and his back shifted fitfully back and forth. A raucous laugh escaped from him and bounced from the stones to echo bizarrely on the ground near us.

When he brought his face up, the smoke-white sun reflected off the sweat and tears as if from a mirror.

"What good is your forgiveness, you hypocrites?" the man cried out.

Father Forsetti froze, a look of confusion and disgust sealed upon his brow.

"I have made my own redemption! I will be saved…" The man's head lolled back and forth and he seemed to have become distracted by something in front of him on the lawn, which remained clear up to where the crowds stood. Everyone had backed up slightly so they could see him; Faith and Helena and I were helplessly moved by the crowd.

Father Forsetti's movements had become much slower and taut with caution. For several seconds, he didn't speak as he crept closer to where the man was perched high above us. The pastor glanced a warning at Theophilus as if forbidding him to pounce.

After a moment, he spoke again, so lowly that we couldn't hear, extending a pacifying hand before him, moving almost as if to clasp hands with the man even with the space in between them. His words sounded even and soothing, but the other man cackled.

"Shut up!" he screamed. "Don't you understand? I will not go to prison until I have made my penance! Then I will know that I am right with God."

Father Forsetti cautiously stepped down one rung, then another. "You don't have to do anything more to find peace with God," he said firmly, his powerful bass voice raising as it did when he was at the pulpit. "His arms are open to you right now. Through repentance-"

"I didn't mean to do it! The first one was an accident!"

The clear evidence that the other man was totally out of touch with what was happening around him sent a slow, dark chill up my spine, reawakening the sweat which had dried.

Father Forsetti lowered himself to the level of his target. "Tell me about it," he was saying, and the rest of his words were lost to us.

For a moment, the wind was all we heard. Then a frantic sob reached our ears.

"I didn't mean to kill him," the strange man

blubbered.

For several minutes, their voices mingled together with the sweeping winds which swirled through the arches and crevices of the cathedral, and we could make out nothing. Father Forsetti's hands were extended, pacifying, but the other man's movements were erratic, vehement, and emotive.

"But then I knew."

The eerie whisper trickled from the parapets of the church to collect in the horrified listening ears below.

"The death of the old priest was a sign to me! I saw that I had to purify the church – to purify it with fire. The hypocrites were the first to go – after the practice round, that is. I chose the prostitutes for that. No one would miss them; they were scum." He chuckled a little too long. "I had to listen and find out who the guilty were, but you helped me – you all helped! With the knowledge of the faithful behind me, it wasn't hard to find sinners in the church – it was hard to narrow it down!"

Father Forsetti's face was white. "It's not your job to punish sinners," he said sternly. But his voice shook.

This drew the man's attention so his head whipped around sharply. "Not my job? Not my job? Not my job?" He shook his head, then began to back away from the priest. His trembling hands felt for the supports behind his back. He almost seemed not to notice when his hand floundered in the air before it rested firmly on solid wood.

He curled into himself for a moment, looking once more like a hunted animal that was trying to fold into a smaller target. Then he snapped back to attention so fast that Father Forsetti jerked and almost lost his balance.

"Not my job?" he said again. His laughter was nervous, a bubbling outlet for emotions as far from joy as his mind was from reason. "On the contrary, it *had* to be mine. I was the one who killed the old priest. He was a good man. He was a good priest. I would never have hurt him. I would *never-*"

His laughter slurred together until it became rapid, muted sobs. Father Forsetti hesitantly approached. He was about six or seven feet away, separated by only two beams and a lot of space. He slowly dropped to his knees.

"So you thought that you had to do something to purify the church in order to save yourself from what you'd done." He slowly raised his arms out in front of him, palms at an angle as if to offer a gentle embrace. His quarry whimpered.

"To save me, to save me," the other man agreed. "To ask for forgiveness!" His hands scrambled up and down the front of his shirt, tugging at loose strings and touching buttons restlessly.

Father Forsetti nodded. "But you said it was an accident." He waited. The other man didn't contradict him. The priest shifted uncomfortably until he was seated on his heels. He made an inviting gesture. "Tell me what happened."

But the other man recoiled abruptly with a snarl. "Tell you! Tell you! You were a hypocrite like the rest of them." Having ascended to a new perch, he resumed the distracted movements of his hands. "You were fighting with the father about something. I don't know what, but you fought him and made him angry, so I knew. The father was a good man, a good priest, and when I knocked over the lantern, I saw his eyes. I saw his eyes, and that was when I knew."

Father Forsetti seemed to slowly freeze, his hands lowered to his knees. Oblivious, the other man went on.

"When I knocked over the lantern, it was like the fire grew into a beast as tall as me, and it leapt up, oh, how it leapt up the sides of the building! It was the vines, the vines that were dead and they caught and it spread! Oh, I didn't mean to!" He buried his face in his hands. This time, Father Forsetti offered no comment. Nothing moved except where the wind flapped at his sleeves and blew through his hair.

When the arsonist brought his face back up, his eyes were as wide as saucers and visible from my place on the ground. "I left, but he kept going back, bringing more and more people out. I hadn't known there was anyone else there – but still he died, and after that I had to do it. I had to make things better."

Father Forsetti's deep voice spoke lowly.

"No, you *don't* understand!" the man snapped impatiently. "You weren't gone for three days, not knowing where you were, and having those smoky eyes follow you everywhere!" Again, he wept. "It was like he was stalking me, his spirit was stalking me. I knew that wasn't possible, and could tell myself so while he was still alive, but once he was dead, this calm fell over me, and I saw those eyes again and I knew what I had to do."

"You killed dozens of people-"

"I was purifying the church-"

"You killed dozens of people and you think that will redeem you for an accident?" Father Forsetti slowly rose to his feet. "You need to stop now and come down with me before you do anything else."

The arsonist raised his chin haughtily. "The old father-"

Father Forsetti's voice was ice cold. "Whatever you thought you saw in his eyes, it wasn't him telling you to do anything like this. Come down at once." He reached out his hand, but this time it was a command. *Take it or force me to do something you won't like.*

But the other man laughed. "Your lies are powerless, you hypocrite! If it had gone as it was supposed to, you would have died in the first fire I set last night!"

Father Forsetti, I've come to realize, is a strong man, but even he recoiled as though from a physical blow at this admission.

Lighter on his feet following this strange and horrible confession, the arsonist turned to make his escape. Father Forsetti glanced down, but by now the distance between them was too great for him to overcome in time.

A flash of light materialized into Theophilus on the same wide beam where the arsonist stood. The entire wooden structure shook as his feet made contact. The arsonist and the priest both swayed on their feet, but without missing a beat, Theophilus had thrown himself against the arsonist, wrapping his arms around the guilty man. Theophilus's weight had thrown them both off balance and allowed him to get a grip on the back of the other man's neck.

"No!" Father Forsetti called out. "Don't hurt him! He will pay for his crimes, but I will not have you commit a guilty act on the very roof of the house of God. I said *stop*!"

One of Theophilus's arms was locked around the other man's throat from behind and bent at a close angle, cutting off the captive's breath. With his other hand, the glassworker gripped the beam above them to balance him easily on his feet. He turned from one to the other, considering the father's words but also the hands which clawed busily at his restraining grasp. When the arsonist's desperate motions became too wild, Theophilus turned and dangled one of the man's feet off the beam on which they stood and the other's hoarse snarls quickly gave way to whimpering pleas.

"Theophilus, enough."

Theophilus's gaze bored into the priest. "Have the others come over here to-"

A screech rent the air, and with a flash of inhuman strength, the arsonist broke free and leapt.

"NO!" Father Forsetti dove onto the beam with Theophilus. He was too late, but still his hands raked the air as if to catch the edge of the deranged man's shirt.

Theophilus caught the priest just in time; for several moments, the father stood with Theophilus's hand pressed against his chest to steady him, gazing in horror and regret over the precipice which ended in the stone parapet below.

The father's voice was too hoarse for me to hear, but his words have since been wildly circulated: "He's gone. And I've got the horrid feeling I knew him."

Theophilus watched him carefully, unmoving. As long as Father Forsetti continued to press forward to follow the culprit with his eyes, the angel-man continued to restrain him. In truth, the priest seemed to have lost track of everything else going on about him.

Perhaps this was why it was only the cries of the other men in the scaffolding which alerted him to the danger.

Theophilus's head swiveled toward the other end of the parapet. Father Forsetti remained as he was. The other men were screaming something, but they were frightened enough that they were shouting over top of each other.

For a second, Theophilus merely stood frowning. Then he gripped the father's shoulders and tried to turn him to face him.

"He's alive!" one of the men managed to scream over the noise of his fellows.

At this pronouncement, Father Forsetti stepped to the edge to look down. At the same moment, a loud snap rang off the stones and the entire structure lurched. Theophilus still had one hand on the beam above them and managed to keep his feet, but Father Forsetti was nearly tossed off the edge. At the last second, he caught one of the supports with his elbow and flung both arms around it.

Another crunch sounded from below them, along with a repeated hacking noise which had been previously masked by the shouting. The two men stared at each other for a moment.

Murmurs flitted through the crowd which pressed

in around us.

"He wouldn't bring the whole thing down on himself, would he?"

"Perhaps he's got hold of one of the workers' tools…"

Soon, our view was almost completely blocked as impatient onlookers forced their way in front of us. Helena clung to Faith's skirts, eyes wide and rolling in terror of being crushed. To me, the shadows of the people seemed almost to block out the sun.

"What's happening?"

"I can't see…"

The force from behind us was like the current of a river, swelling and threatening to wash over us. Faith clenched us both close to her, trying to lift us even though her arms were forced against her at an awkward angle by the tight quarters. Her jaw was clenched so tight that I feared her teeth would crack.

Whack after whack rang out above us, and angry shouts mingled with warning cries from the people both on the ground and above us. A prolonged, horrid creaking sound sang a warning from the quaking scaffolding.

The sensations were too overwhelming, and I had already spent the whole night either walking or fighting the fires. My knees started to wobble, and what little of the sky was visible through the narrow tunnel of faces above me began to whirl before whisking completely out of my view. I went down.

When I was conscious again, I could feel Helena's knees supporting my back and her hands keeping my head more or less upright. One man was yelling too loudly right near us to clear some space for me to breathe, and I put my hands over my ears.

Soon, however, the screams became too loud and too urgent for me to shut them out. Against Faith's admonishments, I gripped my sister's arm and hobbled to my feet just in time to see Theophilus and Father Forsetti fall.

Chapter Fourteen

It wasn't until a few days later that the smoke truly cleared, both literally and metaphorically, and Riversedge began to look like herself once again.

As far as the terror of having an arsonist emerge from among us, the city never recovered. Mrs. Cunningham, especially, never really got over it and has never been the same. She wore the biggest hats she owned, but none was big or imposing enough to hide the shock and shame that aged her more than the years ever had.

But I will get to the reason behind that. First, the end of everything.

Even more traumatic to me than the building which collapsed while we fought the fires was when the entire wooden scaffolding which enveloped part of the cathedral came crashing down. It's so strange; I can awake from another nightmare of the roof falling and immediately fall back to sleep, but the sound of the fall of the scaffolding will forever horrify me. Faith had to comfort me more than once when the sound of some neighbor tossing out a pile of rubbish or some other noise made me shake from head to foot.

For the rest of Riversedge, the aftermath was the worst of it. With so many reduced to homelessness, Faith's blanket project was direly needed in many areas of the city, and she and the ladies' committee worked tirelessly to make sure everyone was warm and tucked away somewhere safe before the swift onslaught of winter.

The other churches began to share resources almost without a word upon the subject; it was deeply felt in the hearts of many that more walls than those of the burning buildings had fallen that night as the city poured out into its streets to help without regard to denomination or creed. Several wells that had been restricted to one neighborhood or the other were opened to their near neighbors, the waterlines having highlighted the absurdity of the arbitrary division.

The death toll came to about a hundred, plus the few that had died in the previous fires and of course, the old priest whom I had never seen. Some bodies were not found for weeks, and the occasional family member's remains appeared up to months in the future, identifiable only by metal heirlooms which had survived the blaze. Some families would search forever.

Mrs. Cunningham was distracted and distant during the recovery, which was odd considering her usual pronounced attendance in every church operation. We were able to track her movements only through hearsay. According to Faith's friend Angeline, Mrs. Cunningham was oddly present each time a body was recovered; she hovered over the rescuers, anxious to guard the identity of the victim. Each time, the moment she knew who it was, she went away. For female victims, her stay was even briefer. To the bedsides of the one or two children, she never came.

At last, one day the heart of the grim mystery was revealed. We had been out and about with Faith and were seeing to a few matters in the cathedral when suddenly there the revered lady was, ashen and leaning on the back of Father Forsetti's wheelchair as he laboriously guided her down the hall. She was breathing as though she would faint, and he quickly secreted her in another room before he reappeared to call for female reinforcements.

For several minutes, Mrs. Cunningham wouldn't let anyone see her, even her friends. When at last her resolve did break, she was inconsolable. Faith's response was to quickly and quietly guide the children and onlookers away and allow Mrs. Cunningham to be comforted only by her own closest friends, who were as distraught and confused as the rest of us.

The truth made its way out soon enough. It was on the day we happened to be at the cathedral that he finally convinced her to confess to him the identity of the one she sought, which was, she whispered as though terrified anyone should hear, a beloved younger brother who had been missing for weeks.

Once she had told her tale, a grim one of a spoiled boy become a weak-minded, selfish, and unpredictable man whom no one in the family had been able to protect or control, Father Forsetti took her to check one more bed for the brother she sought. It was the barred and padded sickroom of the arsonist, and to her great humiliation and misfortune, it was here that her search reached its conclusion.

The details of the matter trickled out slowly, but that was all right; for once, the reception of news by the congregation was manifested as dumbfounded shock instead of an eager quest for particulars. In truth, no one desired to see the great lady brought so low, not even those who feared or envied her. For a loved one to have gone missing at a time like this was one thing; to be forced to recover him in this way was unimaginable. Unfortunately, in her shame, she would allow no one to comfort her, attending church in her regular splendor but more grey and empty-looking than ever.

I used to think we were the only ones with secrets: that nobody wanted me, that Theophilus had once been accused of witchcraft, or that Faith was a lovestruck runaway. Now, whenever I meet someone who seems untouchably perfect, I merely smile. I don't need to know what darkness lies beneath to know that it's there and sometimes to pity the bearer.

Father Forsetti constantly visited the arsonist's infirmary bed, but the nurses said it availed little; the man's mind was as broken as his back and the three bones in his arms, but it was his heart, they said, which was beyond repair. It would be foolish, according to the priest, to attribute his madness totally to crumbling beneath the guilt of the first fire, but still Father Forsetti said little on the subject of guilt; he almost always spoke of forgiveness. He never said it, but everyone knew he blamed himself for the man's mangled brain.

As for Father Forsetti, it is harder for him to get around the hilly, cobblestoned streets now with half of his right leg amputated after his fall. While he was in the wheelchair, he never left the church grounds. Nowadays he gets on well enough with the peg, but he's not a young man and often has to use a crutch. It makes one sad to see his bent back when so often he used to stand with a look of such power at the top of the cathedral, looking out over the city.

The most important moment I have saved for last: when Faith, Helena, and I went searching for Theophilus under the shattered pieces of scaffolding.

He had been near the top of the structure with Father Forsetti when it fell. Most of the wooden framework had fallen over the lip of the parapet and not landed on the men in the lower parts of the scaffolding. The arsonist, who had remained at the other end, had been bent on destroying the supports, and these had pinned him until the workmen were able to free him many long hours later.

It was only seconds after the structure had met its end just beyond the cathedral's stone wall that Faith struggled free from the crush of the crowd and began to frantically circle the scene of destruction. Helena and I had both regained our feet, but Faith's manner scared us. She looked so pale and distraught and seemed for one instant to have forgotten us. Clinging to each other's hands, we darted after her, dodging through the swiftly milling crowd of onlookers.

I remember the tug of Helena's grip as I began to fall behind, but my ears detected nothing for what seemed like several minutes. To my knowledge, nobody spoke, nor did anything move within the nearest hundred yards. We rounded the front of the crowd; there was the bulk of the wreckage. Faith grabbed her skirts and darted into the many pieces of shattered wooden beams.

It was my eyes, not my ears, which alerted me that several people were trying to speak to Faith, but she pushed them all aside and went on. When the two of us were spotted, several well-meaning townspeople did what they could to corral us to keep us from seeing whatever terror lay ahead, but almost without thinking, my sister and I looked at each other and split up, sprinting erratically in opposite directions. It was a trick we had carefully honed during our pirate games.

Helena managed to make her way speedily to freedom, but someone caught hold of me. At last, one word broke from my lips: "Papa!"

A soft sigh broke from several of those behind me, and the unfamiliar hand released me. I ran over whatever track was easiest, dodging between piles of rubble and ducking under beams that rested at an angle.

Instinct bid me follow the massive crush of people that pressed in around one place on the edge of the scaffolding, and I hastened to see from a different angle.

Father Forsetti. They were lifting him up on their shoulders, then to their hands, and carrying him away from the wreckage. Some voices cried, others shouted with hope. His face was bathed in sunlight.

"It's a miracle!"

"Oh, thank God…"

"How did they possibly survive-"

One young man wiped tears from his eyes with the back of his arm. "I saw them come down. The beam they were standing on stayed mostly on the top even when the lot was becomin' a landslide. They couldn't have fallen more than a story on their own."

He succeeded in smearing ashes all over his face, alerting me that he had been among the rescuers of the night, too. Unsatisfied, I kept on.

And then, there they were. Helena and Faith knelt beside a prone form, speaking urgently to each other and shaking their heads. The angel-man lay face-down with his arms bent in front of him as though to defend himself from a frontal attack, but his body was completely still. I ran to them.

A small knot of people had formed nearby but didn't dare come any closer, afraid of what they might hear. When I arrived, someone tried to hold me back and speak to me. It's the only time I remember hitting anyone except for Helena. Before long, I had battered my way through and was standing only a few feet from Theophilus's fallen form.

"Can you move any?" Faith was asking softly. She gently rubbed his back with one hand and rested her weight on the other one, her upper body forming a protective arch above his.

"Yes, please, Papa, try!" Helena agreed, nodding urgently.

"Easy, easy." Faith's lips pinched together. "Just take your time. We don't need to go anywhere just now."

Slowly and with painstaking effort, Theophilus started to move. He rolled over until he was balanced on one side and managed to smile tiredly up at his wife. She released a pent-up sigh and threw herself down to wrap his entire head in her arms and kiss him on his mouth.

Within moments, Helena had decided she was not to be left out and clambered into the narrow space between her parents' two bodies and scrunched into their embrace. They both laughed.

But their relief was lost on me; I was too alone in this moment, too forgotten. I had battled for my life and for those of people I didn't know, and just now I had reached yet another moment I didn't understand. I started to cry. The noise was swallowed up by hundreds of other murmuring or weeping voices.

"Emmy!" the angel-man called. "Emmy, Emmy! Where is she?"

Faith gasped and sat upright, turning this way and that until she saw me. Her face fell when she saw my distress and she opened her arms, but I buried my face in my hands and continued to sob.

"Come here, baby girl!" she said, but for once, I felt as if I really *was* deaf to her words as well as mute to my own.

Helena dashed over to me and grabbed hold of my arm, but I had long ago surpassed being overwhelmed. I was impossible to move for someone her size and stood rooted to the spot, ignoring her urging. I thought I would pass out again and wished I might. I heard a muddied flow of voices but didn't distinguish my own family's.

All at once, the yanking on my arm ceased and I felt a big, warm arm wrap around my waist. I kept crying, but this time a big hand tipped my head into a shoulder that stank of sweat and smoke.

"Hey. Hey, you."

The lips that pressed against my head were gentle, but still I didn't look up.

"It's me."

I batted watery eyes to try and clear them and lifted my head. Those bloodshot eyes didn't look anything like anyone I knew. Then-

"Hey there, Little One. I'm here."

With a quiet cry, I flung my arms around his neck and began to weep afresh, smothered against the remains of Theophilus's ripped and stained white shirt. He hugged me so tight that I thought I would burst, but I didn't want him to ever let go. He only held me with one arm, while the other hung ominously still at an odd angle beside him, but he was on his feet now, turning slowly with me and kissing my hair over and over again.

"Look at us. The night's passed, and we're still here together," he said. He looked around at each of us.

Faith's eyes beamed at him, but her expression was sober as she turned to survey the destruction. "Out of the frying pan, into the fire..." she mused.

Theophilus shook his head, grinning radiantly. "And yet here we are, like Shadrach, Meshach, and Abednego!" he said. With one more resounding kiss, he set me on my feet, then moved to approach his wife.

From beside Helena on the ground, I could see his severe limp and knew he wasn't as well as he made himself out to be. His body had somewhere been broken by the fall.

Nevertheless, he offered his hands to Faith. "Shall we?"

She let out a shuddering laugh. "Right now? But you-"

He shook his head soberly and drew her close against his chest. "Life is very short," he murmured deeply. Then he smiled a little. "And we agreed, did we not-"

"That we would always celebrate what was worth celebrating," she finished. She was smiling now, too.

A hum of voices brought our attention toward the crowd, but before we could look, the subject came to us.

"Look, snow!" said Helena happily.

Theophilus and Faith shared a grim smile. "That's not snow, Nellie," said her father.

"It's ash," Faith agreed. She turned to look away from the cathedral in the direction of the ravaged portions of the city.

Sure enough, what had appeared to be fat white flakes more resembled gossamer rags of the faintest grey, and they crumbled on contact. The wind had picked up from the north and was blowing bits of it everywhere so it appeared to shower down from the sky. I squinted up; with the sun peering through its flashing silver fan of clouds, the ghostly precipitation looked even stranger. Still, their fall was silent, and the little white coating appeared to me just as magical as a winter storm. In fact, its meaning made it better, for-

"It means we won." Faith's ragged voice was lowly

triumphant. She turned again to face her husband, a little smile growing through the grime and ash that coated both their faces.

He proffered both hands and bowed deeply, stopping abruptly partway down to wince in pain. But he smiled and bravely stood once more.

He took her hands, one upon his shoulder and the other in one of his, wrapped his other hand about her waist, and began to turn, slowly at first. Helena giggled softly and stood a few paces behind him, trying to mimic his gargantuan steps with an invisible partner.

The crowds had begun to disperse somewhat, but everyone had stopped in their tracks to watch the ash rain down in silence. Faith's muffled laughter seemed to echo across a frozen plain, and everyone turned in unison to stare at the strange sight, in the midst of all this sorrow, of one grateful couple dancing together.

The first sound I heard was soft weeping, not unfamiliar to my ears in recent times, but now it was a bittersweet tune of both joy and loss, celebration and grieving. Soon, other people were dancing, too. Husbands and wives, mothers and children, siblings, lovers, families of every kind swayed amid the silent fall that proclaimed both our sorrow and our survival. For a little while, Helena and I joined hands with our parents to sway in a circle. Eventually, someone started humming, and within moments, a low chorus of voices had joined in. Then someone began to sing the words.

Helena and I eventually broke off from our parents to spin holding each other's hands. Both of us loved to watch the two of them twirl together, wrapped in an elegant embrace. Once or twice I glanced up at the sky, and at the black hulk of the cathedral outlined against it. It was another of those bright silver days, though it might not have been if it were not for the smoke. I wondered if up above, the sky was pretty and clear, and someone that far up could see nothing but a beautiful, sparkling world.

I spotted movement at the edge of my vision and turned slightly. There, up on the parapet, was a familiar figure. He was propped up by someone else, but still he was watching us. It was Father Forsetti.

And he was smiling.

Toward the end of the refrain, the familiar voices of my parents, which were as beautiful to me as they were dear, joined in to proclaim:

Whatever my lot, Thou hast taught me to say,
It is well, it is well, it is well with my soul.

With this pronouncement, the angel-man suddenly burst into tears and pressed his face gently against his wife's.

"Thank you," I heard him murmur. She only smiled in return.

Chapter Fifteen

For those of us who had been in the heart of Riversedge at the time of the tragedies, the night which dawned into December first was one which changed everything. Sadly, to many others, it was nothing more than a commonplace disaster which created a temporary buzz, then nothing more. Nothing but a surge of fear and a vague sense of societal remorse came and went in an instant, and everyone went about their lives, leaving the shadows of evil to resume stalking the inner rooms of humanity in silence.

Unfortunately, the newfound brotherhood between people of the several denominations within the city was equally limited in its reach. However, we like to hope that this love, kindled in the heart of darkness, will eventually be pumped out from the heart of Riversedge to its farthest extremities. Only time will tell. But, as Father Forsetti is fond of saying, Mama does have a reliable habit of stirring the blood.

Which brings me to one more interesting encounter

between the two of them. It was weeks after that fateful eve of December when a message reached her that the father wanted to speak with her. Since Papa was not yet in any condition to corral us by himself, she was obliged to take Helena and me with her.

We had been so busy helping with various recovery projects that nobody had time to worry about what it was the father wanted. It didn't occur to me until we were ascending the stone steps to the top of that fateful hill and made our way inside.

This time, Faith didn't bother trying to plant us far from their conversation. We were set to play in the hallway just outside the library, the same place where they had had such a terrible row only weeks before. Needless to say, the instant Faith had gone inside, Helena and I were both pressed against the wall, peering around the corner to see.

"How is your leg healing?" Faith clasped her hands in front of her with a hesitant smile.

The father smiled sadly and shrugged. He was seated in a wheelchair, packed in with pillows and blankets. It made him look much older.

"It gets on well enough," he said simply, shifting the wooden contraption which reached up to his knee. A shadow crossed his face as he turned away.

Faith silently sighed and came closer, then took a seat near him across the hearth. Their eyes met, and both awkwardly smiled again. Faith was wearing a plain work dress today; she still had a stray needle stuck through her sleeve from where she'd kept it out of harm's way, and pieces of her hair escaped from the simple braid down her back to curl about her neck and ears.

"Mrs. Gladstone," Father Forsetti began at last, "I believe I owe you an apology, or rather an explanation."

Faith wouldn't have looked more stricken if he had leapt out of his seat and slapped her. She started to say something, but to all of our surprise, he chuckled and waved her away.

"Please," he said. "Allow me to set the record straight, on one point at least, if not many."

He took a leather folder from the table beside him and cleared his throat, then removed a few sheets of paper from it. He glanced over them at her for a second, then sighed and lowered them.

"Faith," he said. All of us started faintly at the familiarity. "We have disagreed on many points, and we have both lost our tempers on more than one occasion. No, please," he said, cutting her off with another wave of his hand. "On a few of those points, we must continue to disagree, but there are others upon which I realize, upon the acquisition of further information, I have made some grievous errors, or at least failed to recognize your unique point of view. Allow me to explain."

Faith watched him intently, chewing on her lower lip. He selected one of the sheets of paper and drew his breath hesitantly.

"'November 29th, New England, township of Reason.'"

Faith's gasp was audible and echoed by both of us. Father Forsetti glanced in our direction but continued to read.

"'To Father George Forsetti of St. John's Cathedral, Riversedge:

'It has come to my attention through various channels that you seek information regarding a certain couple by the names of Theophilus and Faith Gladstone, who have a daughter named Helena. The former two persons are familiar to me; the announcement of the latter I welcome with genuine delight and hope you will give my best wishes to them all.

'It has been some nine years since I have had contact with either of the aforementioned Gladstones, but I can assure you of the legitimacy of their marriage, the strength of their faith, and the uprightness of their character. I am most familiar with the woman – Faith, that is – for I taught her since she was a girl.

'She is a fine young woman, though a bit peculiar, to tell the truth. If you ask me, that will only serve to set her far ahead of her fellows. Theophilus I have met only briefly, but in my short questioning, I found him to be a man of sound mind and good standing. As to their marriage, it was I who performed the ceremony, quiet and somewhat clandestine though it was. I will send you a copy of their certificate in case you should like to see evidence of my acquaintance with the couple.

'I must admit, it surprised me at first to learn the two of them were rooted in a Catholic parish, for if ever a pair were raised to be Protestant heathens (if you'll forgive the jest) it would be these two. However, as long as these two lambs have found a safe pasture, I do not care what type of collar their shepherd wears, if he be a good man. I have made inquiries of my own on that count, and am happy to hear that you are. My condolences for the loss of your senior pastor; it sounds as if he were much beloved and will be sorely missed.'"

Here, Father Forsetti was forced to stop and choke back his own tears. No sound was audible but cinders falling in the grate, and when he swallowed to regain control himself, we could hear this, as well.

"'As to the two about whom you've applied to me, or rather, general inquiries about whom you have cast to the wind, I must warn you I have a strange tale to tell. These two are of no ordinary origins, and have weathered much.'"

Father Forsetti lowered the page. Faith's face was as white as the hands folded tightly in her lap.

"Reverend Alston goes on to say," the father added slowly, looking steadily at her face, "that your husband was accused of a grave crime. That he was convicted and sentenced to death."

Faith sank to her knees before the chair in which she'd been sitting. She watched the priest as though awaiting some terrible pronouncement. Her back heaved with the powerful waves of emotion that washed over her.

Father Forsetti watched her solemnly. "Reverend Alston told me your story, and of how you came to him in the dark of night to ask his aid, and that to this day he believes firmly in both of your innocence." He took a breath. "Faith, I know what happened back in Reason, why your husband confessed, everything you did to save each other. I heard how brave you were."

He smiled at her bowed head, tenderness creasing his usually stony face. "It amazes me that until this point, the two of you have carried it all alone, and it no longer surprises me how you keep to yourselves. I have misjudged you."

When Faith didn't move, he drew a slow breath.

"And now it occurs to me," he smiled ruefully, "that our conversation about my inquiries into the histories of my parishioners must have come across to you very differently than I had intended or ever – in my wildest dreams – anticipated."

Faith tried to speak. "I was afraid- I was *so* afraid-"

He laughed regretfully. "Yes, I know. I know what you thought, or what you were afraid I would think, and how this might have gone differently if your story had been spread all over the parish without anyone to verify the truth. And for the pittance it's worth, I would like to assure you that I wouldn't do that, accuse on so little grounds for a different crime or spread the story before I had thoroughly validated its truth. My intention was to ferret out a possible lead to the source of the trouble, not to strike fear into the hearts of innocent women and men."

Finally, Faith raised her eyes to meet his. He bit his lips and nodded seriously.

"Knowing what I know now, it galls me to realize you thought – and had the reasonable right to assume – that I was taunting you with the terrors of your past, when until this past week I did not even know them. I did not mean to hurt you, and I am truly sorry for having revived this grievous pain."

Her eyes shone with tears. She nodded her thanks

several times. Father Forsetti watched her carefully for a moment before he spoke again.

"There is more news, but I fear you are not ready to hear all of it now, nor would it be kind to force you to receive so much news which is of great personal importance to you in my presence. So I give it to you to read in private with your husband. Let your girls know." He held out the letter, folded and sealed with wax. "I have made a copy for my own records since it was originally addressed to me, but since so much of it is of personal import to you and it was written in the hand of someone you knew, I would offer you the original."

She hesitantly reached out to receive the missive, then quickly stuffed it into her apron and pressed it against her with a clenched fist. She watched him with vulnerable eyes as black as ink, still waiting for something.

He breathed in deeply, then out. "However, Faith Gladstone, there is one piece of news which I wish to convey to you myself, in a way to acquit myself of having brought this dreaded mess to a head."

His eyes probed her reaction, assessing her readiness to hear what he had to tell.

"As I say, there have been many developments since your flight from your old township, and the foremost is this: that four years after you and your husband's escape, that is, roughly five years ago according to the reverend, Theophilus's case was looked into and, upon further inspection and new evidence, he was publicly acquitted."

Faith let out something between a cry of relief and a

wail. She remained on her knees, downcast upon one hand while the other feebly shielded her face as long-repressed tears flowed down. Father Forsetti tried to speak, but his voice was drowned out by her frantic sobs. He waited a moment, then tried again, but Faith could not bring her emotions to heel.

Hesitantly, Father Forsetti drew back the blanket which lay across his lap and used the armrests of his chair to ease himself to the floor so that he, too, crouched upon the flagstones. He gritted his teeth in silent pain and eased his bandage half-leg to a more bearable position, then held out his arm to Faith.

She fell into him, resting her face against his chest while she unleashed the bitter storm brought on by horrific and pent-up terrors held in secret for years. Amazed, Helena and I no longer bothered to try to conceal our presence and stood openly gaping in the doorway at his humbled posture. Gradually, Faith regained control of herself, and it was like the sun shining again after the rain, and I joined in the feeling of newfound relief and gratitude.

Then Father Forsetti turned to look at us, and all at once, it occurred to us that we had been caught. We both froze, debating whether it was too late to dart back to safety, but then his smile broadened, and instead, he beckoned to us.

We needed no further invitation. Helena and I bounded forward to throw our arms around our mother. She started slightly, then sat up and wiped her eyes with a smile and returned the embrace.

Father Forsetti, meanwhile, heaved himself back up into his wheelchair with some difficulty and retreated under the pile of blankets.

"I shall leave you to your news," he said formally, "and bid you good morning."

That was not, by far, the last discussion between Faith and Father Forsetti, nor was it the last of their emotionally charged disagreements. However, from then on, the two came to a new understanding: not, perhaps, agreeing in everything, but ready and willing to see each other as a human with flaws, not the manifestation of everything in Christ's church which vexed either of them. In fact, the two have come to deeply trust each other, and Father Forsetti often turns to Mama for advice, though their conversation is often far from tranquil and usually finds its way back to their core differences of belief. However, the two no longer question each other's faith, merely challenging one another to a better and purer expression of Christ's love. That is, after all, the most important job of the church, and in this, at least, the two are in perfect agreement.

Faith and Theophilus were in for a whirlwind of emotions when that night the letter was opened and an ocean of news poured out. Some friends were married or had moved away; Faith's father had died. But overshadowing all, whether joy or grief, was the knowledge that the truth had at last set them both free.

"So...we can go home now." Faith stared at her hands where they rested on the kitchen table. She and Theophilus had stayed up late to discuss. Helena and I were "asleep" in the next room.

"If you can call it home." Theophilus reexamined the letter for what had to be the thousandth time.

"There's no telling whether public opinion is agreeable enough to prevent them from burning our house down, no matter the official pronouncement." Then he saw the feverish expression in her eyes and his face softened. "But I know you will want to pay your respects to your father, and-"

"And to see my mama. Yes," she said almost in a whisper. She shook her head in despondent wonder. "I never thought we could ever see them again."

Theophilus set the letter on the table and held out his arms for her. She went and sat quietly upon his lap, resting her head against his chest and letting him comfort her and play with her hair.

"The girls have never had a grandfather," she mused.

"Nor will they ever have one," Theophilus solemnly agreed. "Ironic, since my grandfather is all I ever had."

She sat up and looked at him. "You never told me that."

He shrugged and pressed her cheek back down to his chest. "I've told you a little about my past when I can," he remarked. "But you know it's painful for me."

She frowned, then nestled her head up under his chin. "Please tell me now."

He closed his eyes for a moment, wrapping her tighter in his embrace. "My mother was unwed when she had me. My grandfather never even knew who my father was. As for my mum, she died of some terrible disease before I was four years old, and it was three churches before anyone would baptize me when they knew of my origins. My grandfather was the one who kept me."

Faith's eyes were open, and I could see she sensed the unbearable loneliness in him. He went on.

"My grandfather didn't have much to do with children, not even when his own were young. Probably that had something to do with why my mother had turned out so poorly, and he knew it. Thus, he enveloped himself in his business. Of course I didn't know then that it was out of preference rather than necessity, but it taught me always to hope." Here his voice caught.

Faith glanced up. "To hope?"

He nodded. "To hope that one day someone would come along and love me. To hope that the books with which he bombarded me by way of education would one day raise me out of the mire that was my parents' legacy. To hope that perhaps, even though he considered his own unloved child to be a failure, I would be something better and worth loving." He pinched his lips together. "For a long time, all I hoped for was that he would come back, and that someday he would love me. But he died when I was fourteen." There was a long silence. "I've been alone ever since. Or I was until I met y-"

Faith's response was to spring up from under his chin and plant a fervent kiss against his mouth, pressing her face harder and harder against him as if to draw out the years of loneliness like a poison.

For several minutes, they remained like that, caressing one another's faces as if to reassure each other of their presence. When the kiss broke, she still held his face in both hands with a sad smile.

"How could you have survived on so little and not become a monster?" she asked, shaking her head.

Theophilus shrugged. "I don't know. I have no memories of my mother, but I had the vague impression that she loved me. That gave me the faith to believe that one day, someone else would, too." He smiled at her and shrugged once more. "And from there, I took advantage of every opportunity and waited for the sun to shine."

Faith's face was crumpled with sorrow. He pressed a kiss against the wrinkle between her eyebrows and held her for a while longer.

After another long pause, he spoke. "That's why we can't abandon Emmy."

Faith's head shot up. She started to speak, but he cut her off.

"She's family now, Fe. Don't you feel it?" His eyes searched hers urgently, as soft as a child's. "A love like that doesn't appear around every corner. And she and Helena would be heartbroken to part. Let's tell those cousins they can keep the money and that she's staying with us, yes?" He smiled and nodded convincingly, rubbing a few of the strands of hair framing her face between his fingers.

"I love her, too," Faith said carefully. "As much as if she were my own. But what will we do without the money with another mouth to feed? We're not wealthy as it is."

Theophilus sat back and thought for a second. "Perhaps it's time we looked at my paycheck. The father had said it would depend on the quality of my work, so I'm not sure how much to expect."

Faith bit her lip. "Let's do that now."

He placed her on the table while he went through a drawer and came back with an envelope. He sat down in his chair facing her, and they stared at each other for a long moment.

"I think we should pray," she said at last.

"Yes, let's do that!"

They bowed their heads and prayed feverishly in tones I couldn't decipher, then drew back the flap. They were silent for a second.

Then they leapt up with a yell of triumph that sent me running back to my bedroom to hide under the blankets.

Needless to say, I am not the unwilling captive of some mercenary cousins, though we have met them. They were not as conniving as most people in the parish had become willing to believe, but they were, in fact, rather eager to debate the issue of my grandfather's money. The adults discussed it in private for a long time before the angel-man brought me in and put the question to me. Under his guidance, I carved out a portion that was fair to keep my cousins, while leaving myself enough to one day go to school if I chose.

Today we are leaving Riversedge, this time for good. We have lived here together in happy unity for upwards of six years, but now Papa has a commission elsewhere. He has done work for a few other places all from his little workshop downtown, but now we are to depart on a new adventure which will allow us to see the old town of Reason as well as move closer to possible schools.

But there will be no slinking away with just the clothes on our backs and whatever we can carry; no, all week there have been miniature going-away parties and celebrations all over town with each of our friends and this morning with our parish. They have truly become, in their own way, our family.

I am standing before the largest stained glass window, basking in its pool of light. All of Papa's work is fantastic and continues to enthrall visitors with an awe something akin to terror, but this one will always be my favorite. The look of relief on Jesus's face is the look of a person receiving back someone they love. It's a feeling I've come to know well.

Helena comes and stands beside me. She watches the sunlight ripple through the glass for a moment, then tugs on the string of my bonnet.

"Time to go."

I give her a sisterly smile and kick the side of her boot, but follow. We descend the wide stone stairs in silence. The cathedral is blanketed with a weekday hush.

When we get to the main gallery, we gather our smaller parcels and go down the front steps to the little courtyard where we've often played.

Our parents stand with their arms around each other, surveying the garden with the peculiar bliss which has always both pleased and puzzled us.

"Farewell, then."

We turn as Father Forsetti approaches from the narrow doorway in the side wall. In his hand is a bouquet of freshly-picked pink roses, the last of the season. Faith smiles her thanks and accepts them for all of us.

Without another word, the priest accompanies us as we make our way to the front gate. When we step outside, we turn back and survey the old place with misty eyes and grateful hearts.

"It's really beautiful," is all Mama can say.

Father Forsetti smiles. "More so because the two of you have been here." He glances meaningfully from the lovely stained glass to the passel of well-wishers still cleaning up from the party on the lawn. Then his eyes fix on Helena and me. "All of you." He places a hand firmly on each of our heads in blessing.

"Write to us, won't you?" Faith smiles. Then suddenly she throws her arms around him, startling him. "Perhaps you'll be glad to part with this thorn in your side," she laughs through her tears.

He hugs her tightly, then waits till she steps back and meets his eye. "You know, I have communed with many other priests and brothers, but none has challenged me as much as you." He shakes his head as she starts to grimace. "I've come to view that challenge as a good thing. Truly." He smiles. "Though your questions and prodding always take me off balance and sometimes even spark my anger, they have often led me to the questions that ultimately bring me closer to God. And what better gift can a friend offer than that?" He grins and hugs her again.

"I've learned just as much from you," she murmurs. She steps back, smiling. "Though I don't think I shall ever be a truly docile church lady, I intend to be a source of strength and support to my pastor in the future." She raises one eyebrow. "Though I shall not refrain from correction when the necessity presents itself."

Father Forsetti nods several times, considering what she's said. "A new pastor," he muses. Then he pauses. "Give him hell."

Theophilus's laughter echoes off the parapets just as the church bells begin to chime. Then we spot the carriage; it is time to leave.

Helena and I sit in the back, breathless as always with wonder at the haunting tune of the bells. Never was a place so mysterious and full of secrets as this, and yet a certain holiness abides in the shadows, waiting for the right moment to burst forth into radiant light.

"What are you thinking about?" Helena asks me.

I sigh. "I'm wondering what awaits us next." I shrug at her nervously. "I've only ever left to go on a journey once, and it brought me into the midst of a chaos, with rumors and fires and crazy people with hidden agendas."

Helena leans back against her seat and smiles, closing her eyes. "That's the fun of it. You never know where you're going next, or who's around the corner, waiting to spring. But *I* look on it as an adventure." She opens her eyes and takes my hand in hers. "We've made it through everything up to this point, Em. I don't care much where we go, because I know that we," she motions around the carriage and the parents and me, "can make it through anything."

She smiles and nudges me when she sees I'm still not convinced. "Papa survived past his hanging date and the city almost burned around us. I'd say we're up for anything."

Long after she's stopped talking, I watch the scenery slip by. We've left the town far behind us and are rolling through the countryside. The golden fields and rustling wind are glorious, a world far more spacious than any I've known thus far.

We turn a corner, and suddenly it's as if we're in another world.

I gasp. "Look! It's beautiful!"

We have left the high road and entered into a pocket of trees. The cool, blue-sky autumn has set their leaves ablaze, leaving them all red as blood.

The others laugh at me as I sit in awe with my hands clasped to my cheeks. "It's like one of your windows!"

Helena leans out of her seat toward Mama. "It's like the gift that Papa made you."

I whirl around to join her. "Ooh! What was it? I was busy packing and never got to see."

With a secretive smile at Papa, Mama unwraps a small object wrapped in thick cloth and holds it up. Both of us ooh and ah and take it gingerly in our hands; it is a bright red leaf, pressed and encased in glass.

"Didn't you say you picked this up on the night you were married?" Helena prompts him eagerly.

He nods. "Yep. That very night." He shares another smile with Mama. "As we were leaving the clearing, I felt a sudden desperate desire to secure at least one memento from that night, something that wouldn't weigh me down on our journey. I carried it inside a book in my pocket for days. Then, last week, I used the last bits of glass from my shop to encase it. That's why it's so many different colors." He pauses thoughtfully. "It seemed...fitting."

I turn the little orb from side to side, watching as the sunlight breaks through the labyrinth of color in which the leaf is suspended to pool several whimsical shades in my lap. Perfectly imperfect, wild and strange, but still blindingly beautiful, it's perfect for them.

I hand it back to Mama and lean my head on Helena's shoulder, sighing happily. My parents' love story still brings joy to my heart.

Just as we round another bend, a perfect red leaf floats down and lands in my lap. I pick it up and study it. It's not the same kind as the ones from Mama and Papa's story, but it's of the same dark shade.

I twirl it between my fingers, wondering what unsuspecting community the Gladstones will be unleashed upon next. I hope that we're ready to face them, and that whoever they are, they're ready for a good shaking up.

Made in United States
North Haven, CT
27 November 2021